WINTERBOURNE

WINTERBOURNE

ELISABETH WOLF

Black&White

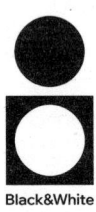
Black&White

First published in the UK in 2026 by Black & White Publishing
An imprint of Bonnier Books UK
5th Floor, HYLO, 105 Bunhill Row,
London, EC1Y 8LZ

Copyright © Alison Belsham writing as Elisabeth Wolf 2026

All rights reserved.
No part of this publication may be reproduced,
stored or transmitted in any form by any means, electronic,
mechanical, photocopying or otherwise, without the
prior written permission of the publisher.

The right of Alison Belsham writing as Elisabeth Wolf
to be identified as Author of this work has been
asserted by her in accordance with the
Copyright, Designs and Patents Act, 1988.

This is a work of fiction. Names, places, events and
incidents are either the products of the author's
imagination or used fictitiously. Any resemblance to
actual persons, living or dead, or actual
events is purely coincidental.

A CIP catalogue record for this book is available from the British Library.

ISBN (HB): 978 1 78530 867 3
ISBN (TPB): 978 1 78530 868 0

1 3 5 7 9 10 8 6 4 2

Typeset by IDSUK (Data Connection) Ltd
Printed and bound by CPI (UK) Ltd, Croydon CR0 4YY

The authorised representative in the EEA is
Bonnier Books UK (Ireland) Limited.
Registered office address: Block B, The Crescent Building,
Northwood, Santry Dublin 9, D09 C6X8, Ireland
compliance@bonnierbooks.ie
www.bonnierbooks.co.uk

For Alyina

Prologue

NEW SCARS OVERLAY THE OLD SCARS. Fresh burns have seared away the ashes of what went before. My mind skitters between the recent and more distant past until, with a deep breath, I drag myself back into the present.

I never think about what the future holds.

Every day, I sit by the open window. I can no longer see what's going on outside. My vision has been reduced to a blur of light and shadow, a drab palette in which nothing can be distinguished apart from an occasional movement. But it's pleasant to feel the light spring breeze on my skin like a cool balm, or a gentle spritz of rain before Fran rushes in and closes the window, scolding me for not taking care. I like the window open. I listen to the street sounds – tyres on the wet tarmac, the metallic clang of lorries going over the speed bump, then the scream of an approaching siren, my anxiety receding once it's passed by. The magpies squawk fractiously at each other in the poplar in next door's front garden. The pigeons grumble, but the blackbirds always seem cheerful. Fran tells me she sometimes sees parakeets in the park, the descendants of pet birds which have escaped and colonised our leafy suburb. She says they're like emerald flashes flitting between the trees. I can hardly imagine them.

I miss being able to watch these neighbourhood birds.

But I don't miss hearing the kittiwakes' incessant chatter, the high screams of the gulls, wheeling over the cliff edges, the cormorant's sharp bark or the haunting, guttural chorus of the shearwaters in the dark. The wind that blows down the man-made canyons of the city might rattle the windows and the doors, but it doesn't howl into the void like the wind on Craigsea Rock, or sneak up behind me to whisper sharply in my ear. It doesn't sweep the voices of the dead across the sand or snake between Winterbourne's granite chimneys with the moans of tortured souls. Instead, I hear a builder shouting to his mate, someone blasting their horn in frustration at the traffic, babies crying and children singing. The clatter of the letterbox and the post landing on the mat.

These sounds anchor me here and stop me from being dragged back to the island, with its brooding skies and the taste of the sea forever on my lips. In this small flat, I turn to other stories. I loved to read. It was my solace. Now I make do with audiobooks. Other people's voices in my ears, their interpretations of the text. But still transporting me to safer places. Fran collects them for me from the library, making sure to avoid anything that she thinks might upset me. I rely on her for so much and I'll be forever grateful to her, as she is to me. We've been through so much together, and I know her time on Craigsea Rock haunts her as much as my time there haunts me.

I hear the tap running as she fills the kettle, and her voice calling from the kitchen.

'Would you like a cup of tea, Anne?'

'Yes,' I say, 'that would be lovely.'

Outside, the sound of a siren crescendos as an ambulance speeds up the street, and before Fran can rush through to close the window, it's carried me back to the horrifying accident just over a year ago which set the nightmare in motion.

One Year Earlier

1

Sirens. Endless sirens. That's almost all I can remember in those few moments after the crash. That, and the blood dripping from a gash on my brother's head, landing on my cheek, running down my chin.

'Malcolm?'

He didn't answer.

I became frantic, saying his name over and over again. I tried to lift my arm to shake him, but a sharp stabbing pain prevented me. It took me a few moments to realise that the car was resting on its side, almost upside down, and I was wedged between the steering wheel and my side window, my cheek pressed up against the glass. The interior looked unfamiliar from this angle. It was only later that I realised it was completely buckled out of shape. All I saw then was Malcolm, unconscious, suspended above me by his seat belt.

I could smell blood and petrol, and I was afraid.

Those first few seconds seemed like hours. Then I heard the sirens, and hands were reaching in for me. I think I passed out. Perhaps I just don't remember. Or maybe my brain's wiped the slate clean for my own protection.

I'd been the driver, and somehow I'd done this.

I woke up in unfamiliar surroundings, though I quickly recognised it was a hospital room. The curtains round the bed, the muffled footsteps and whispered medical terms, the soft, regular bleep of a monitor somewhere behind my head – easy giveaways. I was wearing one of those papery gowns, patterned with the hospital logo, somehow designed to strip you of what little dignity you might cling to in circumstances beyond your control. An ill-judged attempt to raise my head shot arrows of pain in all directions. Every part of me hurt, but most of all my left leg, which was suspended above the bed by counterweights. These were attached to a bolt that went right through my knee.

I panicked, thrashing wildly as I tried to sit up. It went against logic, but I wanted to get out of the bed, out of the room, out of the hospital. I became lightheaded with pain.

'Where's Malcolm? Where's Malcolm?' I shouted. I knew something terrible had happened, and somehow I understood that I was to blame.

Two nurses came running in. One held me still, leaning forward over me, my eyes inches from the rash of acne on her chin, the other injected me, her hands cold and smooth on my arm until I felt the bite of the needle.

Welcome oblivion enveloped me.

The next time I woke up, I looked beyond the horror show of my broken leg to see my mother standing at the end of the bed. She was wearing a black dress with a matching jacket, expensive-looking clothes I'd never seen before, and she must have been watching me sleep. Her eyes were red-rimmed and puffy. I don't ever remember her crying but it looked like she had been. However, now her eyes bored into me.

'Mum?' Anxiety churned in my gut.

She shook her head slowly. 'How could you?'

What did she mean?

'Where's Malcolm?' I was scared to hear the answer.

'You don't know, do you?'

Something bad had happened. I felt panic rising in my chest and I clutched the sides of the mattress.

'Malcolm's dead. You were driving. You had an accident.' Her face darkened. Her voice was tight with anger.

As I struggled to grasp the meaning of her words, a nurse came in. My mother turned and left without another word, and I let out a howl. I couldn't picture a world going forward without Malcolm. I couldn't.

Sedation became my constant companion.

But I couldn't sleep forever. Each day, the hours I spent awake grew longer and the daily routine of the ward gradually became the rhythm of my existence. Breakfast was served stupidly early for people who had nowhere to get to. I began to recognise the nurses who brought my food and who came when summoned with a bedpan. Some tried to chat, but I preferred the ones who were quiet and efficient, getting on with the job rather than trying to be my friend.

I did have to talk to the doctors, though.

'You might never walk again,' my surgeon told me gently. He was an Egyptian man, with grizzled grey hair and sad eyes as he contemplated me from the side of the bed. 'You've suffered a complex compound fracture, with multiple breaks. You're lucky we didn't have to amputate it, and I must tell you that could still be necessary.'

A woman doctor took scans of my head. 'You've suffered a severe concussion. It will probably affect your ability to concentrate, maybe for a long time. You won't be able to read more than a page or so at a time.'

I'm not sure how she expected me to respond, so I said nothing.

Every day, the nurses asked how I felt. I did my best to answer them, but I didn't feel anything. I didn't really care about any of it. It was all insignificant compared to what I'd lost in the crash. A life without walking, a life without books – nothing compared to the prospect of a life without my beloved brother.

I cried, mostly in the mornings, when his loss hit me afresh after the rude awakening of the arrival of breakfast. But also in the night, when the ward was finally quiet, and often all through the day, when I would ask the nurses to pull the curtains round my bed. I know the other patients stared at me, wondering what had happened. One or two of them tried to comfort me, but got short shrift.

I didn't want to interact with anyone. Lost in a morass of grief and guilt, I turned away from human contact. I was happy that I had no visitors. After all, what could I say about what had happened?

I scraped my memories for details of the accident.

I remembered getting up on the day of the accident. Toast for breakfast, with butter and lemon marmalade. A banana, which was overripe. Tea. It was a Saturday. I worked a half-day, finishing at lunchtime. The library was busy and I was in the children's section. When I left the library, I picked up a sandwich at the minimarket opposite. And at that point my memory faltered. I couldn't remember where I ate it. I couldn't remember going back to the car. I couldn't say where and when I picked up Malcolm or where we were going, or had been. It's all gone. I knew what I was wearing – a grey sweater and black trousers, my standard workwear – but I couldn't say what Malcolm was wearing. Or what time it was when we came off the road.

The police came to the hospital and asked me questions about what had happened, over and over again. I wanted to help them, because I needed to know what happened. They told me where the crash happened, on a sharp bend on the road out of town to the north, but I had no recollection of why we were driving along that road. There was no sign of any other vehicle having been involved. No tyre marks, no dents, scratches or paint from another car, no reports from witnesses.

'Your car skidded over the edge of an embankment and fell twenty feet,' said the young officer on what must have been his third visit. 'You're lucky to be alive.'

It didn't feel like that to me.

'Can't you remember anything?'

I shook my head.

'It might come back to you.'

I hoped it wouldn't. Who wants to remember how they became responsible for another's death?

I cried for Malcolm. And with anger and frustration at myself, too.

I didn't see my mother again until the day of my brother's funeral. Overwhelmed by her own grief, I don't think she could face me. Neither of us would be able to come to terms with Malcolm's loss and, while her pain was uppermost in my thoughts, I was glad I didn't have to face her. I had done a terrible thing, and I didn't want to face anyone, her least of all.

I lay curled up on my bed, wretched when I was awake, wishing I'd died instead of my brother.

Mercifully, I don't remember much of Malcolm's funeral. The painkillers did their job, disassociating me from what must surely have been the worst day of my life. I was in a wheelchair, being pushed by a private nurse, and I was mostly out of it.

But there is one memory that stands out. As we came out of the church to follow the hearse to the crematorium, my parents climbed into a huge Mercedes. As the nurse brought me to join them, my mother grabbed at the door and pulled it shut.

'Not with us,' she hissed.

I sat in the wheelchair, awkward and alone in the pouring rain, until a cousin beckoned the nurse to bring me to another car.

And so my mother's persecution of me began.

'How are you, Dad?'

Two weeks after the funeral, I was discharged from hospital. As there was no prospect of my coping on my own with all my injuries, it had been agreed that I would stay at my parents' house. I faced a barrage of therapy and rehab, not only for my leg, broken in four places, but for the substantial burns I'd suffered in the crash and for the PTSD that visited in the form of night terrors that I couldn't remember in the mornings. I'd had to learn to walk again with my leg in a brace and could still only manage a few steps on crutches, gritting my teeth against the pain.

My father came alone to pick me up and helped me into the car in morose silence. I tried to hug him, but he turned away, the rough fabric of his overcoat scratching my face. It was a coat I'd seen him wear a hundred times before, but the world had changed and now it was a barrier between us.

'How are you, Dad?'

He sighed. 'It's your mum I'm worried about.'

He didn't speak for the rest of the journey, and the well of anxiety centred in my stomach grew into a pit of darkness. Things only got worse when I limped into my parents' house, my own childhood home. My mother wasn't there to greet me, and my father hurried to take my case up to my old bedroom. Daunted by the prospect of climbing the steep staircase on my new crutches, I went into the living room.

It wasn't as I remembered it.

It had been turned it into a shrine for my brother. Where a mirror had always hung above the fireplace, there was now a blown-up portrait of Malcolm. His graduation photo. Clean-shaven with a fresh haircut and a mortarboard balanced on top, it wasn't my Malcolm. I'd always hated that photo of him. Underneath it, along the mantelpiece, were more pictures of him, lined up in silver frames. I recognised most of them. Malcolm playing football. Family holidays. Birthday parties. I looked around the room. Framed images of him crowded every flat surface. Familiar ornaments had disappeared. Bookshelves had been cleared. It was all just photos of Malcolm. My parents featured in some of them, along with various of his friends. But my absence from any of them was conspicuous and, I could only conclude, intentional.

I heard the front door open and close, then my mother came into the room. She was still dressed in black.

'You've arrived.' There was no warmth in her voice. Malcolm had always been her favourite, but now it seemed that she'd severed any emotional connection she felt towards me. I was her daughter, vulnerable and injured, physically and mentally scarred, but she had no compassion for what I'd been through.

'Yes,' I said.

She glanced around the room. 'How do you like it?'

True to her word, she wasn't going to let me forget for a moment. As if I could anyway. I knew what I'd done and there wasn't a waking moment that I wasn't agonising over it and wishing I could turn back the clock. I truly regretted the pain I'd caused her, but I was helpless in trying to assuage it.

I tackled the stairs and took refuge in my bedroom. Did she think I didn't hurt too? Did she think I didn't care about what had happened to my beloved brother? Hot, salty tears stung my eyes and the fresh burn scars, livid welts on the right-hand side of my face.

However, the mute condemnation by my father was perhaps even more devastating. He never spoke up on my behalf as, day after day, my mother tortured me in myriad ways. He was a silent and part-time presence in the house, putting in as many hours as he could at work to avoid the sepulchre his family home had become. When he was present, he was a brooding counterweight to the sharp, noisy snipping of my mother's tongue. His pale grey eyes followed me around the room, rheumy with sorrow, and whenever our eyes met, I wanted to cry.

I stayed mainly in my bedroom, apart from when my father drove me in pained silence to one therapy appointment or another. I saw no one. I ignored emails and voicemails, WhatsApp messages and every other attempt friends made to communicate with me. I did my prescribed exercises, which made my eyes water, took my painkillers, and lost myself in a world of books, avoiding my parents at every opportunity. Seeing their continuing pain was a weight too heavy for me to bear.

I ate alone in my room, solitary confinement far preferable to hearing my mother dredging through her memories of 'her darling boy'.

Malcolm and I had been twins. We shared everything – our birthday, of course, but we were also incredibly physically similar. Same hair colour, same eye colour, same bone structure. But on me, the contours of his boyishly handsome face looked anything but beautiful. My jaw was too square, my nose too prominent, my eyebrows too heavy. He was tall and athletic. On me, that same build was tall and gangly, with nary a curve and no feminine softness.

My mother had been enchanted by him. He had an easy smile and had been an easy child to raise. He loved his food, he laughed a lot, he made friends easily. In character, I was almost his opposite, the dark reflection of his lightness of being. As a toddler, I grizzled endlessly. I was a picky eater. I whined. I pushed other children away and was acutely jealous of Malcolm's easy friendships. I can't blame my mother for loving Malcolm more than she loved me, but I can blame her for showing it.

One afternoon she caught me in Malcolm's room. I was lying on his bed, sobbing uncontrollably. I thought she was out, and I must have missed her return.

She slapped me, and from that day on, the door to Malcolm's bedroom was kept locked. It was declared out of bounds to me, though my mother went in there often enough. Lying on my own bed, I would hear her prowling in there and my stomach would churn.

I missed my brother so much. He was my protector. He could deflect my mother's anger in a moment and make her forget whatever she was berating me for. When he was around, she became a better person – she could be kind, even though

I believed it was only to make Malcolm think well of her. He should have gone away to uni, but he chose a college on our doorstep so that he could stay home for me. Bright, beautiful Malcolm. My twin and my guardian angel. And now he was gone.

During the day, I could still hear his laughter ringing through the house whenever my parents were out. I would open doors and peer around corners, hoping to catch a fleeting glimpse of him. And during the night, I heard his panicked shriek when we realised the car was going over the edge of the embankment. Down and down we tumbled, and by the time we reached the bottom he was dead.

2

The longer I stayed in my childhood home recuperating, the more childlike and dependent I became. I made no decisions. As my body slowly healed, my mind stagnated. My confidence circled the plughole and drained away. The job that I had loved before the accident became a something to be feared. No one suggested I was ready to go back to work, and I pushed every thought of a return out of my mind.

Then, eight weeks into my convalescence, I had a visitor.

It was about six in the evening. I was lying on my bed reading when the doorbell rang. I left it for my father to answer, assuming it was some delivery or other, medication for me or something black for my mother to wear. But then I heard my father coming up the stairs. He knocked on my door and stuck his head into the room.

'There's someone here for you. From your work.'

I knew straightaway it would be Marisa. I felt bad for not answering her calls and messages. As well as being my boss, she was my friend and mentor and, as head librarian of the town's three libraries, she'd recently promoted me to be her deputy.

Inside, I panicked. 'I'll come down,' I said.

I took a quick look in the mirror, which was something I'd avoided since coming home from the hospital. Malcolm's pale blue eyes looked back at me, but the rest was a shitshow. My brown, shoulder-length hair was greasy and unbrushed, and my skin looked so pallid it was almost grey. That, however, paled to insignificance as I contemplated the raw, red scar that covered the outer edge of my right cheek and jaw. How could I face Marisa looking like this? The woman at the burns centre had promised to teach me how to camouflage it, but it was still too fresh to plaster with makeup. I was wearing an ancient, baggy tracksuit, split up one leg to accommodate the leg brace I was still wearing during the day. I looked a mess, but Marisa would have to take me as I was.

My hand shook as I turned the door handle to go into the living room.

'Anne!' Marisa swept me into a hug, while being careful of my crutches and my injured leg. 'Oh, it's so good to see you.'

I found myself crying, and I didn't want to let go and step back from her, as then she'd see the full extent of the scarring on my face, and how unsteady I was on my feet.

'I'm sorry I haven't been in touch,' I said. 'It's been … difficult.'

She didn't say anything about my ruined looks, but I saw her take it in as we sat down at opposite ends of the sofa. She rummaged in her bag and placed a box of chocolates on the coffee table.

'Thank you.'

There was an awkward silence as she looked around at all the pictures of Malcolm. My mother had added black ribbon bows to several of the frames, lest I forgot we were in mourning.

Marisa shook her head. *What the hell's all this?* she mouthed at me silently.

My mother, I mouthed back.

'Jesus,' she whispered. 'This is so unhealthy. You have to look at this stuff every day?'

I didn't know how to answer her, so I just looked away.

'How's the rehab going?' she said at normal volume. 'You look way better than you did in the hospital.'

'You came to the hospital?'

'You were out of it.' She opened the box of chocolates and helped herself to one. 'Listen, Anne,' she said, chewing thoughtfully, 'I don't want to put any pressure on you, but have you thought about coming back to work? I had to give Linda the deputy position, though she's nowhere near as competent as you.'

I shook my head, then pointed to my cheek. 'I can't. People will stare and I'll frighten the kids. And besides, everybody knows I'm the woman who killed her brother. I can't face it.'

'Everyone knows it was a terrible accident. No one's blaming you.'

'Apart from my parents.'

She looked around the room again. 'I tell you, my love, you need to get away from here. This is just too grim.'

'My mother wants to make sure I don't forget what I did. I was driving. There was no other car involved. I killed him.'

I don't think Marisa knew how to answer my stark evaluation of the facts. She stood up to leave, waving me down as I struggled to get my crutches.

'There'll always be a job for you at the library,' she said. 'As soon as you're ready to come back, give me a ring.'

I shook my head.

'Then find something else,' she said. 'You're twenty-four and you've got your whole life ahead of you. You need to get the hell away from your mother.'

You need to get the hell away from your mother.

Marisa's words had made me tremble, and for several weeks I tried to push them out of my mind. But they'd taken up residence, because I knew she was right. My parents were suffering, and my mother's answer to this was to make me suffer too. I needed to start looking after myself. But where could I go and what could I do? Eventually, with no real hope, I started to look at the job ads in the local paper.

My mother watched and supressed a small, tight smile. 'It's not likely that anyone will want to employ you.' She tilted her head, arching the opposite brow at the scarred side of my face.

However, the idea persisted. I started sending off job applications. Most of them went unacknowledged. Sometimes I received a polite rejection. I persevered and finally I was invited to an interview. It was for a basic job as an admin assistant in a small firm of accountants. But as soon as I walked into the room, the look on the man's face told me I didn't stand a chance, and I couldn't apply for anything else for weeks after.

I almost didn't apply for the librarian's job at Winterbourne House, but by the time I saw the ad, I was desperate. Furthermore, the job seemed ideal as there would be no interaction with members of the public. It was to work in a private library cataloguing a collection, located on Craigsea Rock, which I discovered was a small island in the Irish Sea. Hundreds of miles away from my mother and her pictures of Malcolm.

I dropped the application into the postbox at the end of the road and waited.

Two days later the phone rang. I was alone in the house and I only just managed to reach it in time because I was a few feet away from it in the kitchen.

'Hello?'

'My name is Janice Allard. May I speak to Anne Adams?' It was a woman who spoke with the sort of clipped English accent that one used to hear in black and white films.

'I'm Anne Adams.'

'You applied for the post of Craigsea librarian.' It wasn't a question.

I took a deep breath, waiting for the apology – that they'd found someone else, that I wasn't quite suitable.

'When might you be able to start?'

'What? I mean, sorry. Could you repeat that?'

'I asked, when might you be able to start?'

'You're giving me the job?'

The woman sighed. 'I asked when you could start. If your answer is satisfactory, we'll move to the next question.'

My head spun. I hadn't really thought about the practicalities. 'Right away. I mean, I'll have to travel to Craigsea . . . and pack . . .'

'You understand that Craigsea Rock is a remote island? Can you work on your own?'

'It's exactly what I'm looking for.'

I told my parents that evening, packed a suitcase and left the next day.

3

THE TRAIN STOPPED UNEXPECTEDLY AND I opened my eyes. We were in a station. I scanned the platform for the place name. Craigross.

Oh, shit!

I pushed myself to my feet, grabbed my jacket, fumbled for my stick and my case and lunged through the carriage towards the door.

Wait, please wait.

If I missed my stop, God knows where I'd end up and when I'd be able to get a train back again.

I pressed the button to open the door, thrust my case out and clambered clumsily from the step onto the platform. I nearly lost my balance and a stab of pain shot from my knee to my hip as I placed weight on my bad leg. I wasn't yet adept at walking with just a stick, rather than crutches and a leg brace. I bit my lip and waited for the pain to subside. The door slid shut behind me and the train pulled away, but at least I'd made it off.

I looked around. I was the only person who'd got out of the train at Craigross. There were three other people in my carriage, and the other ones were just as empty, so perhaps I shouldn't have been surprised. The small branch line served a string of villages along the coast, with just two trains a day in either direction.

The platform offered scant protection from the elements, and a keen wind whipped rain across my face and the scent of the sea into my nostrils. I was glad I wasn't waiting to catch one of the infrequent trains that stopped here as there didn't seem to be a waiting room – or even a bench. It was mid-afternoon, but the light was dulled by a blanket of low, dark clouds. The panic to get off the train had left me momentarily short of breath, so I leant on my stick, looking around for the station exit.

There was just a gap in the fence at the rear of the platform. There didn't even seem to be a ticket office and as I passed through the exit onto the pavement, I saw a sign saying that train tickets could be purchased at the post office. I really had reached the back of beyond.

I'd spoken briefly on the phone with a woman called Janice Allard. It had barely been an interview, but it seemed to satisfy her that I would be right for the job. The instructions I'd received said to go down to the harbour when I arrived in Craigross. At least it wasn't hard to work out which way to go. The station stood at the top of the village. In one direction, the road swept uphill and away from the sea into a landscape of neat hedgerows and rolling fields. I turned the other way and found myself going down a steep hill between two rows of whitewashed cottages. Over their slate-tiled roofs, I could see the flat grey surface of the sea, speckled with white caps, stretching away until it melded with the grim black clouds in the distance. The flat line of the horizon was broken by a low, black island. This was my first view of Craigsea Rock. A smudge of rain connected it to the clouds above, and I shivered, pulling my coat tighter. It was cold here, a stark contrast to the late summer warmth

I left behind. My clothes were light, though thankfully I had more substantial gear in my suitcase.

There wasn't another soul in sight as I limped down the hill. The only noise was the screeching of a multitude of seabirds, wheeling bad-temperedly above me. The sound of my suitcase wheels trundling along the rough pavement drowned them out, and as I passed the first cottage, I saw a lace curtain twitch.

The arrival of a stranger. No doubt word would spread across the village like creeping mist, and even here I would find myself an object of curiosity. But at least nobody in Craigross knew about the crash or Malcolm's death.

At the bottom of the hill there was a junction with the village main street, which curved around a small stone harbour. On one corner stood the post office and village shop, purveyor of stamps, railway tickets and comestibles. There was a pub which was just a cottage, with the words 'Craigross Arms' painted in black above its front door. This was closed. A café advertising internet services stood next to a gift shop with a window packed with porcelain puffins and a bucket full of neon-bright rock-pooling nets propping open the door. A road led away from the harbour at the other end, and further along it I could see a squat red sandstone church brooding over a tiny graveyard. Beyond that, a sign announced the community hall and library, which seemed to be formed out of Portakabins.

But my instructions directed me to the harbour, where I was to look for a RIB and a man called Robert Cooper, who would take me across the ten miles of water that separated Craigsea Rock from the mainland.

All I could see was a storm-battered fishing boat. Three men in grubby oilskins were unloading crates, driving the gulls mad. Every few seconds one of them would swoop down to steal from the crates, and the men would wave their arms at them and curse. I didn't know what a RIB looked like, but I assumed this wasn't it.

I wheeled my case across the street to the harbour's edge, where a set of steps were carved into the granite of the breakwater. At the bottom of these steps, I could now see a large, bright yellow dinghy with a powerful-looking outboard motor. I supposed this was the RIB. In the middle of the boat there was a control console with a wheel and various dials. A man was sitting on one of two seats behind it, studying his mobile.

I went to the top of the steps.

'Excuse me? Are you Robert Cooper?'

The man squinted up at me, raising a hand to his brow to push back a hank of wiry brown hair. 'That's right.' His dark eyes returned to the screen.

'I'm Anne Adams. You're to take me across to Craigsea Rock, I think?'

'That's right.' His voice was deep and gruff, with the hint of a West Country accent. I wondered what he was doing this far north. 'Get on board, then, an' we'll get going.'

I looked down at the stone steps. They were steep and narrow, and from about halfway down wet as well. The worn front edges of each step sloped and even though I was wearing trainers, I was afraid of slipping. There was a rusty chain attached to the harbour wall, but I knew I would struggle with my case and my stick.

'Please, could you help me?'

Robert Cooper's raw-boned features looked up at me again, taking in my stick for the first time. 'Drop your case down.'

My horror at this suggestion must have showed on my face, and he gave a deep-throated laugh.

'Don't worry. I'll catch it.' He stood and moved across to the harbour side of the RIB, making it rock violently. The sound of the water slapping on the inflatable sides didn't inspire confidence and my mother's words sounded in my head. *Are you capable of such an arduous journey?*

I heaved the case over the side of the harbour with determination, then dropped it as its weight threatened to topple me over the edge.

Cooper reached up his long arms, caught it with a grunt and staggered back, falling to a sitting position on the side of the RIB. The boat tilted and a wash of seawater came in over the edge.

'Cripes, girl. You brought the kitchen sink?'

I didn't know how to respond, so I bent for my stick which had fallen to the ground. Slowly I made my way down the steps, one at time, leading with my good leg and clutching the rusty chain which served as a handrail as if my life depended upon it. My progress was slow, but it gave Cooper time to push the case into position behind the two seats and secure it with a fraying bungy cord. As I watched him, I noticed a couple of plastic crates at the back of the boat containing shopping bags and cardboard boxes. One of the crates had 'Winterbourne' scrawled on the side in black marker. The supplies for the island. I wondered how often he made the journey back and forth.

When I reached the bottom step above the water, Cooper came across and offered me a hand – large and bony, with chapped, red skin and knobbled joints. The hand of an outdoorsman. It was only at this point I realised what a giant he was. He towered above me, even though standing on the step I was several inches above the base of the RIB. The rough hand enveloped mine and I lunged forward to step onto the inflated edge of the vessel. The propulsion required to cover the gap between the bottom step and the boat kept me moving, and I landed on my bad leg in the bottom of the boat. Cooper kept hold of my hand to save me from falling, only letting go when I grabbed the back of the nearest seat with my other hand to steady myself.

'Thanks,' I said, manoeuvring myself into a sitting position.

He pulled the sleeves of his heavy fisherman's sweater down, but not before I noticed a bold tattoo, just above his left wrist. It was a small black circle, with eight arrows emerging from it in the directions of the compass. Something to do with navigation, I supposed. He glanced up at the sky. 'Best be heading off now. Tide'll be turning. There's a life jacket under the seat. Put it on.' He spoke nonchalantly enough, but his request made me wonder if he was sensing trouble ahead.

'Is that necessary?' I asked. 'I'm a good swimmer.'

He shrugged. 'Please yourself, but it'll likely be right choppy once we're out the harbour.' He fell silent, concentrating on steering the boat towards the harbour entrance.

In the distance, the grey smudge of rain that I'd seen hanging over the island had become darker, making me wonder if we were in for a squall. I felt underneath the seat and found the life jacket. If anything, it might act as a windbreaker.

'What's wrong with your leg?'

'An accident.'

'And that scar on your face?' He was nothing if not direct.

'The same.' I needed to change the subject. 'How long will it take to get across?'

'Half an hour, give or take.'

'Depending on what?'

He squinted at the horizon. 'We have different weather on the rock.'

I could feel the run of the outgoing tide underneath us as Cooper steered us out of the protective circle of the harbour wall. The wind was instantly stronger and, perhaps because of this, it felt colder than it had on the land. It was also noisier, so I couldn't question him further.

As we cleared the breakwater, the sea became choppy and I gripped the edge of my seat as the RIB slapped harder and harder against oncoming waves. A sudden swell lifted us, then just as quickly we plunged down and my stomach flipped. Cooper revved the engine and as we went faster, we smacked ever harder against the upcoming waves. The tiny Perspex windshield in front of the steering wheel offered no shelter to either of us from the continual splashes of freezing seawater. The saltwater stung my eyes, temporarily blinding me, and the wind whipped strands of wet hair across my face like razor wire. I'd had little experience on the open sea, just a Channel crossing once on a huge ferry. I hadn't realised how different it would be to ride on a small, fast boat across choppy water. Within a couple of minutes, I started to feel sick.

Concentrate on the horizon.

That was the advice for seasickness, wasn't it? I stared forward at Craigsea Rock, still a flat, black lozenge in the distance. It never got any closer. Biting the inside of my cheek, I breathed slowly, hoping that might quell my growing nausea. I glanced across at Cooper. Wet hair plastered his forehead and water ran down his face. But he was smiling.

I wondered who he was. Did he live on Craigsea? Was he the owner of the library? Or did he just deliver the weekly supplies and then return to the mainland? He'd said and done nothing to suggest he was my employer, so I surmised he was either a fellow employee or simply a delivery man. It made me realise how little I knew of where I was going, or the work I was about to embark upon. But at least it took my mind off the wretchedness of the crossing, if only for a couple of minutes.

'Do you live on the island?' I asked.

He turned his head towards me and I heard him shout something above the din, but the wind swiped his words away. I asked him again, but he was facing forwards once more. As I opened my mouth to question him, a blast of seawater hit me in the face. A rush of brine made it to the back of my mouth, forcing me to swallow. I choked and spluttered, raising a hand to my mouth. There was nothing for it. I lunged for the side of the RIB, and crouching low, clutching at the lifeline that ran the length of its side, I vomited over the edge and into the water.

I thought I heard Cooper laughing into the wind, though I hoped I was mistaken. For the remainder of the journey, I crouched low in the bottom of the RIB, mortified by what had happened, ashamed of my own frailty.

When I was finally able to look up again, Craigsea Rock loomed large above us. We were nearly at the island. Gradually the wind dropped as we came into the lee of the land. The waves calmed and a heavy rain rinsed the salt from my hair and face. Gingerly, I clambered to my feet and went back to my seat.

'All right, girl?' said Cooper.

'I'm sorry,' I said. My face became hot with a blush, but Cooper wasn't looking at me.

'You're not the first and you won't be the last.' He grinned. 'Mebbe you'll even get used to it, if you stay with us long enough.'

I'd have to go through this every time I wanted to visit the village shop or go back to the mainland for any other reason? My stomach cramped at the thought. I couldn't see myself repeating this journey unless I absolutely had to, and I couldn't imagine I would ever get used to it enough to feel relaxed about it. I'd dreamt of solitude, away from the prying eyes of strangers. On Craigsea Rock, it looked as if my wish might be granted.

We were skirting south along the coast of the island, in the shelter of which the sea was less choppy. I started to feel better, and I looked across at the land with interest. The shore was mostly low, craggy cliffs, which were alive and humming with a multitude of seabirds. We passed a bay with a sweeping curve of golden sand, which I made up my mind to visit at the first opportunity. At the top of the cliffs, the land sloped upwards towards the centre of the island. Parts of it were cloaked in bracken, but most of it was covered with short, mossy grass that from this distance looked like undulating green velvet. No wonder, if it rained like this most of the time. There were barely any trees and no signs of human habitation, though I was craning my neck for a first glimpse of Winterbourne House. It would be my home for the next few months and I was filled with curiosity, enough so to make me forget my embarrassment.

'Where's the house?'

'Winterbourne?' Cooper raised an arm and pointed vaguely in the direction in which we were travelling. 'On the other side. You won't see it till we've landed and walked up the lane.'

Seeing the island was enough. Despite the dark curtain of rain, my heart soared. My mother and her guilt trip couldn't reach me here.

As we rounded a small headland, a natural harbour between two outcrops of cliffs came into view. There was a low stone jetty built out to provide a breakwater on one side, and beyond it a small hamlet of three squat cottages built of granite with slate-tiled roofs. A quad bike, with a small trailer hooked on behind, was parked on a patch of hardstanding in front of the cottages. Beyond them, before the land sloped up towards the centre of the island, there was a walled vegetable garden with rows of beds and fruit trees trained on the walls. A few other trees stood outside the tended area. They were the first I'd seen on Craigsea. Perhaps the rest of the island was too windswept for any saplings to establish themselves, but this little area was well sheltered and south facing, and as Cooper steered the RIB alongside a small stone jetty, I couldn't wait to take my first step on Craigsea Rock.

A strangled grunting sound close by made me look round quickly, thinking Cooper was choking on something. But it wasn't him. A large black bird was perched on the stone cairn at the tip of the jetty. As I watched, it unfurled its gleaming wings to a span of several feet and stretched its long, reptilian neck, grunting again from deep within its throat. I couldn't tell if it was aggression or supplication. It fixed me with a malevolent glare from one of its sharp turquoise eyes.

I shivered, the bright excitement of a moment ago extinguished.

But Cooper grinned up at it and then made the exact same noise in reply.

4

The creature watched us as Robert Cooper tied up the RIB.

I pointed at it. 'What bird is that?'

Cooper glanced up, a sly grin on his face. 'Cormorant.'

The bird seemed to sense it was being talked about. It flapped its wings and let rip a stream of guttural knocking sounds.

Cooper ignored it this time, and helped me onto the steel ladder attached to the wall of the jetty. It was awkward to climb with my stick hooked over the crook of my elbow, and my backpack seemed heavier than when I'd packed it, but I managed. As my feet clattered on the metal rungs, I heard a dog barking somewhere close by, a deep, gruff roar. Then, as my head crested the jetty wall, I saw it. A huge, shaggy brown dog was hurtling down the harbour wall towards me. Its fur was muddy and bedraggled, but it didn't disguise the powerful chest and long, strong legs. It barked as it ran, and I could see flashes of sharp white teeth in its red maw.

I think I must have gasped. For a moment, my grip on the ladder slipped before I grabbed hold tighter with another sharp intake of breath.

'Loki, sit!' Below me, Cooper bellowed at the hound. 'Sit!'

The dog stopped in its tracks, then sat. Slavering and panting, it stared at me, dark marble eyes under a wet fringe. Its chest heaved as it panted noisily.

As I restarted my climb, it barked again.

'Don't mind Loki. He don't see many strangers, so the sight of you has him excited.'

Even though the dog had obeyed his master immediately, I was shaken as I clambered onto the top of the breakwater. Loki was still giving me the evil eye, and I'd been nervous of dogs since the accident, scared that they'd jump up and topple me over on my unsteady leg.

Behind me, the cormorant let out a last raucous grunt and flew away, and for reasons unknown I felt relieved at this. I stood for a moment looking around, leaning on my stick for stability. The clouds were lower and heavier than they had been, and though it was still a couple of hours from dusk, it felt as if the evening was drawing in. I was thankful for the low cliffs on either side, sheltering us from the wind. I waited nervously for Cooper to come up. Only he could put an end to my standoff with Loki. He was unfastening my case from behind the seats. Then he hauled it up the ladder, holding on with one hand, the case hanging from the other. He grunted noisily as he heaved it over the edge of the jetty. Loki growled and stood up.

'Sit!'

The dog ignored him and, emboldened, came forward to sniff at my case.

'Loki!' Cooper's voice was low growl, and the dog growled in reply. So much for it being obedient.

'Bend down and hold out your hand,' he said. 'Let him get to know you. He don't bite.'

I didn't trust Cooper or the dog, but I squatted down.

'Loki? Here, boy.'

Cooper disappeared back down the ladder. The crates of supplies were still to be brought up.

Loki studied me. He was close enough for me to smell the rank odour of his matted fur and the stench of his dog breath. I'd never been good with animals, and I didn't find him adorable. I didn't really want to be his friend. He came closer still, sniffing the air to pick up my scent.

'Good boy.' My voice sounded nervous, but I knew I shouldn't show any fear.

Loki let out a low rumble. Then he sniffed my trembling hand. I flexed my fingers to scratch him under his chin. The fur was wet and greasy, but he raised his head for more. His tail started to wag and, unexpectedly, he flopped over and showed me his belly.

'There now,' came Cooper's voice as he reappeared balancing one of the plastic crates in the crook of his elbow. 'At least you've got one friend on the island.'

I straightened up, pondering this statement. So Cooper didn't consider himself my friend? But I didn't think on it for long, as another cry came to us from the far end of the jetty.

'Robert Cooper, get that bloody dog in its kennel.'

A middle-aged woman in jeans and a fleece was hurrying along the harbour wall towards us. She wasn't tall, but she looked strong and capable.

I heard Cooper curse under his breath as he struggled up the ladder with the second crate.

'Loki, bed!'

The woman said it first, and Loki ignored her, looking up at me pleadingly, still hoping for a belly rub.

Cooper repeated the command, and Loki begrudgingly rolled onto his front, then stood up. He growled at Cooper, and as the woman reached us, he set off at a trot along the jetty, back towards the land. The woman stroked his back as they passed each other and Loki tossed his head, snapping at her hand.

As she reached me, I heard her muttering under her breath. 'Damn dog.' She had a gaunt face, with cheeks almost as ruddy as her husband's. Her iron-grey hair sported a mannish cut, and there was no trace of makeup around her eyes or on her lips. There was a drip at the end of her nose, which she self-consciously wiped away with her wrist.

'I'm Anne Adams,' I said.

'I know who you are. We don't get unexpected visitors out here.' She remembered to smile a couple of seconds after she finished talking, then stood watching as Cooper shoved the second crate onto the jetty.

'Sorry . . .' I said. I felt stupid. 'I don't know who you are.'

She turned back to me, rolling her eyes. 'I'm Mrs Cooper. There's only me and Robert Cooper here on Craigsea, so I thought you'd know who I was.'

'I didn't know that,' I said.

She picked up one of the crates and set off along the jetty. 'Come on, let's get you out of this rain.'

As we got closer to the cottages, it became evident that only one of them was lived in, and this was the one she led me to. The other two were run-down, with cracked windows and woodwork in need of painting, but the exterior of the Coopers' cottage was spruce and tidy, with potted plants on the step and a windchime hanging by the front door.

Inside, there was nothing new or interesting about the house. The front door opened directly into a tiny living room, and an archway without a door led to the kitchen beyond. It was clean, but the furniture was dated and the wallpaper faded. I looked around. There was no evidence of Loki, so I guessed his kennel was somewhere outside the house. This seemed just as well. The living space was cramped as it was, with no room for a large, dirty animal.

'Would you mind taking your shoes off?' said Mrs Cooper.

'Of course,' I said. I tucked my case up against the wall and complied with her request. Meanwhile, Mrs Cooper filled a kettle at the kitchen sink. 'Is this where I'll be staying?' I asked. The other two cottages certainly didn't look habitable.

'Lord, no. There are only two bedrooms in here. One's mine and one's his. And you don't want to be sharing a bedroom with Robert Cooper, believe me.' She laughed.

I didn't.

'So where will I be staying?'

'Up at the big house. Winterbourne. That's where you'll be working, in his library.'

Who was the he she referred to? The owner of the library, presumably the owner of Winterbourne House. I had so many questions, but Mrs Cooper seemed to expect me to already know all of it. I had set out on this adventure without doing my due diligence. I hadn't asked Janice Allard the right questions, or in fact any questions on that very short call. It had hardly qualified as an interview, just some minor fact gathering on her side. And it made me suddenly wonder why I had been offered the job. But I'd been so desperate to escape my mother, I hadn't given it a second thought.

It wasn't until I took the first mouthful of sweet, milky tea Mrs Cooper brought me that I realised how long it was since I'd last eaten. I was famished. She had me sit down at the kitchen table, then offered me slices of a fruit loaf spread thickly with yellow butter.

'We'll let Robert Cooper take the supplies and your suitcase up to the house, then I'll walk you up the track and you can get settled in.' She was sitting opposite me, nursing a mug of tea, though she didn't have anything to eat.

'Is there a lot of work to be done?' I said, between mouthfuls.

'In the library? Don't ask me. I keep house for Mr Broussard, but I don't know anything about his work or his books.'

'Mr Broussard? Is he the owner of Winterbourne House?' I vaguely remembered Janice Allard referring to someone of that name.

She nodded. 'It's been in the Broussard family since it was first built. About a hundred and fifty years, or thereabouts.' She cut me another slice from the loaf. 'The first Lucien Broussard bought the island in the eighteenth century, using some of the fortune he made in spice shipping, but it wasn't till years later that his grandson, another Lucien, actually built the house.'

'Will I meet Mr Broussard this evening?'

'No, he don't live here. He visits a couple of times a year, usually with a new consignment of books for the library. We don't see much of him.'

'Where does he spend the rest of the time?'

This was apparently a question far enough. Mrs Cooper frowned and abruptly cleared the mugs and my plate. She placed them in the sink. There was no dishwasher here. Modern technology appeared to have bypassed the Coopers' cottage. I wondered what things would be like in Winterbourne House.

'So it'll just be me in Winterbourne House?'

'You're a big girl. You don't need me staying up there with you, and you certainly don't want Robert Cooper up there with you of a night.' She laughed, but it sounded bitter.

This unsettled me. It was the second time she'd made a disparaging remark about her husband.

She must have seen the concern in my face. 'Don't worry. There ain't no ghosts up there.'

There was a clatter at the front door and Cooper appeared. He had one of the plastic crates that he'd brought up from the RIB.

'Here's our stuff, Mrs,' he said, bringing it into the kitchen and putting it down on the table. Rainwater pooled where he set it down.

'Shoes, Robert Cooper.'

'I'm going straight out again.' They were tetchy with each other. Hardly surprising if it was just the two of them on this island for months at a time.

Mrs Cooper frowned, but then just as quickly smiled. 'Ever seen a ghost, Bob? Up at the house?'

'Stuff and nonsense,' he said. He didn't smile. 'Don't you let her go filling your head with rubbish like that, Anne.'

'I don't believe in ghosts,' I said.

Mrs Cooper rolled her eyes. 'You gonna get that case up the lane?'

'I told you I was going out again.' He glanced back through to the living room and spotted my case standing close to the front door. 'The yellow bedroom?'

'Of course,' said Mrs Cooper. 'Where else?' I didn't miss the warning look she gave him as she said this.

Cooper disappeared and moments later I heard an engine starting. The quad bike, I assumed, with my suitcase in the trailer.

I helped Mrs Cooper with the washing up, scant as it was.

'I'll take you up to the house now,' she said, taking the tea towel from my hands and hanging it across the rail on the front of her range.

She'd put my wet jacket on a hanger above it, but it was still sopping.

'Wait a moment,' she said. 'You can borrow one of Robert Cooper's waterproofs.'

She opened the kitchen door and went out into a small storm porch, where a row of jackets hung on wooden hooks. The rain had become, if anything, worse while we'd been in the cottage. The wind was flinging it hard against the windows, as if throwing pebbles to attract our attention. It moaned and screeched around the corners of the cottages and, beyond, the dull roar of the sea added its own bleak chorus.

The coat Mrs Cooper handed me was like the yellow oilskins I'd seen the fishermen wearing at Craigross harbour. It smelt of sweat and earth, and the rubberised fabric was cracked in some places and scuffed in others. The bright yellow was faded by grime and oil stains.

'It's his old one,' said Mrs Cooper by way of explanation as I looked at it.

It was much too big, swamping me as I did up my shoes. My backpack felt damp to the touch, and I hoped my laptop hadn't suffered. When Mrs Cooper was ready, she picked up a torch from a small table near the front door and led me out of the cottage.

Outside, a blast of rain whipped my hair across my face. Though barely dusk, it was as good as dark already, thanks to the cloud cover. Mrs Cooper snapped on her torch and shone it on the ground in front of us as we started across the hardstanding side by side. The oilskin had a hood which I quickly pulled up, though it flopped forward so far over my forehead I could barely see where I was going. Not that it mattered. I just had to follow the beam of light at my feet.

We set off along a narrow, tarmacked track that wound its way up the bluff behind the cottages. Mrs Cooper was clearly used to the climb. She strode out and before long a gap had opened between us. I was having to use my stick to push up with each step as my injured leg simply didn't have the strength to raise my body weight up the hill. It took a while for her to realise that I was falling behind, or at least to show that she realised it.

I immediately flagged that thought as uncharitable. She had welcomed me into her home and given me refreshments, and now she was taking me up to Winterbourne House. Even so, there was something about her that put me on edge. I wasn't sure I could warm to her, and this was a worry if I was to spend months on the island with only her and Robert Cooper for company. I needed to get on with them.

She waited for me at the top, and I stopped alongside her for a few seconds to catch my breath after the climb. I looked around. The sky was a sludgy grey and the landscape was virtually the same. The top of the island stretched away from us to the north. There was a steep hill in the distance, to one side, and various stone walls, but I could see no sign of human habitation.

'How far is it?' I said.

"Bout a mile or more, beyond Beacon Hill there.'

More than a mile in this weather? I was already exhausted from travelling all day. My spirits fell and my body slumped as I leant harder on my stick.

'You'll be all right?' said Mrs Cooper, as if she'd only just noticed I needed a stick to walk with.

'I'll be fine.' It came out sounding sharper than I intended.

We set off again, driving into an ever-stronger wind, the rain lashing against us. The going was either flat or sloping gently upwards. Never downhill. Below the hem of the oilskin, my jeans were soaked through, and my feet squelched in wet socks. My bad leg complained bitterly, and I knew I would pay for it in pain for days to come. We didn't talk. We would have had to shout to hear each other over the gale, and the exertion was stealing me of breath as it was. But Mrs Cooper slowed her pace to match mine, making sure that I could at least see the rutted surface of the track stretching out ahead of us.

After about half an hour, I spotted a light coming towards us in the distance. I paused for a moment.

'It's Robert Cooper coming back,' said Mrs Cooper.

I wondered why she always used his full name. People who live in isolation become idiosyncratic, I supposed.

'I said to him we should have got a golf buggy with two seats, but he wasn't having any of it. The quad bike can go over rough land and that's what he needs it for most of the time.'

I supposed visitors weren't high on his list of priorities.

Eventually we could hear the engine over the wind, and then he was upon us.

'He could take you the rest of the way in the trailer.'

'It's fine. I'm fine. I assume we're almost there?'

'Surely.'

Then I would carry on walking. I didn't need to suffer the final indignity of being towed to my new home in a baggage cart.

They exchanged a few words, and we carried on walking.

But it seemed like forever until we rounded the base of Beacon Hill and the lights of Winterbourne House finally came into view.

5

Winterbourne House stood before us, a black silhouette against a slate sky. Even from several hundred metres, it seemed vast. Outlined against the sky I could see gables, chimneys, parapets and a crenellated tower. Dark windows glinted across the sweeping walls. A few were lit, but I could make no sense of how many floors there were. It seemed as if different wings were on different levels. In the centre of the side we were approaching, there was a huge archway. A small light shone beyond the arch, but the shadows were too long and too deep for me to see much.

As with the cottages, trees had been planted around the house, but up here at the top of the island, they were stunted and bent one direction from bearing the brunt of the wind. The ground around them was strewn with boulders and shrubs and I could see paths leading off in different directions, though there was no formal garden.

I stopped, and leant on my stick, drinking in the details. This was to be my home for the next few months and I felt immediately overwhelmed. I'd never set foot in a private house this big. It was as large as my old school or the rehab centre where I'd learnt to walk again after the accident. I couldn't fathom how one family could need so much space.

'Just wait till you see it when the sun's shining,' said Mrs Cooper, turning back to me once she'd realised I'd stopped. 'But I'll skin that bloody man for leaving all those lights on. Some days I think Robert Cooper doesn't have a brain in his head.'

Secretly, I was pleased he had. It would have looked less welcoming, positively austere, had it not been for the golden squares and rectangles of the lit windows.

We set off again and, ten minutes later, I found myself following the beam of Mrs Cooper's torch through the great stone arch. It led into an internal courtyard, surrounded on three sides by wings of the house, with another similar archway leading out on the opposite side. The light I'd seen in the distance came from a small brass lantern hanging above a large oak door.

'This is the kitchen entrance,' said Mrs Cooper, 'and it's the one we use every day.'

We went inside, then through another, smaller door and came into an expansive, old-fashioned kitchen where the warmth enveloped me like a welcoming hug. I dropped my stick and struggled out of the dripping oilskin. Mrs Cooper took it from me and hung it out in the small entrance foyer, taking off her own waterproof coat at the same time.

I looked around, feeling as if I'd quite literally stepped back in time. There was a range along one wall, about twice the size of the range at Mrs Cooper's cottage, with an open fireplace to one side above which hung the turning apparatus for a spit. The kitchen table was almost as big as a football pitch, and the blue plastic crate marked 'Winterbourne' stood on it, waiting to be unpacked. On the opposite side of the room to the range, a row of giant white Belfast sinks with wooden draining boards sat under a wide window overlooking the courtyard. Copper saucepans in every size and well-worn griddles hung from hooks on the walls, and glass-fronted cabinets were full to bursting with white china plates and cups, glassware, jugs, teapots and more.

Mrs Cooper straightaway put on an apron and started fiddling with the controls on the range. I wondered if I was supposed to be watching and learning, though she didn't explain what she was doing. I cleared my throat.

'Give me a moment,' she said, shooting me an annoyed glance over her shoulder. 'I'm setting this up to make sure you have hot water in the morning.'

'Thank you.'

She finished and turned around. 'This is how things work around here. When someone's staying at Winterbourne, you in this case, Robert Cooper and I come and take our meals up here, even though we stay down at the cottage. I do all the cooking and that leaves you to get on with whatever Mr Broussard has asked you to do.'

That was a relief. The sight of the range worried me. I wasn't an experienced cook and it looked somewhat challenging. I wondered if Mrs Cooper was a good cook. If the fruit bread I'd had earlier was homemade, then I suspected she was.

'I'll show you round quickly before I get on with tea. We eat here in the kitchen. If Mr Broussard comes to stay, he eats in the dining room. He'll let me know if he wants you to eat with him or not.'

It seemed that I wouldn't get a say in that. But I was more than a little interested to meet Winterbourne's owner and I hoped he'd put in appearance while I was here.

'How often does he visit?'

She shrugged. 'It varies, and he doesn't consult with me. I just hear it from Mrs Allard, a day or two before he arrives.' She took off her apron and folded it over the back of one of the chairs. 'This way.'

The house seemed even bigger on the inside than it was on the outside, if that was possible. We went along a corridor that obviously still counted as part of the servants' quarters. Like the kitchen, it had white tiled walls and terracotta tiles on the floor. Exposed pipework ran the length of the ceiling.

Mrs Cooper noticed me looking upwards. 'You might not believe it, but Winterbourne was one of the first houses in the country to have a centralised heating system and electric lights in all the rooms.'

'Doesn't look like it's been modernised since,' I said. This earnt me a look of reproval, but I hadn't seen a microwave or any other mod cons in the kitchen.

At the end of the corridor, she pushed open a heavy door and flicked a light switch. A vast dining room was flooded with light from a chandelier that made me think of the Christmas tree in Trafalgar Square. Everything about Winterbourne was on an unreal scale. The dining table could seat thirty when all its leaves were in, Mrs Cooper told me proudly. The inglenook fireplace was roomy enough to have cosy wooden settles on either side of the fire. Even the logs laid ready in the grate were size of tree trunks. At the centre of the limestone fire surround was a painted bas-relief coat of arms. It featured a shield surmounted by a knight's helmet and a blazing tower, surrounded by acanthus leaves. In the middle of the shield, which was divided into red and yellow quarters, sat a black scorpion, tail up and ready to strike.

'That's unusual,' I said, pointing at it.

'The Broussard family crest,' said Mrs Cooper. 'They originally hailed from somewhere in France, but they added the lighthouse at the top when they came here. There's a lighthouse at the far end of the island, though it's not in use anymore.'

There was so much to learn about my new home.

We passed through a series of rooms, identified by Mrs Cooper as the drawing room, the morning room, the Japanese room, the garden room, most impressively the ballroom, Mr Broussard's study and more. I wanted to linger in each one of them. The morning room was elegant and airy, with an ornate desk and pale blue satin drapes. The Japanese room lived up to its name with glass display cases of oriental objects, Edo-style prints on the walls and a magnificently ornate Chinese rug on the floor. The ballroom had a parquet floor, which must have been sprung – I felt as if I was bouncing as we walked over it. In the study, there were portraits of interesting-looking men on the walls, curios in cabinets, bookshelves and display cases, and in another room I spotted an instrument which I thought was a harpsichord, which definitely merited further investigation. I stopped to peer at a glass-fronted shelf that contained a collection of what looked like shrunken heads, but Mrs Cooper seemed to be on a mission to get round as quickly as possible. And I suppose that was fair enough. She must have seen all these rooms a thousand times before, and she needed to get on with cooking the evening meal. And I would have plenty of time to explore in the coming weeks.

'I'm a little worried I won't be able to find my way back to the kitchen,' I said, as we rattled from one end of the ballroom to the other. 'Perhaps I should have left a trail of breadcrumbs behind me.'

'Don't even joke about it,' she said, frowning. 'I'm in a forever war with the mice as it is. Bloody varmints.'

I hadn't quite believed her, until she pointed out a couple of mousetraps left in strategic positions near the skirting boards in one of the hallways.

We'd reached a grand wooden staircase that twisted up from the double-height entrance hall. The oak banisters were incredibly ornate and on the top of each newel post sat carved baboons holding tall beacon-shaped lamps. The walls around the staircase were wood-panelled and hung with yet more illustrious portraits.

'We didn't see the library,' I said, suddenly remembering my purpose in the house.

'It's on the first floor,' she replied. 'I'm taking you there now.'

We came to an imposing mahogany door and stopped. Mrs Cooper felt in her trouser pocket and pulled out a steel key ring, heavy with keys. She unclipped it and took one off, using it to open the door. Then she handed the key to me.

'Mr Broussard likes the library to be kept locked at all times, so here's your key.'

I stashed it in my own pocket.

'Why?' I asked.

'Lord knows,' she said with a shrug. 'It's not like Robert Cooper's going to sneak up here and snitch a book.'

We went in and she flicked on the lights.

I audibly gasped as I registered the size of Winterbourne's collection. Floor-to-ceiling shelves lined all the walls, and there were multiple alcoves along every wall, allowing further shelving. Miles of books, leather-and cloth-bound in red and green and blue and yellow and black, with black and gold and silver lettering on the spines. Bibles, encyclopaedias, atlases, histories, almanacks, compendiums, serials, novels, bound magazines ... My head spun as I took it all in. The room was located above the ballroom and was easily as large, if not larger.

'This is amazing,' I said, my eyes darting from shelf to shelf. I could have tarried in there for hours.

There was an old wooden plan chest under one of the windows. Lecterns with books open. Three large round tables, laden with newspapers and magazines, piles of books and ledgers, stood in a row down the centre of the room. A wooden cabinet contained handwritten index cards. And, of course, there was a fireplace, with a pair of comfortable armchairs on either side, where I could imagine sitting and reading for hour upon glorious hour.

This is where I'd be working, and my heart felt fit to burst.

'Come on, I'll show you your bedroom. Then I need to be getting on.' Mrs Cooper clearly wasn't a book lover.

As we came out of the library, she reminded me to lock the door. I slipped the key into my pocket, where I could feel its weight against my thigh, a secret passport to another world. The key to my happiness.

'Your room is on the second floor. Mr Broussard indicated that you should stay in the yellow bedroom.'

I wondered how many bedrooms there were, and if they were all colour-coded. I assumed Lucien Broussard stayed in the master bedroom when he came to the house.

We went up another ornate set of stairs, above which sat a series of bronzes portraying strapping young Greeks engaged in heroic endeavours. On the half-landing, there was a stained-glass window but, without daylight, I couldn't make out what was depicted. There was so much more to see over the coming days that I felt giddy.

The yellow bedroom was as different as it possibly could be from the childhood bedroom I'd just vacated. Mrs Cooper hurried across the room to close the curtains as I looked around. It was elegant and spacious, and there was no mistaking why it was called the yellow bedroom. The wallpaper was primrose and white regency stripes, with curtains to match, while the series of Persian rugs that covered the floor all had yellow as their dominant colour. The bed was a half tester, with a gold silk coverlet and yellow drapes hanging around the head. There was a pretty marble fireplace, by which sat a small, two-seater sofa, and under the broad row of windows was a chaise longue, both upholstered in mustard velvet.

I would feel like a princess in a room like this.

'Your case is in here,' said Mrs Cooper, pointing.

A small archway led through to a dressing room. A dressing room! With wardrobes and drawers, and a dressing table with an oval mirror. I didn't have enough stuff to fill a quarter of the storage space. Beyond it, there was a small bathroom with a rolltop bath, above which a modern rainfall shower had been installed.

'This is lovely,' I said.

Mrs Cooper smiled, finally pleased by my appreciation of something. 'Just wait till you see your view in the morning. The master bedroom might be bigger, and have two bathrooms, but I think this bedroom is the queen of the house.'

I hadn't seen any of the other bedrooms, but I suspected I would agree with her.

'Right, I'll leave you to settle in. Come down to the kitchen to eat at seven. It will usually be six, but I'm running a bit late today.'

The look she gave me told me this was my fault.

'I hope I don't get lost,' I said.

'You won't. Straight down these stairs, then you'll see the grand staircase to the hall. The dining room will be on your left and you can come through there to the kitchen. Or you can go the other way, down the servants' stairs.'

'Thank you,' I said.

'Welcome to Winterbourne,' she said, slipping from the room.

'Welcome to Winterbourne indeed,' I said out loud to myself, as her footsteps disappeared. It was a place for new beginnings.

Outside the wind had dropped and I heard a noise. The strangled grunt of a cormorant. I wondered if it was the one from the jetty.

6

MRS COOPER'S COOKING DIDN'T DISAPPOINT. Robert Cooper was already eating by the time I found my way back to the kitchen, stripping the meat from a lamb chop bone with his teeth and once done, helping himself to another from a platter in the centre of the table. There was creamy mashed potato, a rich gravy and a selection of crisp, fresh vegetables. The Coopers drank steaming mugs of tea with their supper. Mrs Cooper offered me a cup from a brown earthenware teapot, but I fetched a glass of water instead.

Neither of the Coopers spoke as they ate, so it fell to me to start the conversation.

'What sort of dog is Loki?'

'The bad sort,' said Mrs Cooper sourly.

'I mean, what breed?'

'Otterhound,' said Robert Cooper through a mouthful of broccoli.

'I've never heard of that,' I said.

'Supposed to be good for hunting in water,' said Mrs Cooper. 'So he's always wet and he always stinks.'

'Do you use him for hunting?' I fired this question at Robert Cooper. I wanted to know what wildlife there was on the island.

Robert Cooper carried on eating, having apparently run out of words.

'North of Winterbourne,' said Mrs Cooper, 'there's a wall, the Halfpoint Wall, that divides the island in two. You'll see it from the upstairs windows. Loki isn't allowed beyond the Halfpoint.'

'Why not?'

'That's where the deer are, and the sheep. He'll take one down if he escapes north of the wall, and then we have to butcher it, whether we need meat or not.'

Cooper woke up from his lamb fat-induced reverie. 'You keep those gates in the Halfpoint Wall shut if you go walking.'

'Of course,' I said. I didn't want to be held responsible for a massacre. 'Anything else I should be aware of?'

'You told her about our Jenny?'

'Good point,' said Mrs Cooper. She was clearing our plates. I got up to help her and she gave me an approving nod.

As I stacked them in the sink, she opened one of the range's large ovens. A cloud of apple-scented steam filled the kitchen.

'Eve's pudding,' she announced, carrying a white dish with a sponge topping across to the table. 'Your favourite, isn't it, Robert Cooper?'

Cooper grunted.

She dished out portions into bowls, then passed round a jug of thick yellow custard.

'Something about Jenny?' I prompted, once we were all eating.

'Oh, yes. Watch you don't burn your tongue on that apple. I honestly think I prefer it once it's cold.' She set down her spoon in her bowl. 'Winterbourne, and the rest of the island, gets its power from a generator, our genny. It runs on diesel, which has to be delivered from the mainland twice a year.'

A genny, not Jenny then. 'I see,' I said, though I wasn't quite sure why I needed to know this.

'We run it from six in the morning until midnight, but between twelve and six the following morning it's switched off.'

'There's no power in the night?'

'That's right. At midnight, the lights go out, and if you're still up and about, you'll need to have a torch with you. There's one in your bedroom.'

'Yes, I saw it.' I'd assumed it might be for the occasional power cut. Not for a nightly outage.

'There are lots in here,' she said, pointing at one of the cupboards, 'and plenty of spare batteries. And you'll usually be able to find one in most of the rooms.'

Great. Never more than three metres from a torch.

Robert Cooper let his spoon drop into his bowl with a clatter, pushed his chair out and disappeared through the door to the back porch.

'That's him gone.' She ate another spoonful, then fixed me with a serious gaze. 'I don't know if you're a night owl or not, but my suggestion to you would be to get to bed before midnight, and not go wandering about the house when the genny's off.'

'Any reason why?'

'I wouldn't want to come back here in the morning and find that you'd fallen down the stairs in the dark or summat.'

Why did she think I might fall down the stairs in the dark if there were torches everywhere? It struck me as a little odd.

'Just one more thing, before you go,' I said.

'Yes?'

'The internet password?' Books were much more my thing than computers, but I liked to catch up with the news every now and again, and check my emails.

'We don't have that here. Neither me nor Robert Cooper has a computer.'

'Please tell me I can get a mobile signal then?'

She shrugged as if she wasn't even sure what that was.

'So how do you communicate with Mr Broussard? How did you know I was arriving today?'

'Down in the cottage, we've got a satellite phone that he gave us. We can use it to call Mr Broussard or if there's an emergency. If you need to get in touch with someone urgently you could use it. If you want to go on a computer, you could go over to Craigross with Robert Cooper. There are PCs in the library, and one of them internet cafés.'

Wow. I really had landed in the back of beyond.

'How do you get the news?'

'Robert Cooper goes to the mainland once a week. He brings me back a newspaper.' She got up from the table and went towards the sink, where the supper dishes were still piled up.

I quickly stood up. 'I'll do the washing up. It's only fair, as you did the cooking.'

Mrs Cooper smiled at me with genuine warmth. It was the first time I'd seen her smile reach her eyes. 'Thank you, dear. I'll get going back to the cottage, then.'

I didn't envy her that long walk on her own in the dark.

I was alone in the house.

It was like being the only guest in a swanky hotel. Or maybe the only member of staff, I thought to myself, as I set about washing up the supper things. It took me a while to get it done. First off, I couldn't find a tea towel, and after that I had to work out where everything went. I wasn't entirely sure I'd got it right, but no doubt Mrs Cooper would inform me of any errors.

I explored some of the cupboards and shelves in the walk-in larder, searching for coffee. My last caffeine hit had been a distinctly underwhelming takeaway coffee I bought in hurry when I changed trains, and that already seemed a lifetime ago. I found a jar of instant, half full, and by the way the granules had coagulated and stuck together, it looked as if it had been opened and abandoned in the distant past. It wasn't even going to compete with the railway station coffee.

Perhaps I could ask Cooper to pick up some ground coffee and a French press when he next went over to Craigross. Although possibly that was expecting a bit much of the village shop.

I made my coffee and took it with me up to the library. I wanted to explore the collection and get a handle on what needed doing in terms of cataloguing. After the warmth of the kitchen, the rest of the house seemed cold. There was a slight smell of damp as I walked along the servants' passage, and I shivered as I climbed the grand staircase. I could feel a cold draught sliding down as I went up, coming from the windows on the upper landing. So much for the early adoption of central heating. But maybe I couldn't expect the whole house to be heated when there was only one person in it.

The library, by contrast, was almost as warm as the kitchen. This surprised me. All the walls were lined with shelves and there were no radiators. A potted plant stood in the fireplace instead of a grate. Damp books deteriorate quickly, and mildew is a serious issue in libraries, but the air in here was warm and dry and the distinctive smell that marks out badly managed libraries and second-hand bookshops was missing. I bent down and placed a hand flat on the carpet. It was warm to the touch. Underfloor heating. Broussard understood how to look after his books.

The card index I'd noticed earlier was an old-fashioned wooden cabinet with sixteen drawers, arranged four by four, and each drawer had a small brass frame nailed to the front, in which a label identified its contents with letters of the alphabet. The cabinet stood on a small stand to the left of the door, and nearby, jutting out into the room, there was an antique pedestal desk, complete with a brass banker's lamp and ink-stained blotter.

This would be my desk while I worked here.

I put my coffee cup down on the blotter. I didn't want to leave a heat ring on what might or might not have been a precious piece of furniture. Then I took a walk around the vast room, taking in how the books had been organised, which was something I'd been too giddy with excitement to notice before. I quickly concluded that there was very little organisation at all. There were some books shelved together as they should have been, including the entire works of Shakespeare, and several shelves away, all of Dickens' novels. But on the shelf above, I found a mixture of fiction and non-fiction, while the shelf below housed mainly art books, though there were other topics mixed in among them.

Sets such as encyclopaedias were shelved together, but there didn't appear to be any sort of cataloguing by subject or even author. I found James Joyce novels in at least four different bookcases.

My work was cut out for me. With my librarian's eye, I estimated that there must be at least fifty-thousand books in Winterbourne's library, maybe more. I went to the card index and opened one of the drawers at random. The cards were packed in so tight I couldn't flick through them. Instead, I had to force my thumb and forefinger down between them to grip a small selection and yank them out so there would be room to scroll through the rest.

I looked at the cards in my hand. I could tell from the grime and dog-ears along their top edges that they were old. They had been filled in by hand, the blue or black ink faded now, and I could distinguish the writing of at least three different people. I'd opened the drawer marked 'H–K', but apart from being by authors whose surnames fell under these three letters, they weren't in alphabetical or any other logical order. I flicked through the rest of the cards still in the drawer. It was the same. Fiction and non-fiction, mostly by the author's surname, but there were also multi-author history books that had simply been filed by title, most beginning with *A History of . . .*

The amount of information on each card varied. Some, usefully, gave a shelf location. Or, I thought it was useful until I checked, but the books must have been moved as the library expanded over time, as none of the locations given led me to the books in question. I shoved the cards I'd taken out back into the drawer and closed it.

My coffee was cold now, but that was no great loss.

I sat at the desk, wondering how I was going to tackle this gargantuan task. It would be a challenge, but I was totally up for it. I couldn't have wished for a better, more satisfying job. Just me and a roomful of books. My only problem would be trying not to read half of them while I worked.

I remembered Janice Allard telling me that I would receive instructions once I arrived at Winterbourne. Lucien Broussard wasn't here, so maybe he'd left written instructions. I opened the top drawer of the desk's left-hand pedestal. Stationery. Pencils, lined up and sharpened, a fountain pen, a steel ruler, a bottle of dark blue ink, a silver paper knife with a pale blue enamelled handle, treasury tags, a stapler with a box of staples. Whose fountain pen was it? The rest was general stationery, but in my experience fountain pens were personal. Broussard's maybe? I took the lid off it and tried it on the blotter. It was dry. Nobody had written with it recently. I put it back and closed the drawer.

I opened the top drawer on the other side. There was nothing in it but a rectangular envelope, with my name, Anne Adams, written in a calligraphic hand on the front. I picked it up. The ivory paper was thick and heavy, and I weighed it in my hand, guessing there were several sheets inside. My instructions, hopefully. I was about to rip it open when I remembered the paper knife in the other drawer. It's not the way I would usually do things, but somehow such exquisite stationery deserved to be treated with more respect. It felt satisfying to slip the blade of the knife into the top corner of the envelope, then slice it open neatly along the top.

I pulled out a single sheet of creamy white vellum and unfolded it. A small key slipped out onto the blotter, but I was more interested in the letter. It was written in the same hand as the envelope, in black ink, all the letters perfectly formed and every line completely straight. I admired the penmanship. I flipped the page over to see who it was from, and wasn't surprised to see that the signatory was Lucien Broussard.

I turned it back over and started to read.

Dear Miss Adams,

Firstly, welcome to Winterbourne House. I hope you will have a pleasant stay while you are working for me, but of course if there are any problems that Mrs Cooper can't solve for you immediately, please don't hesitate to get in touch with me directly.

I wasn't sure how to do this. I read on.

Regarding the work you've been employed to undertake, as I hope Mrs Allard explained to you, your primary task will be to catalogue Winterbourne's extensive library.

Over the years that the collection has been assembled there have been several attempts to keep track of it. I'm sure, as a trained librarian, you will already have seen our card index. This outdated system only covers about half the books and the shelf locations are no longer accurate. The previous librarian in my employ made a start on an electronic catalogue, but unfortunately had to leave. It is up to you to finish the work she started.

You will find a laptop in the top drawer of the plan chest by the window. The username is BROUSSARD and the password is 53khm37. The enclosed key is for the plan chest. Keep the laptop locked in there whenever you are not using it, and it absolutely must always remain in the library.

As you will soon discover, many of the books in this collection are rare beyond value. It was established by my great-great-grandfather, Lucien Broussard, and all the Broussards since have been avid book collectors. Now, however, it is becoming unwieldy, and I find that I need to divest myself of at least a part of it to keep it manageable. Cataloguing the collection is the first step in this process.

You will remain employed until the catalogue is complete. I do not wish you to feel enslaved, and I only expect you to work on the catalogue for four hours each day. The rest of your time is for you to do as you please. Explore the library, explore Winterbourne, explore the island. It is a rich environment in so many ways.

I very much look forward to meeting you, Miss Adams, when I next come to Craigsea Rock. Mrs Allard spoke highly of you, and I trust her impeccable judgement.

Yours, with the best of intentions,
Lucien Broussard

I put the letter down on the desk and picked up the key. What a peculiar way to sign off. With the best of intentions? What did he mean by that? Anyway, the fact that someone else had already started the work took decision-making out of the process. I could just follow the previous librarian's lead with regard to how the books were to be catalogued and what information to include on each book.

Cataloguing books can be monotonous work, and Broussard seemed to recognise this by only requiring four hours from me each day. I appreciated his invitation to explore Winterbourne and the island at large. It was something I'd intended to do anyway, but it was good to have the owner's blessing. The library was like an Aladdin's cave to me. I could never grow bored even if I was confined to just this one room. However, if the clouds ever parted and if the sky turned blue, I would take my exercise out of doors. I needed to walk regularly to continue building up the strength of my injured leg and the rough tracks and undulations of the island would be perfect for that.

Now I knew more about what I would be doing, I was ready to relax for the rest of the evening. I had a book in my suitcase which I was halfway through reading, but that didn't prevent me from wanting to start something new, like a diner whose eyes are too big for her stomach. I had my pick of fifty-thousand titles. Where to begin? With no order to the shelving, I started to browse at random. I wanted a novel, something meaty and satisfying that I could sink myself into over the long quiet evenings. All the classics were on display, from Tolstoy and Twain to Dickens and Nabokov, as well as recent titles by Atwood and Mantel. I'd read a lot of them, of course, but then I came across a book I'd been meaning to read for as long as I could remember. *Catch 22* by Joseph Heller. It was a beautiful clothbound, hardback edition, red with gold embossed lettering, in pristine condition. I took it across to one of the armchairs by the fireplace, and tucked up my feet underneath me.

I opened the book with that familiar frisson of excitement that greets every new read. It was an American first edition, published in 1961 by Simon & Schuster. On the title page it had been signed by the author in a free-flowing hand in bright blue ink.

For my dear friend Lucien,
my very best wishes to you,
Joseph Heller

This made me gasp. I was holding in my hands a signed first edition of one of the most celebrated novels in the American canon. How much must it be worth?

'No spilling tea or greasy fingerprints on this,' I said out loud. My voice echoed around the empty library, and for some reason I experienced a moment of discomfort, as if someone might have heard what I'd said in private to myself. I lowered the book to my lap and looked around. Everything was still. Everything was quiet. Until a sudden gust of wind rattled the window casements and I jumped half out of the chair. The book clattered to the floor, and splayed face down on the carpet. When I picked it up, I saw that two of the pages had been crumpled in the landing. I smoothed them out as best I could and slid the book back onto its spot on the shelf. They would press flat overnight, and I could start reading it another time.

I looked around for something else, and quickly settled on an old favourite, *The Life of Pi* by Yann Martel. It's the story of a boy and a shipwreck and a tiger, which I'd first read while I was still at school. This, too, was a first edition, from 2001, and it was also signed, in a diagonal spider scrawl across the title page.

> *Happy reading, Lucien — you know you remind*
> *me of Richard Parker!*
> *Yann Martel*

Both books personally dedicated to my employer. One in 1961, the other forty years later. How old did that make him? He must have been an adult by 1961, to be reading *Catch 22* and to be counted as a friend by Joseph Heller. Suffice to say, he must be very elderly by now. And if the first two books I pulled from the shelves were signed, how many others were also signed? Of course, I'd have plenty of time to find out as I catalogued the collection. What an extraordinary place I'd come to.

I settled back into one of the armchairs and lost myself in the familiar story, skipping forward quickly until I came to my favourite part, when the eponymous hero, Pi, is trapped on a life raft with a Bengal tiger named Richard Parker.

Then the lights went out.

It was midnight, and I was alone in the dark.

7

There was a torch in nearly every room. That's what Mrs Cooper had said. I had that horrible, panicked feeling that a sudden surge of adrenalin brings on. My breath was coming in short gasps and all my muscles were tightly contracted.

Calm down. Big breaths. Slow breaths.

I forced myself to stay sitting in the armchair as my eyes became accustomed to the dark. I pictured the whole room in my mind's eye, trying to work out whether I'd seen a torch anywhere. Nowhere obvious, like on the tables in the centre of the room. Not on the desk or anywhere around the card index cabinet. The surface of the plan chest had been clear.

I blinked a few times as the dark silhouettes of shelves and furniture made themselves known to me. I stood up and started to feel my way around, sweeping my hands left and right to feel for any shelf or cabinet or flat surface where a torch might have been stowed. As the shock subsided, I began to feel angry. Who'd come up with this stupid rule that meant there was no power supplied to the house through the darkest hours of the night? How much did they hope to save by turning off the generator during the hours when no one was using much power anyway?

I worked my way around the room, wishing I had the benefit of moonlight from the windows. But although it had finally stopped raining, the clouds hugged the island like a dark blanket, blotting out any natural light and, consequently, the library was a stifled black. None of the objects which my hands located were a torch, so when I reached the door, I didn't hesitate to step out onto the wide first-floor landing. It was just as dark.

In fact, if anything it was darker. No light came through the stained-glass windows above the grand staircase, which was somewhere to my left. Mrs Cooper's strange comment about me falling down the stairs in the dark suddenly sprung into my mind. Had it happened before? Wasn't that an argument enough to keep the generator running through the night? Of course, if I'd had my phone on me, I could have used it as a torch, but I'd left it in my room, seeing no point in carrying it around in a place that had neither phone signal nor internet. However, I seemed to remember seeing a console somewhere against one of the walls and possibly there had been a torch on its bottom shelf.

I felt each step forward by sliding my foot along the floor, so I would know if I came to the edge of the stairs. It would be too easy to lose my sense of direction in the dark in an unfamiliar house. I wanted to reach the other side of the landing, where I thought I would find a torch, but as I took each step, arms outstretched in front of me, I felt nothing. The space seemed much larger than I recollected. I spun round, trying to make out any solid objects in the darkness, but all I did was lose any sense of where I was, or where the library door was, or where the staircases, up or down, began.

A door slammed somewhere in the bowels of the building.

I heard myself shriek.

I thought I was alone.

'Who's down there? Who's there?' Fear put a tremor in my voice and raised its pitch. It seemed to echo through the empty house.

Nobody answered, but a floorboard creaked. Was there someone on the stairs?

Panic made me run, heedless of where I was going.

My foot hit something hard and my momentum carried my body forward. My hands crashed into what I immediately realised were the stairs leading up to the next floor, but not before my face had also smacked into one of the steps. I sprawled, winded and terrified in the dark, fighting for breath and listening to the house.

There was nothing but the sound of my own laboured breathing, followed by a couple of loud sobs until I managed to get a grip of myself.

Everything was okay. There was no one else here. Old houses make noises. Draughts slam doors. As if to confirm it, I heard the wind whistling around the building, along with the rattle of the nearest windows. And I'd fallen up the stairs, which was better than falling down them. I raised a hand to my mouth and tasted blood. My top lip was already swelling, but as I ran my tongue around my teeth I was relieved to find they were all intact. At least my hands had broken my fall enough for that.

I climbed slowly to my feet and reached out to find the banister. At the top of the stairs, I knew which way to turn, and I felt along the wall until I reached the door to my room. There was the torch on my bedside table and, at last, a beam of light in the darkness. I carried the light through to the bathroom and shone it on the mirror, so I'd be able to see the extent of the damage to my mouth. My top lip looked puffy, and there was a small cut. I splashed it with cold water for several minutes, and things didn't feel so bad. I'd learnt my lesson. I would make a note of where every torch was, and I'd make sure that wherever I was in the house after dark, I had a torch by my side.

In the bedroom, I found my phone and turned on its torch. With both sources of light propped up on opposite sides of the room, I could see what I was doing. I found my pyjamas and changed, then found the book I'd been reading before and climbed into my new bed. I was tired, and after ten minutes I couldn't keep my eyes open. I switched off my phone, then the torch, making sure both were within easy reach in case I woke in the night. It wasn't likely. I couldn't remember such a long and eventful day, and not even the drumming of the rain on the glass, the howl of the wind, the low roar of the distant sea or the throaty cry of the cormorant were going to keep me awake.

I woke up to a symphony of gold and yellow, as sunlight streamed through the primrose curtains and bathed everything in a soft glow. For a split second, I thought I'd died and gone to heaven, but then I remembered where I was. Winterbourne House, Craigsea Rock. And this beautiful bedroom was mine to call home for the foreseeable future.

I pressed the switch on the base of one of the bedside lights and it lit up. The power was back on. Not that I needed a light. The clouds must have shifted during the night, so the first thing I did was rush to the window and pull back the curtains. I wanted to see my new world in the sunshine. Such had been the level of my disorientation the evening before that I had no idea which way my bedroom window faced and what part of the island I'd see.

The rain had blown through and the wind had dropped, and I realised from the rhythmic thrum of the waves that the sea was closer than I'd thought. Much closer. In fact, looking out, water was all I could see. Not the slate-grey choppiness of yesterday's crossing. This morning the sea was mottled blue and teal, reflecting the sky, where there wasn't a single cloud to dampen my excitement. I leaned forward so I could look down directly. Under my window there was a wide terrace, then a few feet of grass, sloping down to a crumbling cliff edge. All my life, I'd lived just about as far from the sea as was possible in a country that was an island. Of course, I'd been to the sea for days out, even a weekend in a bed-and-breakfast in Southend, but I'd never spent an appreciable stretch of time at the ocean's edge. I'd never slept so close to the water, but from here I could see the spray cresting the top of the rocks and hear the gulls calling to one another as they wheeled above the no-man's-land between the tide marks, searching for something to eat.

I threw open the window to take a huge gulp of cold air and I immediately tasted the salt on my tongue. Leaning out, with my elbows on the windowsill, looking to the left I could see Beacon Hill. It rose, gently at first, then more steeply, from the moorland at the top of the cliffs. At the peak there was a cairn and next to it, a column with metal basket on the top, the beacon after which the hill was named. I craned my neck in the other direction to look to the north. The island stretched away to the horizon. I could see ploughed fields close to the house, that bounded what must have been the Halfpoint Wall. It was a sturdy drystone wall, about four feet high, that ran from the cliff edge I could see, cutting across the land no doubt all the way to the opposite coast. Beyond it, the moorland became more desolate and wild, stretching away as far as

I could see. On a distant slope, I spotted a handful of sheep, but there was no sign of any deer.

I wanted to get out there and run along the top of the cliffs or find my way down to the rocky shore, to climb Beacon Hill and venture north of the wall. To hell with a shower, to hell with breakfast, I wanted to explore, at least as well as I was able with my weak leg.

I threw off my pyjamas and hurriedly dressed, grabbing my stick as I left the room. I assumed that Mrs Cooper would be in the kitchen making breakfast, so rather than getting waylaid by her, when I reached the bottom of the grand staircase I crossed the hall to the wide front door. It wasn't locked and seconds later I was outside, standing under the stone archway of a mighty porch. This was on the opposite side of the house to where I'd come in the previous evening by the kitchen door, so the first thing I did was walk out onto the driveway and turn around to see Winterbourne House from the front.

All I'd seen the previous evening was the silhouette of the rear elevation, and that had taken my breath away. From the front, Winterbourne House was spectacular. Nestled on a gentle slope above the cliffs and surrounded by its grove of wind-sculpted trees, it was without doubt the most beautiful house I'd ever seen, the most beautiful house I could ever have imagined. Built of grey-pink granite, with mullioned windows and ornate gables, it towered for three floors above me with a forest of chimneys amid which a spectacular tower stretched up towards the azure sky. The granite glinted and sparkled in the sunlight, and the stained glass in the windows above the grand staircase made the house seem studded with emeralds and rubies. And from under the eaves, a legion of carved gargoyles grinned, gurned, frowned and leered at whoever walked below. I was completely charmed.

I walked to the corner of the building to see the long façade that overlooked the cliff edge. This was where, on the ground floor, the ballroom opened out onto the wide flagstone terrace, and above it I recognised the long row of windows of the library. Craning my neck to the next floor, I could see my own bedroom window, left open, the yellow curtains flapping in the breeze. And above that rose the tower. I'd forgotten about the tower once I was inside the house. I squinted at its top, raising a hand to shield my eyes. There were two small arched windows and a small balustraded balcony facing out over the sea. A room in the tower had to have the best views in every direction. A movement at one of the windows made me squint harder, but it was just the reflection of a passing cloud. It would make a glorious place to sit and read, and to watch the weather rolling in. I decided there and then that it would be the first part of Winterbourne's interior I would explore.

What a house, and what a multitude of treasures lay inside, waiting to be discovered. As far as I was concerned, it was the most gorgeous place in the world. I was delighted by every aspect of it.

'Thank you, Marisa,' I whispered. If it hadn't been for her suggestion that I needed to get away from my mother, I would never have come to Winterbourne. And I would never have encountered Lucien Broussard. But, of course, I'm getting ahead of myself.

8

I WALKED AROUND THE CORNER onto the terrace and stared in through the windows, hardly daring to believe that I now lived in a house grand enough to have a ballroom. I tried to imagine what it would have been like, the balls that might have been held here over the years. Elegant women in Victorian ballgowns gliding around the floor, then later hot girls in flapper dresses doing the Charleston to newfangled jazz music. When had it last been used?

The terrace was bordered by a low stone balustrade. There was an opening in the centre where six or seven worn steps led down onto the shallow lawn at the edge the cliffs. I went down the steps. The grass was wet underfoot and the crash of the waves on the rocks sounded much louder. Of course it was. I was much closer to the water. I could smell the stench of drying seaweed and, as well as the shrieks of the gulls, I heard other bird calls which I didn't recognise.

At the corner of the lawn, a stony path dipped over the edge and as I came closer to it, I could see that it wound its way between the rocks to a small sandy cove at the bottom. It was steep and gravelly, not ideal for someone with a stick, but I was desperate to get right down to the sea. I slipped and skidded, using my stick as a brake, and bracing myself against the rocks with my other hand. A stone dislodged by my foot skittered down the crag, sending a pair of black and white oystercatchers chuntering into the air with fright.

I paused for a moment. I needed to be careful, so I slowed down my descent but, finally, five minutes later, I was standing on the small apron of golden sand at the bottom. I threw my arms up and shouted my glee into the wind, scuttling backwards as an incoming wave threatened to drench my feet. From down here, the house was out of sight, and I could have been entirely alone on the island.

When a counsellor told me, shortly after the accident, that grief was non-linear, I hadn't really understood what they meant. But now I did. It crashed through me like a tidal wave.

Malcolm.

I had never felt so entirely alone and lonely. The space my brother used to take up in my life had turned into a black hole, sucking in all the joy, all the oxygen, all the hope.

Malcolm.

He would have wanted me to feel properly alive, but some days it was difficult.

Fighting back tears, I picked up a couple of flat stones and tried to skim them across the water as my father used to do when we were kids on the beach, before he became the silent repository of my mother's resentment. The stones sank without trace. It reminded me of a particular day at the beach – I can't remember which beach, I was only eight or so. I was trying so hard to impress my father, chucking stone after stone with no technique, all of them sinking.

'Teach me how to do it,' I pleaded.

But he just walked away to look at something my mother was pointing at. It broke my heart. So for the rest of that week, Malcolm took me to the beach before breakfast every morning and taught me how to skim stones across the surface. On the last day of the holiday, I showed my father my progress. He was still unimpressed, but it would always be my favourite remembered holiday because of those precious hours spent with Malcolm on the deserted sand.

I tried again. One bounce, then the stone dipped under the water. I'd forgotten the technique. It didn't matter. I squatted at the edge of a couple of rock pools and watched sea anemones shrink away from the tip of my finger, while tiny fish darted in the crystal water.

Then the surface of the rock pool rippled and the sun vanished. I looked up to see a black mass speeding across the sky, a telltale smudge of rain slanting in its wake. The air became chilly and before I'd even grabbed my stick and straightened up, I felt the first drops of rain on my cheek. The squall moved in and the waves reared up aggressively. My feet were soaked by a sudden rush of water over the rocks. It was time to go back.

There are people that swear climbing down is just as hard as climbing up, but on this particular morning that was not my experience. My weak leg didn't have the strength needed to raise my body weight, so I had to step forward each time on my good foot and follow with the weaker one. This put all the burden of the climb on one leg, already fatigued by the long walk of the previous evening. The rain became heavier, almost horizontal, stinging my face and hands, and soaking through my clothing. A torrent of water rushed down the path, making the larger rocks slippery and turning the gravel into mud. I stumbled and had to save myself by grabbing at a handful of ferns which ripped away in my hand. My good knee smacked hard against a boulder, making me wince, and the rain in my eyes made it hard to see where I was going.

How had the weather changed so quickly?

By the time I reached the top, I was dripping wet, panting and in considerable pain. The trip down to the beach hadn't been one of my best ideas, but nothing had suggested it might end like this. I hurried back into the house, leaving a trail of water across the entrance hall. I headed straight for the kitchen. At least I'd be able to warm up in there.

The smell of bacon made my mouth water as I limped down the servants' passage. Though my breakfast was usually just a coffee and a croissant, the climb had left me ravenous.

'Morning,' I said, as I came into the kitchen. Mrs Cooper was in her apron at the range, tending to a sizzling pan. Robert Cooper was at the table, already wolfing down a full English breakfast, with a mountain of toast stacked on a plate to one side.

'You been out?' said Mrs Cooper, eyeing me over one shoulder.

'Just down to the shore. It was such a lovely morning when I woke up.' I raked my fingers through my wet hair to draw it back from my face.

She gave a wry laugh. 'Got caught out? We get three or four seasons' weather every day here. I think it'll be blowing in for the rest of the day.'

I hoped she was wrong. The sunshine had lifted my mood immensely after the travails of getting here.

Cooper grunted as he finished his food and, grabbing a couple of bits of toast, took his leave.

When he was gone, Mrs Cooper cleared his plate and a moment later set down a large plate of bacon and eggs in front of me. 'Eat.'

I didn't need asking twice.

She sat down opposite me and poured herself a mug of tea. Then she fixed me with a frown. 'You left the library unlocked last night.'

I was surprised by this. Why would she have gone up to the library before breakfast? Checking up on me? 'I'm sorry. I got caught out by the generator shutting down and I couldn't find a torch.'

She shook her head. 'No telling some folk, is there?'

'I was reading and I lost track of time.'

She wasn't impressed.

'It won't happen again. I'll go and lock it now.'

'It's all right. I locked it.' She slid the library key across the table to me. I'd left it on the desk the previous evening and had forgotten all about locking up in my panic over the lights.

I cleared my plate and started washing up.

'If you need anything from Craigross, just let Robert Cooper know. Or . . .' she lowered her voice '. . . if it's women's things and you feel embarrassed to tell him, just write a note for Mrs Unwin, the shopkeeper. She'll package things up for you to spare your blushes.'

I supposed she meant sanitary protection by 'women's things', and she was right. It wasn't something I'd want to discuss with Cooper. Or maybe she was sparing his blushes. I was sure he would find a conversation about tampon sizes excruciatingly embarrassing. However, I'd brought plenty with me, and my periods had been scant to non-existent since the accident anyway. But it brought it home to me that there was no popping out to the shops from here or ordering things from the internet, and it made me understand just how reliant I was on the Coopers' goodwill.

'Thanks,' I said, letting the water out of the sink. 'I'd better go and get started in the library.'

'You do that. I'll leave you a sandwich out for your lunch, and supper will be at six.'

That hadn't been the best start, but forgetting to lock the library door on the very day I'd been told to do so was very much in character. As I made my way up the grand staircase, I resolved to do better. I could feel the weight of the library key in the pocket of my jeans. I just had to remember to use it.

Mrs Cooper must have come up to the library to clean it while I'd been down at the beach. The book I'd been reading the evening before was back on the shelf and my letter of instruction had been put back in its envelope, which was set squarely in the centre of the blotter. There was a vase of fresh dahlias on the middle of the three reading tables. They must have come from the Coopers' walled garden. They were my mother's favourite flower. I hated them.

I looked around my desk for the little silver key for the plan chest. It was back in the envelope, with the letter. I wondered if Mrs Cooper had read the letter, or if she already knew of its contents anyway. All of this locking things away seemed an unnecessary level of secrecy and security to me, but I had to admit that it was an astonishingly valuable collection of books. It was just that there wasn't anyone on the island to steal them.

I went across to the plan chest to get the laptop. Outside, the squall seemed to have turned into a gale. The trees were throwing their branches this way and that, and as I got near to the window, I could hear the wind whistling around the corners of the house and twisting itself between the chimneys. At least I'd sampled fresh air when I could.

The plan chest was fitted with a wooden batten down one side that blocked the drawers from opening. When I unlocked it, it folded back on hinges to allow access to the contents of the chest. I opened the top drawer. Inside, I found a new-looking MacBook Pro, along with a charging cable. I brought it back to my desk and opened it. It was almost fully charged, and I was able to log in using the details Broussard had provided.

There were only two items on the desktop. One was a file of notes the previous librarian had made about how the books were to be catalogued, and the other was the catalogue itself. He or she hadn't made much headway into the actual cataloguing of the collection, but the notes were useful. They set out how the books were to be divided and subdivided, and what information should be included for each entry: title, author, publisher, publication date, edition, ISBN for those books new enough to have one. However, as far as I could see, most of the collection predated the use of ISBNs, so in most cases this cell would be left blank.

I looked at the initial entries in the catalogue and saw that the cells for shelf location were also blank. It appeared that whoever had started the work hadn't begun to reorganise the shelves in line with the catalogue. That would be a gargantuan task, but I believed that it was part of the remit. And with that came the realisation that rather than the months of work I'd envisaged, if I was to complete the job, I might be living at Winterbourne for a year or more.

I pushed my chair back and went across to the nearest window. I took a few deep breaths. I really wasn't sure how I felt about this. Even if I sped up the job by working more than four hours a day, I would still be here forever. I wondered if that realisation was why the previous librarian had barely scratched the surface of the job. Of course, they might have left for some other reason altogether. I decided I'd ask Mrs Cooper about them. It seemed a little odd to have left a job before it was properly started.

The rain didn't let up its drumming on the windows, and though the wind rose and fell, its sighs and moans were a constant chorus. However, the library was warm and dry, and as I settled into the work, a feeling of contentment washed over me. I was doing what I loved and there was no one here with an agenda of constantly reminding me of the accident and of what I'd done to Malcolm. I had escaped from my mother and now, maybe, I'd find some peace.

9

Although I went down to the kitchen to fetch a cup of coffee, and again later to eat my sandwich at lunchtime, I didn't see any sign of either of the Coopers for the rest of the day. Once or twice, I heard a door opening or closing in the distance and I certainly heard a hoover being used somewhere, but with the library door closed, it was difficult to tell where the noises were coming from.

I interspersed my time working with the natural urge to dip into the books I was cataloguing. It was such an easy distraction. This library was a treasure trove of the rare and the unusual. There were books about literally everything, as well as huge number in languages other than English, the only language I'm fluent in. These would be more difficult to catalogue, particularly those in Cyrillic, Arabic and a host of other scripts. But I had more than enough to work on, so I could leave that issue for later.

I set a couple of books aside for my evening reading. A large, illustrated book of birds, so I could learn to identify all the seabirds I'd seen when I went down to the beach, and a book on how to draw and paint landscapes. Perhaps I could ask Robert Cooper to bring some art supplies from the mainland. The idea of taking up drawing as a new hobby seemed appealing, given the hours I'd have with no television or internet to entertain me.

After lunch I became lost in the work. It was engaging and engrossing, and I certainly worked longer than my four hours that first day. Dusk fell and I hardly noticed, until I felt something brush softly against my cheek. I looked up from the screen and a shadowy form passed in front of my eyes. I raised a hand and a gasp of shock escaped me.

A moth. A huge moth was fluttering around my head.

My heart practically smashed its way out through my ribs. Since childhood I'd been terrified of moths. I stood up, kicking my chair over behind me, arms flailing, as adrenalin flooded like ice through my veins.

As the moth settled on the keyboard of the laptop, I took three or four steps back, panting. My back came up against the closest bookcase and I grabbed hold of the middle shelf on either side of me, clenching my knuckles.

'Calm down, Anne.' I spoke out loud. 'Just a moth. Can't hurt you.'

I stood staring at the creature as I waited for my heart rate to drop back to normal. It was just a bloody moth, after all.

On the moth scale of things, it was a giant. Its fat, hairy body must have been three inches long, and as it rested, wings open, I guessed it had a wingspan of about five inches. From a distance it was mottled black and gold, but as my interest overcame my fear I crept forward, so I could see it in more detail. The body was mostly black, with partial gold stripes, a little like a wasp. The forewings were black with small flashes of gold, like watermarks, while the hindwings were gold with two black bands on each. At the front of its head, two antennae quivered like thick gold wires.

I took another step closer. The was no mistaking the image on its thorax. A human skull marked out in golden tufts of hair. It was a death's-head hawkmoth, something I'd never seen for real before now, but which had haunted my childhood imaginings and flooded my heart with fear.

As I stared, slack-jawed, breathing hard, the creature manoeuvred itself around on the keyboard and let out an angry scritch.

I ran to the library door and out onto the landing, slamming it shut behind me.

Leaning against the wall, I gave myself a good talking-to. It was just a moth. Yes, a big one, that could apparently make a noise. But it wasn't malevolent and it didn't want to harm me. Moths don't bite, I told myself. I tried to convince myself. But I was sure I'd heard somewhere that an angry hawkmoth could nip, and this one was huge.

The house was silent around me, but somehow it seemed to be breathing with me too. I felt dizzy, so I squatted down and put my head between my knees. Somewhere, in the distance, floorboards creaked.

Another noise made me jump, but I realised it was just the cormorant outside. A cormorant. Not necessarily the one I'd seen on the jetty. They all looked and sounded the same, didn't they?

When I felt calmer, I went up to my bathroom and splashed cold water on my face. How stupid was I to get scared half to death by a moth? I pressed the towel against my eyes, straightened my hair in the mirror and took a deep breath. Hopefully it would have gone by the time I got back to the library, but if it hadn't I'd simply open one of the windows and shoo it out with a rolled-up newspaper.

The house was still quiet as I made my way down the stairs, the atmosphere heavy. I felt nervous, but I was determined to overcome my fear. I put my hand on the library door handle, pushed it down and swung open the door.

This time I screamed, using up all the air in my lungs.

There wasn't just one hawkmoth. There was a multitude. A black cloud of moths, dancing in the air, filling the room with the soft whisper of beating wings. They were settled on every flat surface and crawling on the spines of the books. They perched on the flowers in the vase and flitted round the light fittings which hung from ceiling. As the draught from the moving door alerted them to my presence, some of them started to make the same scritch noise that the first moth had made when it landed on my keyboard. Now there was a cluster of moths on the keyboard and more crawling up the screen.

I slammed the door shut and screamed again. Then I ran as best I could without the aid of my stick towards the stairs. Clutching at the banister, I took the stairs two at a time. Mrs Cooper was opening the kitchen door just as I arrived on the other side of it, and I barrelled into her, making us both stagger back against the big table.

Mrs Cooper grunted with the impact.

Robert Cooper, who was sitting at the table studying a newspaper, looked up. 'What's the matter, girl?'

I fought for breath, stepping back from Mrs Cooper, who looked me up and down as she straightened her apron.

'Moths,' I gasped. 'The library's full of hawkmoths. Hundreds . . .'

The Coopers stared at each other for a second, two seconds.

'It's a sign—' said Cooper.

Mrs Cooper cut him off. 'Robert Cooper, go up there and flush them out, please.'

Cooper gave a mock salute, the bitter sarcasm of which was unmissable, but he pushed back his chair and ambled out of the kitchen.

I looked at Mrs Cooper. 'What did he mean, it's a sign?'

Mrs Cooper turned away from me. She had something bubbling in a pot on the range. 'The stuff and nonsense that comes out of that man's mouth.'

'But ...'

'Go and help him, Anne. It'll only take a couple of minutes to get them out. Can't let them stay and nest.'

I caught up with Cooper at the top of the grand staircase and grabbed the top of his arm from behind.

'What did you mean?' I said as he turned to look at me. 'What sign?'

He pulled away and carried on walking towards the library. I hung back. I didn't want to see the hawkmoths again. I'd hardly stopped shaking from the first encounter. He opened the door and stepped inside.

'Nothing here,' he said with a raised voice.

I went to the open door. Cooper was standing in the middle of the library and he was right. There wasn't a single hawkmoth to be seen. I grabbed for the door handle, unsteady on my feet.

'What the ... ?'

'Look.' He pointed at an open window. Rain was coming in at a slant and there was a considerable wet patch on the carpet beneath. 'If there were any in here, they've gone now.' He turned back to me. 'But you shouldn't leave the window open like this. Them books are valuable. Mr Broussard's particular about not letting damp in here.'

I shook my head, dumbfounded. Of course I hadn't left the window open. It had been closed all day. It was closed when I saw the first moth and I could have sworn it was closed when the moths were swarming. So how could it be open now? And where were the moths? Had they all just flown out of the window, into the pouring rain?

It didn't make sense.

Cooper closed it.

'Thank you,' I said. Although he hadn't really done anything.

'Hundreds, you say?'

I nodded.

His eyebrows went up. He thought I was lying.

'Look, I didn't imagine them. They were here. I saw them, and I heard them.'

He was already walking away down the landing.

I stood in the centre of the library and spun around. Not a single moth, anywhere. I went over to my desk.

I hadn't imagined it. On the keyboard of my laptop there was a light dusting of gold powder that the moth had left behind. The hawkmoths had been real. They had been in here. And Robert Cooper had believed me when I'd told them in the kitchen.

I left the library and started to make my way slowly downstairs. It was almost supper time, and the library didn't seem quite the haven it had before. On a whim, I tried one of the doors along the corridor that went in the opposite direction at the top of the grand staircase. It was locked. Piqued, I tried another. Also locked. What was Winterbourne hiding from me? A door on the other side of the corridor opened. It was a bedroom. I turned on the light so I could have a look round. The blue bedroom, I supposed, as the furnishings and wallpaper, curtains and carpet were in shades of blue. It was bigger than my room and not quite so feminine. More portraits of imposing men, and none of any women. It was something I'd noticed throughout the house. There were very few pictures of women, if any at all. On the grand staircase, the entrance hall and the myriad of downstairs reception rooms, all the portraits were of men. Of course, there were other pictures. Landscapes and seascapes, hunting scenes, faithful hounds and prized steeds, but the women of the Broussard family were distinctly lacking, while the men were on full display in military uniform, court dress and tailcoats.

Where are the women?

I went to the window and peered out into the rain-lashed dusk. Somewhere below, I could hear the waves pounding the rocks at the foot of the cliffs, but it was too dark now to see the sea. It was virtually the same view as my room had on the floor above.

On a small occasional table by the window, there was a round silver salver upon which sat decanters of liquor and cut-glass tumblers. There were bottles of aftershave on the chest of drawers, and a political biography lay at an angle on one of the bedside tables. It was a man's bedroom.

Lucien Broussard's?

The thought made me feel like a trespasser, and a footstep outside in the corridor froze the blood in my veins. I didn't want to get caught somewhere I shouldn't be by one or other of the Coopers. I quickly switched out the light and waited in the dark room until the footsteps had passed by. Then I opened the door a tiny crack and peeped out at the receding figure. It was Mrs Cooper. Wasn't she in the middle of cooking supper?

She certainly was when I got down to the kitchen some five minutes later.

10

For the next couple of weeks, the weather alternated between the balmy days of an Indian summer and the blustery onset of autumn. Mrs Cooper could read the sky and she became my weather oracle at breakfast every morning, advising me with remarkable accuracy of when it might be best to take my walk. I'd got into the habit of spending at least half my day, on days when it was fine, exploring the island.

Although I'd never been much of an outdoor girl in my previous life, I'd developed a taste for the windswept moors north of the Halfpoint Wall. They were a mix of short, tufty grass, bracken, gorse and heather, forming great sweeps or pretty patchworks of green, rust, purple, brown and yellow. Standing on high ground, I would drink in the landscape stretching out before me, always ending in a fringe of cliffs or a tumble of rocks before the flat grey-green sea raced away to meet the sky. If I looked east on a clear day, I could sometimes see the mainland, with the little white boxes of Craigross staring back at me. In the opposite direction, there was nothing but the vast expanse of the water. Maybe, if I could climb somewhere high enough, and take a telescope, on a crystal clear day I'd be able to see Ireland.

But it wasn't just the landscape that drew me north of the Halfpoint Wall. Kept away from the danger of Loki's snapping jaws, there was a feral herd of ancient Soay sheep. They were different to the white puffballs that formed my childhood image of sheep. These beasts had brown or piebald fleeces, and long curled horns. They were sturdy and muscular, and they stared out at me through golden eyes with strange bar-shaped pupils. They weren't afraid of me, but they weren't tame either.

Unlike the Soay, the Sika deer were skittish, and always ran for cover if they noticed me approaching. There were fewer of them than the sheep, and they tended to cluster on the lower stretches of land, where they could find shelter in small spinneys and banks of rhododendrons. Mrs Cooper had served venison stew more than once since my arrival on Craigsea, as well as a lamb hotpot with a distinctly muttony flavour, and I supposed we were eating meat from animals that had lived and been butchered on the island.

I was also learning about the myriad of birds that shared the rock with us, mostly seabirds, but there were also some that I knew from home, including blackbirds, robins, sparrows, thrushes and tits. Occasionally I even saw a pair of magpies, who nested in the tumbledown ruins of a small church just south of the Halfpoint Wall.

Robert Cooper had unexpectedly presented me with a tall thumb stick for my rambling. It was made of pale, gnarled wood, and had a small V-shaped bifurcation at the top in which I could rest my thumb. It was far more practical for walking the uneven land than my usual stick, and it made the going easier as I clambered up hills or down steep stony paths to the shore.

I found that I was getting fitter. My injured leg gained strength and I was able to venture further and further each day. Some days I took a small backpack with me, holding a sandwich, a bottle of water, a book on birds and a sketchpad. I'd taken to stopping and making quick drawings of the plants and animals I encountered, or sketching the rock formations on the coast and outcrops in the centre of the island.

I felt happier and healthier than I had done in such a long time. My appetite had returned, my body was growing stronger and my dreams were becoming less troubled.

'Today'll be the last of it,' said Mrs Cooper, squinting out of the kitchen window at the square of blue sky above the courtyard.

'Last of what?' I said, spooning ground coffee into the cafetière that I'd finally managed to have Robert Cooper source in Craigross, with the cooperation of Mrs Unwin in the shop.

'Last of the good weather. You'd do well to take advantage today, as you won't be seeing the sun for months to come.'

I wasn't sure I believed her, but I did realise the exceptional run of good weather we'd had was bound to end sometime. And, yes, we were on an island surrounded by water, so rain was a given, but I could also hope for the odd cold, bright snap through the winter. Anyway, in the short term she was invariably right, so I decided to take her advice and spend the day outside. I could easily do my four hours of cataloguing after it got dark.

I quickly packed a day bag with a sandwich, fruit loaf, a Thermos of tea which Mrs Cooper made up for me and my sketchpad and charcoal. From maps of Craigsea in the library, I had located the sweeping, sandy cove I'd seen from the boat. I hadn't been there yet, as it was a long walk for me, but I was determined to get there. This was the day, while the weather was still good, and there were enough hours of daylight for me to get there and back before dark.

'Where are you off to today?' said Mrs Cooper. She was the only one who took an interest in where I went and what I got up to. Robert Cooper was a silent, brooding presence, who excused himself from the kitchen before he'd even finished his last mouthful of food.

I told her of my plans. 'Do you think I'll be able to see seals up there?'

'Not on the beach, but if you keep to the coastal path, you'll surely be able to see them sunning themselves on the rocks.'

I set off, reflecting that it must be one of Craigsea's most glorious days so far. Loki lolloped alongside me as I followed the path that led from Winterbourne to the nearest gate in the Halfpoint Wall. He was ever hopeful that he might join me on my walk, but I was particularly careful not to let him accompany me north of the wall. While he was mostly obedient to Robert Cooper, I certainly wouldn't be able to control him if he started worrying the sheep.

'Not today, my friend,' I said, chucking him under the chin as I came to the gate.

He dropped to his haunches, gazing up at me through his bedraggled fringe. He knew the drill. I went through the gate and closed it firmly behind me, and he whimpered a little. The poor creature seemed starved of affection. Robert Cooper simply viewed him as a working dog, and he was kennelled outside. He never got to lie in front of the fire or share a bite of human food.

'See you later.' I turned my back on him and started along the narrow path that would follow the coast all the way to the beach. My destination was about three miles away. It would be one of the longest walks I'd attempted, but it was a fine day and I had my lunch with me. If I became too tired, I could always turn back early, even though I was determined not to do so.

I settled into a steady rhythm, and sticking to the dirt path that ran the length of the clifftops was far easier than walking across country on the moors. I tested myself on identifying the birds I saw along the way. There were cormorants, herring gulls, guillemots, razorbills and gannets, though their numbers were already fewer than when I first arrived, as the winter migration got underway.

But my reward for remaining watchful came some two miles into my walk. The path followed the edge of a dip in the cliff line, bringing me almost level with the rocky shore along a series of tiny, secluded bays. As I came around to the second of these bays, I saw to my delight a plump adult seal stretched out on the top of a flat boulder that was half in the sea, half out. As I came further round, I saw that her body had been shielding a much smaller baby seal from view, also lying sunning itself on the rock. These were grey seals and the mother's coat was a beautiful mottled velvet of silver and brown. In contrast, the pup's fur was almost white and looked wonderfully soft and fluffy.

I perched on rock a few feet above them and watched them doing nothing but soak up the warmth of the sun's rays. Then the mother woke up and sensed my presence. She let out a short, harsh bark, and pushed herself up onto her front flippers, nudging her offspring with her nose.

I quickly retreated to the path. I didn't want them to feel they had to hide away. I wasn't going to harm them. I was simply sharing a moment in the sun with them. I fixed the image in my mind for a sketch later, and went on my way, thrilled that I'd seen them at all.

Another hour of walking brought me to the beach I'd seen from the boat. The sky was an intense azure above, with nary a cloud, and the sea within the sandy horseshoe of the bay reflected its colour. The white sand was pristine. No footprints. No litter. Just soft and powdery sand, stretching away from me for at least a mile. Along the highwater line there were tangles of seaweed and jumbles of shells and driftwood. The tide was galloping in, and gulls were picking the beach clean of anything edible, screeching at each other as they argued over every morsel.

But by now, I was exhausted and sweating heavily. I'd shoved my jacket into my backpack, so I was walking in just a T-shirt and jeans, but with virtually no wind, I could feel the heat of the sun on my skin. I flopped down onto the sand and pulled out my flask of tea. At least that would be lighter to carry on the way back. I got out my sketchbook and attempted to draw the seal and her cub, while taking bites of my sandwich at the same time.

After a while, my pencil dropped from my hand and I let my head fall to rest against my backpack. I covered my eyes with one forearm and let sleep claim me like the incoming tide.

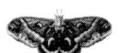

When I woke up, the sun had moved, though it was still high the sky. The tide was slipping out now, and the exposed patches of my skin prickled with heat. My mouth was dry. As I finished the lukewarm tea, I gazed out at the water. It looked so inviting, shimmering, so blue, and I hadn't been swimming since I'd come home from the rehab centre months ago.

Without a second's thought, I ripped off my T-shirt, my trainers and my jeans, and ran into the water in just my underwear.

The shock of the cold inching up my legs as I waded deeper made me gasp. My last swim had been in a heated, indoor pool. But I fought the urge to run back onto the warm sand, and once the sea level had reached the top of my thighs, I plunged forward with a shout of triumph and started swimming. It was so unexpectedly cold, which is stupid really. But my body was used to twenty-five degrees in the pool, and this was way lower.

It made my muscles feel stiff, so I swam hard to loosen them up. As I pushed out from the shore, the feeling of shock wore off. It was cold, it was bracing, and I knew I couldn't stay in for long, but it was also incredibly refreshing after the long, hot walk.

It was only when I decided to make the turn back to the beach that I realised how far out I was from the shore. I'm a slow swimmer, especially since the accident, but as I looked around the land suddenly seemed a long way off. I'd swum far further out than I'd imagined. Then, as I trod water, assessing the distance, I understood what had happened. I was being carried out by a rip current.

A moment of panic had me flailing, arms and legs thrashing in every direction. My head went under, and a gulp of seawater made it down my throat before I was able to bring myself under control. Coughing and spluttering, I pushed my head upwards and angled my body so I was floating on my back. It took me several minutes to bring up all the water and feel that I was breathing normally again, and while I did this I was being dragged even further out to sea.

The water in the curve of the bay had been relatively flat, but as I was swept beyond its bounds, the sea became choppy. I had already been in too long. My body ached with the cold. I racked my brains trying to work out what I needed to do to escape the current. I couldn't swim back to the shore against it, so what was the alternative? Panic tightened my chest and made my stomach cramp. My muscles were stiff, and it was all that I could do to stay afloat, holding my body rigid, with my face out of the water. The ability to swim was evaporating fast and I was still drifting further out. Fatigue was setting in, despite the punch of terror-induced adrenalin.

'Help! For God's sake help me!' My pointless screech was carried who-knows-where by the wind. There was certainly no one within earshot to come to my aid.

The island seemed far away now, rising and falling on the horizon as the swell lifted me to the crest of each wave, then dropped me down the other side. The sun had gone and drops of rain had started to spatter on the surface of the water. My tears added to the salt, stinging my cheeks as I gave up the fight.

They say drowning isn't the worst way to die. I was about to find out.

In the maelstrom of the waves, a sense of peace washed through me. I thought of Malcolm. He'd be righteously furious with me for getting into this predicament. I'd been careless with his life, and now I'd been careless with my own.

I didn't have energy to hold myself rigid, so I let my head fall back in the freezing water. I just wanted to sleep.

'You!'

Who was the voice talking to? Me?

'Hey, wake up!' It was a man's voice.

Something hard poked me in the shoulder. The shock of pain kicked me out of my stupor. I raised my head, my body moving to vertical in the water. I put one hand up to feel for the thing that had hit me, turning towards it.

A boat hook on the end of a pole.

I grabbed for it, relief flooding through me. It was real. I wasn't imaging things. At the other end of the pole, two male hands. A man I didn't recognise, leaning over the side of the

RIB. And Robert Cooper, watching over one shoulder as he held the RIB steady in the water.

The man pulled the pole in with me on the end of it until I was able to grab the guide ropes on the RIB's side. Then, with Cooper's help, he dragged me into the boat. Half drowned, delirious with cold, I landed on the bottom, breathing hard, unable to speak. But I was safe.

The man stood above me, staring down at his catch. I felt sure I'd met him before. I recognised the long straight nose, the almost-black eyes, wide set under heavy brows. The wide mouth with its sculpted Cupid's bow. All topped by a sweep of blue-black hair that glistened as darkly as a cormorant's wing feathers.

'Who are you?' he said.

'She's Anne Adams,' said Robert Cooper with a knowing grin.

'You?' I said, my teeth chattering so hard I could barely speak. Then I spewed a gallon of seawater around his feet.

'I'm Lucien Broussard.' His tone was cold, his voice haughty.

Now I knew why his striking face was so familiar. He was the spitting image of all the men in Winterbourne's portraits. The latest in a long line of Lucien Broussards. Handsome, stern-faced men with troubled expressions. And lying in the bottom of the RIB, in nothing but my grotty underwear, with all the livid scars from the accident in plain sight, was not how I'd envisaged my first meeting with him.

Broussard took off the black windcheater he was wearing and squatted down to place it around my shoulders as I struggled to sit up.

'My clothes ... on the beach.' I tried to point to the shore, but my arm was shaking and I could hardly raise it.

'We're heading for the shore anyway, and damn lucky for you that we are. If we'd stayed on our normal course, we would never have seen you in the water.'

'Thank you,' I said. I felt mortified.

'You shouldn't have been in the sea. You clearly don't have the experience, and to go in on your own like that was idiotic.'

Behind Broussard, Robert Cooper looked highly amused by the turn of events. Inside my cold chest, my temper flared.

'I'm a good swimmer, but I got caught in a rip.'

'Point proved,' said Broussard. 'You don't know these waters and you've no business taking unnecessary risks that could put others in danger.'

I had to bite my tongue because, of course, he was right.

'And I suppose it was you who left the gate in the Halfpoint Wall open?'

I must have looked puzzled.

He pointed at the beach. 'Loki. That's why we were heading to the shore. We heard Loki before we saw you in the water.'

Now I could hear the dog barking over the sound of the waves and the outboard. He was running back and forth across the sand excitedly. He'd seen the boat.

'No, I was careful. I shut the gate. I made sure of it.' I knew I had. Hadn't I? I tried to remember but I couldn't seem to get my mind into gear.

Broussard looked away from me. I didn't think he believed me, so another reason not to be impressed with his new employee. I pulled his jacket tighter around me. I was freezing and exhausted. I couldn't believe I'd ever feel warm again.

Cooper manoeuvred the RIB up onto the sand and Loki ran over to us, planting his front paws on the side of the boat. Now that he was close, I saw to my horror that his snout and the front of his chest were stained red. It was blood. He'd killed something.

'Down, Loki,' roared Cooper.

Broussard climbed out of the RIB on the other side, and Loki immediately ran round to him. The dog jumped up in greeting, even though Broussard stretched out an arm to push him down.

'Call your damn dog off.'

'Loki, down.' Cooper was off the RIB and grabbed Loki by the collar. He raised an arm to strike the beast.

'No! Don't you dare.' I clambered out of the RIB, but my legs couldn't hold my weight, so I collapsed onto the sand.

Loki escaped Cooper's hold and came over to me, pushing his face into mine, sniffing and panting. He stank of blood and I wanted to retch. Broussard dragged him off and took him to the water's edge. Loki struggled against him, but Broussard was strong. He dunked the dog's face into the sea and used his free hand to wash the blood from Loki's fur. Meanwhile, Cooper pulled the RIB higher onto the beach to stop it drifting away.

I sat up and looked round for my stuff, spying it a couple of hundred metres further up the beach. Testing my legs, I stood up gingerly. I was still shivering violently. Wet sand clung to my body and Broussard's jacket was soiled with seawater and blood from Loki's chin. My injured leg was excruciatingly painful, and I doubted I would make the distance to my clothes. But I couldn't face the two men, so I set off away from them, gritting my teeth and refusing to cry, even though the lump in my throat was as big as the world.

I hadn't gone far when I heard the thud of footsteps on the sand behind me. I turned to see Broussard bearing down on me.

'Wait,' he said. 'Let me help you.'

He caught up easily and immediately pulled me into a tight embrace, rubbing his hands vigorously up and down my upper arms to create friction. The heat he created on my skin was as agonising as the cold, but I leant against his body, unable to break away.

After a few minutes he stopped and pulled back from me. 'Your clothes will be damp.' It was still drizzling. He pulled his black turtleneck over his head and thrust it towards me. 'This will have some warmth and give you a dry layer under your jacket.'

I stared at him, unable to even raise an arm to take the garment from him. His torso was lean and muscular, olive skinned with a sprinkling of black hair. But what caught my attention was a small tattoo on the inside of his left forearm. It was the same as the one I'd seen on Robert Cooper's wrist. A small black circle with eight arrows pointing outwards from it. How weird. Why would they have the same tattoo?

He realised I was incapable of helping myself, so he helped me out of the jacket and pulled the warm, dry sweater over my head, as if he was dressing a child. It was an awkward struggle to get my arms into the sleeves, but we managed. Then he fetched the rest of my clothes from further up the beach and helped me into my jeans and trainers.

I was still shivering. I still felt terrible. But his kindness felt like a warm duvet being wrapped around my battered body.

Down by the RIB, Cooper had Loki under control and was watching us with his habitual look of amusement.

'I'm sorry about all of this,' I said through chattering teeth. 'I'm so sorry.'

He rubbed my arms some more and guided me back to the boat.

11

When I woke up the next morning, my skin felt as if it was on fire, my bones ached and every muscle felt shredded. My jaw hurt and my teeth felt sensitive, and I was suffering from a raging thirst. I remembered getting up in the night and being sick, but I couldn't remember how I'd got from the RIB up to Winterbourne or how I'd ended up in my own bed.

Daylight penetrated the curtains, but it wasn't bright and gave me no clue as to how long I'd been sleeping. I reached for my mobile on the bedside table and read the time. Eleven thirty-five. So I'd missed breakfast, probably scoring another black mark with my employer.

I struggled out of bed and saw that I was in my pyjamas. Another horrifying thought. Who'd changed me out of my wet clothes and into these, before putting me to bed? God, I hoped it had been Mrs Cooper and not Lucien Broussard. My face burnt with shame. Now everyone on the island had probably seen the ugly scars that criss-crossed my body. Scars from the accident, scars from the operations that had followed. Still bright red and hardly faded, though nearly a year had passed since it had happened.

And they must be wondering about the cause. I limped to the bathroom, my leg more painful than usual. This was the life I faced. Gauging my pain each morning. Paying for the previous day's activity with further impairment. I understood that I would, for the rest of my life, be considered disabled, rendering me invisible to most of the population, apart from those who stared. Who would then pretend they hadn't seen me the moment I might need any sort of assistance. I'd been like that too, perhaps. Now, karma was paying me back.

As I was cleaning my teeth, there was a knock on the bedroom door. I quickly spat and wiped a hand across my mouth.

It was Mrs Cooper, bearing a tray with tea and scrambled eggs on toast.

'How are you, Anne?'

I glanced down at my hands, which looked red and raw like the rest of my skin. 'Worn out.'

She put the tray on a small occasional table next to the chaise longue. 'Mr Broussard said he thought you would have drowned within minutes if they hadn't come across you in the water.'

I was filled with shame. How could I have done something so stupidly reckless. 'He saved my life – I suppose I owe him everything. And Loki, too. If he hadn't been on the beach, they wouldn't have veered closer to the land and found me.'

'Bloody dog. He killed one of the sheep and injured another that Robert Cooper had to finish off.'

'I promise you, I shut the gate behind me.'

She didn't say anything. After all, who was the most likely person to have let Loki escape? One of the two people who'd been living on the island for years, or the one new arrival?

'Maybe he jumped over the wall.' I was clutching at straws.

'Eat your breakfast,' she said. 'If you're up to it, Mr Broussard would like you to join him for dinner in the dining room this evening. I'll serve it at seven.'

'Of course.'

The tea made me feel half human again, and the buttery eggs were the food of the gods. I stayed in bed until late in the afternoon. Then I got up and went to work in the library. Despite a hot shower and my warmest jumper, I still felt cold, even though the library was well heated. But at least my hands had stopped shaking and I was able to get on with a couple of quiet hours of cataloguing.

At half past six, the library door opened and Lucien Broussard stepped into the room. He was in clean clothes, not a hair out of place. He couldn't have looked more different to the man who'd helped me on the beach the day before. He nodded at me.

I stood up. 'I need to thank you. You saved my life.'

'Of course we did. We wouldn't have left someone drowning in the water.' He sounded sharp. 'Please don't mention it again.'

'But . . .' That hardly seemed adequate, given the enormity of what he'd done for me.

He frowned at me, then walked around for a couple of minutes, examining the shelves. I'd made a tentative start on relocating the books according to the cataloguing, but there was still a long way to go. But my first move had been to put all the various sets of encyclopaedias together as the start of the non-fiction section.

'Presumably fiction will be housed on the opposite wall?'

I left my desk to join him in the centre of the room. 'It will. I thought I'd start it in that corner shelf, close to the window, and give it that entire wall.' I pointed to where I meant. Only about a quarter of the books in the library were fiction, and my plan was to arrange them alphabetically along the end wall that housed the fireplace, furthest from the door.

'Get Cooper to help you move the books.'

I murmured a non-committal reply. I really didn't want Robert Cooper invading what I'd come to view as my own personal space.

'Come and join me in my study for a pre-dinner drink.' He swept out without waiting for my answer, so I shut down my laptop and followed him.

I'd seen the study when Mrs Cooper had given me the whistle-stop tour on my first evening at Winterbourne, but I hadn't been back into the room since. It was wood panelled, with a row of three leaded windows which overlooked the carriage drive at the front of the house. Since the glorious weather of the day before had taken a turn to something more autumnal, I was glad to see a fire crackling in the grate. The only other light came from the desk lamp, and that was so feeble that I could barely see the corners of the room. It made it seem like a cave, but a warm and welcoming cave.

'Sit,' said Broussard, pointing at a pair of armchairs by the fire.

I did as instructed and watched him as he poured two glasses of something red from a decanter. Once again, he was dressed all in black, and with his black hair and dark eyes, there was something of a sense of drama to the way he looked. But I'd been expecting someone old. Old enough to have known Joseph Heller in the sixties. However, the Lucien Broussard in front of me didn't look more than forty, and I realised that the one addressed by Heller must have been his father or maybe his grandfather.

'Madeira,' he said, handing me a glass and taking a seat opposite me.

I'd never tasted Madeira before. I wasn't much of a drinker. In the firelight, the liquid glinted ruby. It tasted richer and more complex than red wine, but it was syrupy, and I wasn't sure that I liked it. I set my glass down on the low table between us. Broussard held his glass up in front of the fire, twisting it on its stem to catch the light. He took a sip, savouring the liquor in his mouth before he swallowed. I studied his hands, strong and tanned. He didn't wear a wedding ring, and there was no telltale ring of pale skin to show that he ever did.

'Mr Broussard, despite what you said in the library, I must insist on thanking you properly. You saved my life yesterday.'

He waved a hand as if to bat away my words.

'If you must,' he said with a sigh. 'But I should apologise to you. I was ferocious with you, wasn't I?'

'It was no more than I deserved. It was a stupid thing to have done.'

'You're all right now?'

I nodded and took another sip of the Madeira. 'I'm sorry too about Loki. I'm sure I shut the gate behind me, but maybe it didn't catch.'

'Cooper won't have it, but I think Loki can jump the wall. There's a section where the land slopes up steeply on our side. A dog that size could take a run at it, and Loki's a sly beast. Knows better than to let Cooper see him do it.'

I wondered if he was saying this to make me feel better.

'I should pay you the value of the dead animal.'

'Nonsense. You'll be eating most of it over the next couple of months. And stop calling me Mr Broussard. Lucien will do.'

I wanted to ask him all sorts of questions, like how long he would be staying, where he lived the rest of the time, what he did for a living. But I couldn't think of a way to bring them up without seeming nosy.

He emptied his glass. 'Come on, Mrs Cooper will be ready for us.'

I put my drink back on the table. I'd only drunk half of it, but it had left a slightly bitter taste in my mouth.

'Oh, for God's sake,' he said, as he entered the dining room ahead of me.

I peered round him to try and see what was wrong. He strode to the far end of the table and gathered up the place setting and glasses. Mrs Cooper had laid up at each end of the table, meaning that we would have been miles from one another. Lucien reset the cutlery in front of the chair next to his, and gestured for me to sit down.

'That's better. No one wants to shout while they eat.'

There was a bottle of red wine, already uncorked, next to his place. He picked it up and made a move to pour some into my glass.

I moved my hand to cover the glass. 'Thank you, but I'm not really a drinker.'

'No worries. Let me know if you change your mind.' He poured a modest measure of the wine into his own glass and put down the bottle.

There was the sound of wood cracking against wood and the door swung open to reveal Mrs Cooper pushing her way in behind an old-fashioned butler's trolley. On the top level were two plates covered with silver domes. She parked the trolley next to the table, frowning slightly when she saw that the place setting had been moved.

'Evening, Mrs Cooper,' said Lucien. 'What delights have you brought us?'

Mrs Cooper ceremoniously placed one of the plates in front of Lucien and raised the dome with a flourish. A puff of steam rose from the plate.

'Navarin of lamb with roasted root vegetables.' I noticed that a flush of pink had also risen in her cheeks.

It smelt delicious, but I suddenly felt a little pang of guilt. Was this the poor sheep that Loki had killed?

Mrs Cooper fetched the second plate from the trolley and placed it in front of me. It was certainly far grander than our kitchen suppers, and instead of the white kitchen crockery, this meal was served on a much finer pale blue china. A lot of extra effort for the boss.

'It looks wonderful,' I said. 'Thank you.'

Lucien nodded in agreement, and she practically simpered.

'Right, your dessert's down there.' She pointed at two bowls on the lower level of the trolley. 'I'll be off home now. Anne, you can manage coffee yourself, can't you?'

'Of course.'

'Mrs Cooper,' said Lucien, 'can you ask your brother to come by my study tomorrow morning after breakfast?'

'I'll tell him,' she said. 'Good night.'

'Goodnight,' said Lucien.

I waited until I felt sure she was out of earshot. 'Her brother? Is he staying with her?' I hadn't seen anyone else anywhere on the island.

Lucien gave me a puzzled look. 'Robert Cooper.'

'He's her brother?' I pondered this for a moment. 'But she's Mrs Cooper, so she married someone called Cooper, and his name's Cooper . . .'

'She never married. She reached a point when she decided she was too old to be Miss Cooper any longer.' Lucien laughed and his eyes danced, but there was warmth in his voice. They must have worked for him for a long time.

Brother and sister. That certainly explained some of her caustic comments about Robert Cooper. It also explained why they didn't have children.

We ate in silence for a few minutes, then Lucien topped up his glass.

'Tell me, Anne Adams, what was the first book from my library you started reading?'

I thought back to my first evening in Winterbourne. '*The Life of Pi*, one of my all-time favourites. Have you read it?'

'Of course. It's a stunning work, totally deserving of all the accolades it received. But what do you think – was Robert Parker really a tiger or was Pi's second, less palatable, accounting the truth?'

'I've always wanted to take his story at face value. He was on the boat with a tiger.'

'You'd rather think of the tiger eating the other animals, than cannibalism at sea? Animals are allowed to do things that are unacceptable behaviour in humans?'

'That's what makes us human. We have morals and values, beyond our animal instincts. Surely you believe that too?'

Lucien took a sip of his wine and pushed his chair back from the table to consider my question. After what seemed a long time, he spoke. 'I've seen plenty in my life that gives me reason to doubt that. But those are stories for another day. Let's see what Mrs, or really Miss, Cooper has left us for dessert.'

We spent the rest of the evening talking about the books we loved. Broussard was very well read. There wasn't a book I mentioned that he didn't know, and they were by no means all classics, while he mentioned lots that I hadn't heard of and I made a note to look up some of them in the library the next day. I surprised myself by accepting a small glass of wine. Then, we were both surprised when the lights cut off at midnight, but he easily located a couple of torches, then found matches to light three large candelabras on the table.

'Can I ask you something?' he said as he took his seat again.

'Go ahead.' I was expecting another bookish question.

'In the boat, I couldn't help but notice your scars. What happened to you?'

He caught me completely off guard. It was so direct. I wasn't used to people asking about the accident. I wasn't used to people at all, since I'd hidden myself away in my parents' house. I sat staring into my wine glass.

'Anne? Have I offended you?'

'No. No, of course not. It's just not something I really talk about.'

'Maybe it would help if you did.'

'It won't turn back the clock.' I didn't manage to hide my anger.

He frowned at me. 'I apologise if you thought my question inappropriate.' He didn't sound sorry. 'I'm just always interested in what makes people tick and how life has shaped them.'

'I'm sorry. I was in a car accident. I'm sensitive about it because my twin brother died.'

'You were driving?'

It was an assumption, but he was right. I barely nodded.

'I'm so sorry. That must be a terrible burden.'

It was, but no one apart from Lucien Broussard had ever acknowledged it before.

I didn't want him to see me cry, so I mumbled some excuses and took one of the torches to light my way up the stairs. I stumbled at the top of the grand staircase and dropped my light with a clatter. The beam of light swung across the landing floor as the torch rolled away from me. A movement caught the corner of my eye, something scurrying, no, gliding across the floor and disappearing into the dark shadows beyond the light.

I sprung to my feet and grabbed the torch, wielding it frantically from side to side, trying to catch whatever I'd seen in its beam.

But there was nothing there.

The thing had gone.

Another beam of light joined mine. It was Lucien, coming up the stairs behind me.

'Are you okay?'

'I stumbled,' I said, by way of explanation. 'Too much wine.' But it had only been one glass, hadn't it? 'I thought I saw something, scurrying away into the shadows.'

Lucien shone the beam of his torch into all the corners of the landing.

He laughed. 'Just a mouse. Mrs Cooper's supposed to keep on top of them.'

'Maybe it was a mouse.' It had seemed bigger than a mouse and had moved differently.

'Perhaps we should have a cat in the house,' he said.

The thing that slithered into the shadows, the cormorant with its turquoise eyes, sounds of the old house moving. They all kept me awake that night. Loki's mouth, dripping with the blood. Robert Cooper's sly grin. And most of all, the memory of Lucien Broussard's broad chest as he stood in front of me on the beach, offering me his sweater.

It was almost dawn before I slipped into Morpheus's embrace, and even then the peculiarities of Winterbourne haunted my dreams.

12

Alcohol lets the mind play tricks on you. When I woke up the next morning, I realised this. My dreams had turned the cormorant into a malevolent beast that was half human, half bird, but it was just a bird. The slithering black shape, which in my dreams had grown into an insatiable demon, had been nothing but a mouse, slipping away when my light disturbed it on the landing. How foolish I must have looked to Lucien Broussard, scared of my own shadow, tripping on the stairs.

Although it disappointed me, it didn't surprise me that there was no sign of him at breakfast and Mrs Cooper served me in the kitchen. I felt dehydrated and tired. Such vivid dreams were hardly restful. I lingered over my tea, watching Mrs Cooper making bread. I had so many questions about Lucien, but I didn't want to be the first to bring him up. However, Mrs Cooper was engaged in her task, with no apparent need for conversation, so eventually I took myself upstairs to the library to work.

My concentration was lousy. I was listening for Lucien at the door. I heard footsteps, his, I'm certain, going along the corridor outside, but he didn't come in. Later, I spotted him through the window, walking up towards the gate in the

Halfpoint Wall, Loki at his heels. Richard Cooper caught him up, carrying a couple of shotguns. So, they were going hunting, presumably for deer. I wished I was out there with them, even though the clouds were low and there was drizzle in the air.

I ate lunch alone in the kitchen. Later in the afternoon, when I went down to get myself a cup of tea, I heard voices in the butler's pantry. Mrs Cooper and Lucien, talking about a couple of deer carcasses from what I could hear, but neither of them came into the kitchen when the conversation finished. I took my time, eating an extra slice of Mrs Cooper's excellent fruit bread, but the house was quiet again. It felt like I was on my own.

I returned to the library, even though I'd done more than my required four hours. I was too restless to settle down in one of the armchairs and read a book. I paced the shelves, running my finger along the spines, pulling books out, fanning the pages and putting them back again. For a while, I pored over the pages of a Victorian world atlas. The maps were beautifully rendered, with sea serpents coiled in the oceans and colourful borders of plants and animals from far-off shores. But the repeated images at the bottom of each map of Britannia, straddling the globe with her shield and trident, left a bad taste in my mouth, while maps of the shipping routes served as an unpleasant reminder of the three-way trade that had underpinned the empire. Mrs Cooper had told me the Broussard fortune had been built on the spice trade, and now I realised that must have been a euphemism. It surely meant that at least part of the great fortune that had built this house had been derived from slaving.

Of course, this was the case for virtually all the grand houses built by the Georgians and the Victorians. Even once slaving had been abolished, the fortunes endured and the ruling class continued to benefit from the bounty born off misery and death. What did Lucien Broussard live on? Family wealth or did he make his own money? I realised I knew nothing about the man except for his ownership of Winterbourne and this extraordinary collection of books.

But I wasn't destined to find out more. Over the next few days, all I saw of Lucien were fleeting glimpses, out of windows, disappearing down corridors, or his voice overheard conferring with one or other of the Coopers. Was he actively trying to avoid me? What had I done? It seemed strange after our shared evening. I thought we'd been getting along fine, but perhaps he thought I was dull and ill-read compared to whoever he usually spent time with. I was just an employee, I supposed. So I got on with my task, feeling suddenly lonely, which I hadn't before he'd arrived on the island.

One morning, after Robert Cooper had scarfed his breakfast and bolted for the door, I decided to tackle Mrs Cooper.

'What does Mr Broussard do for a living?' I asked, as I cleared the used plates to the sink.

Mrs Cooper was preparing blackberries to make bramble jelly. 'He's a businessman.'

'What kind of business?'

She shrugged. 'Business. Money and companies and stuff.'

She didn't know. 'Is he married? Kids?' I tried to keep my voice casual.

She turned slowly towards me and gave me the sort of withering look she usually kept for her brother. 'Don't you be getting thoughts like that into your head, Anne. Not unless you want to enter a world of pain.'

I bristled. 'It was an innocent question. How long have you worked for him?'

She shrugged. 'A dozen or so years.'

'Don't you get bored of the isolation?'

'Mr Broussard needs me. It would be too difficult for him to find someone else.' She frowned at me. 'That's enough with the questions, Anne.'

'He's my boss. I'm just curious about him.'

'Well, don't be.' She turned back to the berries.

Conversation over. I'd been put in my place. She seemed very protective of him – something he surely hardly needed from her. I finished the washing up as quickly as I could and retreated to the library. But I found it difficult to settle down to my work. Instead, I gravitated towards the window and stared vacantly towards the horizon. How could the sea look so smooth and flat from here, when all the while, if you were on it in a small boat, the swell would be approximating a roller coaster ride? A tanker in the distance seemed to glide by effortlessly. Was it too big to feel the swell?

The day was fresh and there were rare glimpses of sunshine between the clouds. If I didn't feel like working, I could go for a walk. On days like these, I loved to watch the shadows of the clouds chase each other across the high moorland at the centre of the island. I hurried downstairs and grabbed my waterproof off the row of pegs by the kitchen door, driven to get out there before the weather took a turn. Loki greeted me excitedly in the courtyard and ignored my commands for him to stay put. He trotted by my side as I climbed the path to the Halfpoint gate, using my thumb stick to help me up the steep slope.

'Go home,' I said again, once we reached the gate.

He whined at me, imploring with huge dark eyes that seemed to promise he'd be on his best behaviour. Then a low grunt from behind me sent him running off back down the path. I turned, expecting to see Robert Cooper, but it wasn't him. The cormorant had landed on the Halfpoint Wall and was sitting with its wings outstretched. This was as close as I had come to it and it stared at me, unblinking, with its disturbing turquoise eyes.

How could I tell if it was always the same cormorant? This might be a different bird.

It croaked again and flew away.

Loki was nowhere to be seen, so I quickly went through the gate and shut it firmly behind me. Now that I knew the path and my leg was getting gradually stronger, I could walk at what was, for me, a decent pace, even though the land sloped gently upwards. A mile along the track that ran along the backbone of the island would bring me to the top of the moor, the highest point after Beacon Hill. The perfect place to blow away the cobwebs of my fuzzy head, with glorious three-hundred-and-sixty-degree views of the entire coastline.

After a brisk start, I slowed to a more comfortable pace, taking time to soak up the scenery which was an ever-changing tapestry, depending on the weather and the light. As autumn advanced, the bracken had all turned to rust and the last of the summer flowers were rapidly disappearing, though gorse and heather still gave bright splashes of colour here and there.

A dip in the land brought me past a small copse of sycamore and beech. The trees, though hardy, were stunted by the relentless wind and owed their meagre existence to the shelter afforded by a sweeping rise of the cliffs just beyond, protecting them from the worst of the weather.

Just as I reached the point where the path came closest to the trees, a guttural bark made me jump. I stumbled on a stone and dropped my stick. The sound came again, along with a rattling of branches and the thundering of hooves on the ground. Grabbing for my stick, I skidded to my knees, just as a huge rutting stag emerged from the sycamore trees. It galloped towards me, lowering its antlers, and in that second I was thrown back to the moment when a similarly huge stag had crashed through the undergrowth and onto the road directly in front of the car my brother and I were in. I'd steered one way, Malcolm had grabbed for the wheel and pulled it the other way. Our combined effort made the car skid. The stag leapt to one side, narrowly avoiding us, but by then our trajectory was fixed. We mounted the grass shoulder at the edge of the road, smashed into the low crash barrier, then rolled over the top of it and down the steep embankment beyond. The world became a juddering blur of pain. I thought my chest was caving in, my head so shaken that my neck could have snapped. The noise was deafening. I screamed. Malcolm shouted. The engine roared.

Then there was silence. I was hanging upside down, and at some point, everything went black.

I blinked. I wasn't in the wreckage of the car. I was on Craigsea Rock, sprawled on the path leading to the top of the island. The stag was still bearing down on me. I used my stick to pull myself quickly to my feet. I waved it and shouted, awkwardly moving backwards, away from the path, away from the trees, up the bare slope on the opposite side.

The deer rushed on along the path, still bellowing as it passed me, apparently satisfied that I was in retreat and no threat to its does. I turned and clambered as fast as I could up to the top of the open moorland. At the crest, I looked back. The stag had disappeared and I was alone. I dropped to my haunches, shaking like a leaf. I'd never relived the crash with such clarity of detail before. I'd thought I'd imagined the stag as a way of exonerating myself. The accident report never mentioned a stag, because there was no trace on the car of having hit the stag. I came to accept its non-existence, and the longer I'd believed that the stag wasn't real, the more I'd blamed myself. But now my memory was clear. The stag bearing down on us, my evasive action, Malcolm's panicked response. I couldn't conclude that I wasn't to blame. But it was more complex than I'd thought. Our combined reactions must have been responsible, and neither of us could have anticipated what the other would do.

I was panting. My chest was heaving. I kept rehearing Malcolm's scream as we rolled over and over down the embankment and I felt my heart breaking all over again. I needed to calm down before I had a full-blown panic attack. I had to get back to the house. The encounter with the stag had shocked me, and had thrown the past into stark relief. My therapist had warned me that I hadn't fully processed events, but now I had no choice but to face up to what had happened.

I pulled myself to my feet and set off across the open moor back to the Halfpoint Wall. I didn't want to drop down to the path in case the stag returned along it. It was difficult to find a way through the heather and the bracken, and my leg suffered all the more for walking over such uneven ground. It took me twice as long to get back to the gate, and by the time I reached Winterbourne, the heavens had opened.

I limped into the kitchen, leaving my stick in the vestibule. I sank into a chair, head in hands. Mrs Cooper was at the range.

'Was that you?'

Her voice sounded sharp, so I looked up. She was pointing at a pile of broken china in the centre of the table. I didn't recognise what it was.

'N-no. What is it?'

'Valuable is what it was. It came from China.'

I studied the pieces, still dazed from my experience up on the moor. 'I've never seen it.'

'Someone broke it,' said Mrs Cooper pointedly.

The inference was that I was responsible. Was that possible? Could I have brushed past it and knocked it over without realising it?

'You look like you've seen a ghost, Anne.' Lucien appeared as if from nowhere.

'I'm sorry.' I stood up, gripping the back of the chair. 'I appear to have broken something valuable.' I nodded at the debris on the table. Now I would be sacked, and sent back to my mother's house, where I would have all the time in the world to relive the accident over and over.

'Sit.'

My head was swimming.

'Mrs Cooper, sweet tea. Now.'

He sat down opposite me. 'I broke the vase on purpose. It wasn't you.'

I heard Mrs Cooper's sharp intake of breath. Lucien turned to her. 'It wasn't Anne.'

'But why?' said Mrs Cooper. 'That's one of the treasures your grandfather brought back from Japan.'

Lucien gave her a scathing look and turned back to me.

'Do you know the meaning of *kintsugi*?'

I shook my head. I wanted to leave the kitchen and hide out in the library until my mind had stopped racing, and until Malcolm's cries had stopped ringing in my ears. Mrs Cooper set down a steaming mug in front of me on the table.

'It's the Japanese art of repairing things using gold to fill the cracks. It imbues a certain power to the object.'

I had no idea what he was talking about, but now I felt even more stupid. I would have let Mrs Cooper blame me for something I had nothing to do with. I sipped the tea, hiding behind the mug. It was horribly sweet, but I supposed that would help.

'Are you okay?' he said, when I failed to respond to him.

I gathered my thoughts. 'I'm fine. I was surprised up on the moor by an aggressive stag, that's all.'

'I'm sorry. I meant to warn you. The deer are rutting just now and that can make the males particularly aggressive. Did it hurt you?'

I shook my head. 'Nothing like that. I think I'll feel better once I've rested.' I finished the tea as quickly as I could and left the kitchen. I could feel Lucien's eyes on my back as I left, and I willed him not to follow me out. I had to get away from questions and solicitous glances and other people's expectations about what I was feeling, just as it had been right after the accident.

I limped slowly up the grand staircase, remonstrating with myself.

It wasn't anything like the time after the accident, and I was being stupid. But the encounter with the stag had disturbed my fragile equilibrium.

Exhausted, I flung myself down on my bed as soon as I reached my room. Within minutes I was asleep. I missed dinner. When I was woken by footsteps hurrying past my door, the room was dark. I rubbed my eyes and sat up. I couldn't make out the dial of my watch, so I went over to the window. The sky was clear and the moon more than half waxed. It allowed me to see the time. I'd slept from 5 p.m. to just after midnight. Seven hours. And now I was wide awake. I couldn't see how I'd get back to sleep for the rest of the night.

The moors and the sea were painted silver and mercury in the moonlight and, for the first time since I'd arrived on Craigsea, there was a dusting of frost, glittering like ground glass. I shivered. My bedroom was cold, and I'd been lying on top of the bed rather than under the duvet. A door slammed somewhere above me. In the tower? The sound reminded me of the footsteps that had woken me. Lucien, prowling through the dark house, up to what?

A guttural shriek, followed in close succession by another one, made me jump. I couldn't tell if it was animal or human, or where it came from. I flung open my window to look down onto the terrace, letting a blast of icy air into the room. But outside, everything was silent. Nothing moved, and there wasn't even a breath of wind.

I heard the sound again. From somewhere within the house?

Was there someone there or was I imagining things?

I felt lightheaded. A drink and some food would bring me back down to earth. I hadn't eaten for hours. The kitchen would be warm and there was a gas lamp in there.

I grabbed my torch from the bedside table and quietly opened my bedroom door. As I did, the door from the servants' staircase opened just as quietly and a beam of torchlight emerged. I melted back into my room, leaving the door open a crack so its latch wouldn't make a sound. I didn't feel like bumping into Lucien and explaining why I was up and about.

But it wasn't Lucien who came down the corridor towards my room. It was Mrs Cooper, who surely shouldn't have been here at this hour. In one hand she carried the torch that was lighting her way. Her other hand clutched a large steel basin. There was something inside it, a mound of something, but I couldn't make out what.

Then I saw. The light of her torch skittered back and forth as she walked. As the light bounced back at her, reflected from a mirror, the contents of the bowl flashed clear. It was a pile of rags. Bloody rags. And there was blood on the hand that carried them.

13

I DIDN'T GO DOWN TO THE KITCHEN. I retreated to my bed and hid under the covers. I was awake for hours, but stress is exhausting, so eventually I slept again, though not well. I woke up several times thinking I could hear the half-human cries I'd heard earlier. But each time I raised my head in the dark to listen, the house seemed remarkably silent. No cries, no footfall on the stairs or creaking floorboards. At times I wasn't sure if I was awake or dreaming, and when I finally surfaced into the sunlight flooding the room through the open curtains, I didn't feel as if I'd rested at all.

What had been going on during the night?

The kitchen was deserted when I went down for breakfast, properly starving as it was almost twenty-four hours since I'd eaten. I was a little later than usual, but Mrs Cooper was usually there for most of the morning. Robert Cooper's breakfast things were in the sink, but there was no sign that Mrs Cooper had cooked anything for Lucien.

No matter. I was perfectly capable of getting my own breakfast. I made toast and scrambled a couple of eggs. I fried a rasher of bacon for good measure and made tea.

'Perfect,' said Lucien, appearing in the doorway without warning just as I was carrying my plate to the table. 'I'm starving.'

He sat down and I put the food in front of him, returning to the range to make more.

'Thank you, Anne.'

He looked fine. Vigorous, with a healthy flush to his cheeks. Not like someone who'd lost God knows how much blood in the middle of the night. How could I frame a question that would tell me without letting on what I'd seen?

'Last night,' I said slowly, as I sat down opposite him with my own breakfast.

He glanced up warily.

'Last night, I heard a horrible noise, like someone howling. Did you hear that?'

His expression relaxed. 'You mean the shearwaters. Like a child being throttled?'

'Exactly. It made my blood run cold. But they're just birds?'

'You'll get used to them.' He smiled. 'Haven't you heard them before?'

I shook my head.

'They're at it most nights. I sleep through it now. When you know what it is, it becomes much less disturbing.'

So much for the noises. But the shearwaters didn't explain Mrs Cooper's presence in the night, or the bloody rags she carried, or her absence now for that matter. Did I dare ask?

'Mrs Cooper's gone to the mainland with Robert Cooper this morning,' said Lucien.

I almost choked on the piece of bacon I was chewing. It was like he could read my thoughts. 'Oh.' Was it something to do with the events of the night?

'She has some family business to attend to. She'll be back in time to cook tonight's dinner. Though judging by this, you'd make a perfectly good job of it.'

His praise made me blush. It was so long since anyone had complimented me.

As I spent the morning working in the library, my mind kept wandering into thoughts of Lucien Broussard. The man was an enigma. Most of the time he was remote, acting as if I hardly existed. He barely nodded to me if I passed him in a passageway or came across him walking to or from the gate in the Halfpoint Wall. At other times, though rare, he was kind and solicitous. I'd felt so safe in his arms when he'd rescued me from the sea. I thought about the dinner we'd shared the day after he arrived on the island, and how we'd talked about books long into the night. That evening, we'd shared a certain intimacy, but since then he hadn't come into the library once and showed no interest in the work I was doing. He was either out and about, hunting with Robert Cooper, or closeted away in his study with the door firmly closed. I still had no idea what, if anything, he did for a living, or where he lived when he wasn't at Craigsea.

I decided I would try harder to engage with him. Not that I was lonely on the island. I'd always been happy with my own company and certainly wouldn't look to the Coopers for friendship. But I'd been effectively alone since Malcolm's death. I craved the companionship of another like-minded soul. Lucien was erudite and interesting. Dare I say it? I found him fascinating.

The plan to win his friendship, however, went nowhere. Over the next week, I saw nothing of him, quite literally. Once or twice, I heard his voice as I approached the kitchen, but he'd always disappeared by the time I reached it. Sometimes his footsteps would ring on the stairs. A few times I saw Mrs Cooper carrying trays to or from his study, but she rudely rebutted me when I offered to help. Since her trip to the mainland, she was sullen and hardly engaged with me during mealtimes.

I heard or saw nothing of Lucien at night, after the Coopers had gone back to their cottage. It was as if I was living at Winterbourne all on my own again, and it pulled me down into a darker mood. The days were all the same, one after another, working in the library, reading in the library, watching the weather rolling towards us across the water. The long-held fantasy of having a library all to myself was tarnished. What was the point if you couldn't share your bookish discoveries with others? For the first time, in all the weeks I'd been here, I began to wonder if it had been right to take such a remote job. Sure, I'd escaped from my mother, but it wasn't the way to escape my own demons, and I found myself spending more and more time thinking about Malcolm. I still felt to blame for the accident, and the memories that had returned were now keeping me awake at night.

A break in the weather gave me the chance to shake myself out of my malaise. Having seen a blue sky busy with birds from my bedroom window, I decided a day outside would press the reset button. I filled up at breakfast with extra bacon and toast. Then, as soon as I'd finished the washing up, I went out to the back vestibule to pull on my walking boots.

'And where are you off to?' said Mrs Cooper, appearing at the kitchen door.

'To take advantage of the day,' I said. 'I've a mind to climb Beacon Hill. I want to see the view from the top.'

'Then stay on the east side, in the sun. There'll be ice on the shaded side, making the pathway slippery.'

'Thanks.' It was a good tip.

Frost crunched underfoot as I set off along the track that led from Winterbourne to the Coopers' cottage and the jetty. The short grass glittered with it and the fronds of the bracken were rimed with hoarfrost and unexpectedly beautiful. My breath preceded me in swirling clouds as I set off at as brisk a pace as I could manage with my stick. My leg ached from the cold, but I was still pleased with my increasing strength and fitness.

Loki bounded up to me, barking with joy. I hadn't seen him for several days and, as I was walking on his side of the Halfpoint Wall, I'd brought some bacon wrapped up in my pocket. I tossed him a piece of it. His tail wagged and he danced round me, chewing happily.

'Eh, you'll spoil that damn dog.'

I looked up. Robert Cooper was coming up the track on the quad bike.

'Everyone deserves an occasional treat.'

'That so?' One of his eyebrows went up, and I realised he was reading more than I meant into the comment.

I gave Loki the rest of the bacon and carried on walking, relieved when Cooper revved the quad bike and went on his way. Realising that the bacon was all gone, Loki gambolled after him, his own panting breath creating clouds of steam in the cold air.

When I was almost level with Beacon Hill there was a path that split away from the track and wound around its base. I looked up at the climb ahead of me. The hill was steep but the path on this side swung from side to side in a series of hairpins to make the walk less precipitous. There was bracken and gorse growing up the side of the hill, but the path marked a clear passage between them, and though the ground was rocky and uneven, the climb wasn't particularly difficult, even for me.

I made steady progress, not hurrying, but keeping a good rhythm to my steps when the way allowed it. On the shoulder of the hill, there was a rocky outcrop of several huge boulders, tumbled against each other. It would make the perfect fort and I thought of how it would have delighted Malcolm if we'd come across a place like this as children.

The path cut through a narrow gap between two of the giant stones, with a waist-high step that led into a short, narrow passage. I pushed my stick up into the space, then turned my back to the step and pushed myself up to a sitting position on its edge. After that, I was able to swing round onto my knees and almost stand. The passage wasn't full head height, but after three or four steps it opened out onto a flat, gravelly patch behind the stones.

I stopped for a moment to catch my breath. I'd been on the island a month and I felt certain I couldn't have attempted this when I first arrived. But now the top was within reach, so I carried on. The path was steeper on the final section and gravel slipped under my boots, but fifteen minutes later I stood triumphantly on the summit, leaning back against the stone pillar of the beacon and stretching my arms up towards the sky.

'I did it!'

It felt like a real achievement. Maybe not much of one for someone fit and healthy, but it was for me. After the accident, I'd had three operations on my leg, and it was held together with titanium plates and pins in several places. The surgeon had warned me early on that I might never walk again, and at that time I was in such a dark place, I hadn't really cared. But now, having made it to the top of Beacon Hill, I appreciated how much I would have lost if it hadn't been for his good work and the help of all my therapists since.

I pulled off my backpack and, sitting at the base of the cairn, I drank water so cold that it felt like a blade slipping down my throat. The sky above was deep azure and the air sparkling clear. I could see all the island like a map below me, and across the water, there was Craigross, bathed in sunshine, as pretty as a postcard. Winterbourne sat like a majestic jewel in the landscape, and I could hear the murmur of the sea rolling against the rocks at the base of the cliffs.

In the distance, there was a whisp of smoke coming from the chimney of the Coopers' cottage, only just visible where the land dipped down to the bay. I could see the jetty and as I watched, Cooper rode out along it on his quadbike. There was something in the trailer. I squinted, bringing a hand up to my brow to block the sun. It was a suitcase, and he lowered it down the stepladder into the RIB. A few minutes later, Lucien arrived and climbed down onto the RIB. He said something and Robert Cooper threw back his head with laughter. Lucien laughed too. There was an easy camaraderie between them, and I felt jealous. Why would he choose to be Robert Cooper's friend but not mine?

It was the first time I'd seen Lucien in days, and if the case was his, it appeared it would the last time as well. The RIB pulled away from the jetty. He was leaving the island.

I watched for a few minutes longer as the RIB struck out into the open water. Part of me felt a little bereft, even though the man had hardly offered me any company. Now it would be back to just me and the Coopers. I couldn't help but wonder when he'd next visit the island. Winter was coming and a small rock in the Irish Sea might not seem so hospitable when it was dark and cold. But at least I'd be warm in the library, and I'd never run out of books to read.

The RIB was almost too small to see now, so I turned to take in the rest of the spectacular 360-degree view that the summit of the hill afforded. It was like looking down at a map of the island. I could see the Halfpoint Wall, slicing the plateau across the middle, and beyond it, the rough moorlands of the northern half of the island, dotted with granite outcrops and candytuft sheep. At the northern tip, there was a lighthouse that I hadn't realised was there. I suppose it made sense, given that the shipping route between Belfast and mainland Britain passed somewhere to the north of Craigsea. But why wasn't it operational? Perhaps satnav meant ships no longer needed lighthouses.

Looking down the other side of the hill, there was a ruined church that was hardly visible from the track to Winterbourne. It must have been used in the years when the house was first built, but I could see from my vantage point at the top of the hill that its roof had fallen in, and the graveyard that surrounded it looked unkempt and overgrown. There was a path leading down this side of the hill that went past the deserted building, so I put away my water bottle and picked up my stick.

This was on the shaded side of Beacon Hill and the path went almost straight down, unlike the meandering climb on the other side. No matter. It was downhill this time, and I was able to use my thumb stick as a break when necessary. I nearly slipped a couple of times. As Mrs Cooper had predicted, there were still pockets of frost and ice on this side of the hill. I didn't want to jeopardise my injured leg, so I made my way slowly, looking carefully as I placed each foot to avoid any slippery patches. Walking in the shade made me realise how cold it was, but the sky was still blue above and it felt good to be outside.

When I got to the low wall which surrounded the church and its graveyard, I sat down for a rest. It was a tiny building and while its four granite walls remained intact, the roof had gone and what looked like the remains of a bell tower had fallen to the ground at one end. The doorway was empty, as were the windows, and the grass around the tombstones was longer than any I'd seen on the island, sheltered from the sheep and the scouring wind.

There was a gate in the wall, but it was padlocked. However, it was easy enough to swing my legs over to the other side where I was sitting. I wanted to explore, to see who was buried here and whether any of the interior of the Broussard family chapel had survived.

As my steps sounded on the stone path that led from the gate to the door of the church, there was a sudden clatter of wings. A pair of magpies flew up, disturbed by my presence. They squawked angrily at me, settling on the stump of the bell tower at the far end of the building. I saluted them. One for sorrow, two for joy. My father had taught me the rhyme and when I was a child I believed that any sighting of a magpie was lucky. Maybe I still did.

Inside, the tiny church was just a husk. The flagstone floor had slumped and cracked in places and there was no sign of any pews. Perhaps someone had removed them to salvage the wood for other uses. I could see a rectangular mark on the floor where an altar had once stood, and the outline of a cross on the wall above it, but nothing remained. Black streaks on some of the walls and a few pieces of charred wood suggested there might have been a fire, though wind and rain had scoured most of the traces away. Close to the empty doorway, there was something scratched on one of the flagstones, a circular mark of some sort. I guessed it was where the font would have stood, but that too was gone. But looking at it more closely, it reminded me of the symbol tattooed on Lucien's forearm.

Standing in the shadow of the hill, it felt bleak and austere. Not the sort of place earlier inhabitants of the island might have come to for comfort.

The magpies shouted at me again, as if to tell me I was trespassing. I went back out into the graveyard. There were about twelve or fifteen tombstones, some standing straight, others tilting or cracked. The land sloped down towards the top of the cliffs, and the prevailing wind came in from over the sea. The stones were worn, scrubbed by sand and salt until the carved letters were hardly legible.

The largest of the tombs was covered by a granite slab at the head of which stood the ghost of a statue of an angel. The sandstone statue had been so eroded that the angel's face was gone and the one wing that remained was worn smooth of any feathers. The other wing lay broken on the ground next to the tomb. I squatted by the side of the slab and used my forefinger to trace the shallow letters and numbers. I could just make out a woman's name, Aisla Hamilton. The year was seventeen-something, but the other details were indecipherable. There was another name below hers. David Hamilton. I couldn't read the date. Perhaps her husband, or maybe her son. Maybe I would be able to find the church records somewhere in the library. I wandered round, peering hard at the other gravestones. Most of the writing had worn away, though on some there were enough letters to guess at a name. A couple more Hamiltons, certainly, and a Douglas or two. But, try as I might, I couldn't find a single gravestone with the name Broussard on it. So all those splendid gentlemen in the portraits had died and were buried elsewhere.

It seemed strange, but maybe Winterbourne was no more than some sort of beefed-up holiday cottage for them. A private place where they could get away from everything to hunt and shoot, and throw balls and parties. It was hard to imagine a lifestyle more different from the lives of my mother's and father's families, who were solidly middle class and who had all worked for a living.

I'd reached the furthest corner of the churchyard when I made an unnerving discovery. Hidden out of sight, behind three slumped-sideways tombstones, I stumbled across a long, rectangular slash of bare earth cut into the grass. I knew what it was straightaway. A fresh grave. I couldn't tell how fresh. The earth was tamped down, not mounded up as it sometimes is immediately after burial. I looked to either end, but there was no gravestone, not even a wooden cross to mark the place where a gravestone would go.

Could someone have died on the island recently? Some time before my arrival?

I shivered as a breeze stirred the cold air around me. But it wasn't the wind. It was the cormorant, settling on the graveyard wall, just a few feet from where I was standing. It gave one of its singular barks. I turned away. I found there was something deeply unsettling about the bird, and I didn't want to make eye contact with it. I could picture it flying back to Robert Cooper and telling him exactly what I was doing and where I'd been.

A nonsense of course, but it was time to get going. There were clouds bubbling into existence to the west and the temperature seemed to be dropping fast. I'd missed lunch and it wouldn't be long until the gloaming fell like a cloak across the island.

14

Spooked by what I'd seen at the graveyard, I hurried back along the track towards Winterbourne. I felt exhausted. Perhaps climbing the hill had been a little too much for me. My leg, already aching, succumbed to a sharp stab of pain that almost toppled me over. After that, I slowed right down, limping as I used my stick to bear half my weight.

The sound of something scurrying behind me made me catch my breath, but it was just Loki, as pleased as ever to see me in the hope of more bacon scraps.

I stopped walking and bent to scratch him behind his ears.

'I've nothing for you, lad.' But it was nice to have company for the rest of my walk back.

When I reached the kitchen door, he dropped to his haunches and whined. He knew he wasn't allowed into the house.

'Sorry, you'd better get off home now, Loki.'

Mrs Cooper appeared in the doorway. 'Scram,' she shouted at him. 'Go find Robert Cooper.'

Loki took one look at her and skulked back towards the archway.

'But Robert's gone to the mainland,' I said, as I followed her inside.

Mrs Cooper gave me a questioning look.

'I saw the RIB leaving from the top of Beacon Hill.'

'And Loki can go wait by the jetty,' she said. 'You look famished. I'll make you some eggs.'

Mrs Cooper occasionally surprised me with small acts of kindness like this. Most of the time she was a taciturn presence in the kitchen, doing what she needed to without chatter or any warmth. Sometimes I thought it was a sign that she disliked me being at Winterbourne, but then she'd do something like this, making me realise it was just the way she was.

Five minutes later, I was tucking into beans on toast with a poached egg on top, accompanied by a mug of strong, restorative tea. Mrs Cooper sat down opposite me and sipped from her own mug of tea.

'Can I ask you something?'

She shrugged. She couldn't really stop me.

'There's a new-looking grave in the graveyard by Beacon Hill.'

Her face was blank.

'Someone's been buried recently. Who was it?'

Then she frowned. 'No one's been buried in the Michael Kirk's graveyard for decades. Maybe a hundred years or more.'

I shook my head. 'No, there's a grave that's much more recent. In the far corner. The earth's been disturbed.'

'No one's died here. No one's been buried. Might be that Loki went digging for bones.' She smiled, but not with any real feeling.

I knew that what I'd seen wasn't the result of Loki digging for bones. It was a precise rectangle cut into the grass, not the frenzied digging of an overexcitable dog. But I also realised I wasn't going to get any more out of her. Was that because she wasn't telling or because she didn't know? There would be no point asking Robert Cooper about it, and Lucien had left the island. It would remain a mystery.

The weather drew in that evening, and a heavy, wet fog kept me indoors for several days. I worked diligently in the library, cataloguing books and rearranging shelves. The work was methodical, and it allowed my mind to wander. As I typed away on the laptop, part of me was exploring Winterbourne and the island, looking for answers to the questions that kept on repeating themselves in my brain.

I searched for books that might give me the answers. A history of the Broussards perhaps, the parish record of the ruined church. But I couldn't even find a reference to the church's name. There was no local history, which seemed strange. When the Coopers had gone back to their cottage in the evenings, I searched the kitchen for household paperwork. I don't know what I expected invoices and shopping lists to tell me, but they told me nothing as I didn't find any. There was a small room off the kitchen, the butler's pantry, where Mrs Cooper sometimes worked at a desk, but the drawers of this were empty and there were no household ledgers from earlier times on the shelf above it.

Perhaps Lucien's study would afford me some answers, but the door was locked. I searched everywhere for a key to it, over a couple of evenings, but I was thwarted in this too.

Looking out of the windows, I could see nothing but the pale grey miasma. It was as if Craigsea Rock had been swallowed by a cloud. The house was completely enveloped. The wind had dropped, and the fog barely stirred. The roar of the waves and the cries of the gulls were muffled. All I could hear outside were heavy drops of water falling from the gutters and gargoyles onto the terrace below my window. And at night, the sound of shearwaters, their cries even more haunting when everything else was silent. They sounded closer than they had done before, as if they were huddled on the roof of the tower or down in the rock garden at the side of the terrace.

I ventured out only once while the fog was so heavy. After days indoors, I started to suffer cabin fever. The air in the library seemed stale, and I wanted to smell the tang of the sea and feel the soft sponginess of the grass beneath my boots.

Mrs Cooper cocked an eyebrow at me as she saw me preparing to go out.

'Don't get lost out there, Anne. Robert Cooper won't appreciate it if he has to go out searching for you.'

'Just a breath of fresh air. I won't stay out long.'

She was mothering me. But at least, unlike my real mother, she wasn't reminding me of what I'd done to Malcolm.

Outside, it was much colder than I expected. I'd maybe thought the fog would act like a blanket over the island, but that wasn't the case. I could hardly see across the courtyard to the archway, and when I reached it I found myself staring out at a blank expanse of dirty white. All I could see was the track at my feet, so I took the decision to stick to it so I wouldn't get lost, or worse, walk over the cliff edge.

Within minutes, tiny droplets of water clung to my jacket and my trousers. My hands and my cheeks felt wet. But at least it gave me the chance to stretch my legs. I walked as briskly as I could manage, trying to burn off the excess energy that had built up from the sedentary days in the library.

The fog made everything silent, apart from the sound of my own feet. The house was between me and sea, and I couldn't even hear the waves. And as I walked on up the track, the shadowy outline of Winterbourne disappeared behind me. I could see nothing ahead, or to either side. I felt completely alone, and I could have been anywhere on the island.

Suddenly, something whistled through the air close to my cheek. At the same time, I heard a loud crack. Gunfire? Someone was out here shooting, in the mist?

I dropped instinctively to my haunches.

'Who's there?' My voice sounded loud and confident, though that wasn't how I felt inside.

'What the hell are you doing out here, girl?' Robert Cooper loomed towards me from the side of the track.

I used my stick to pull myself upright again. 'I could ask the same of you,' I said, 'but I don't need to. It's clear what you're doing. Taking random potshots.'

'I thought you was a deer come over the wall.'

How could he have thought that? 'If you couldn't see the difference between a deer and human, you had no business to be firing your gun. You nearly killed me.' I would never normally have raised my voice at Cooper, but I was furious. His bullet had missed me by an inch. The man was a dangerous idiot.

I stared at him defiantly, but he stood his ground, his shotgun now hanging broken over his forearm. I'd noticed that when Lucien wasn't here he behaved as if the island was his own private fiefdom. He glared at me for a moment, then he laughed.

'Mrs Cooper told me you was asking about the fresh grave in the Michael Kirk.'

'I was. I wanted to know who was buried there.' At least he didn't seem to deny its existence.

'Wasn't a person. There's a dog in that grave. Loki had a sister, Daruka. I buried her there to stop Loki digging her up. Dog was mad with grief. But I never told Mrs Cooper. She wouldn't hold with burying a dog in the churchyard.'

'What happened to her?'

'She got in a row with a goat, north of the Halfpoint, and was gored.'

Standing still made me feel colder and I realised my clothes were drenched through. I gave Cooper a sharp nod and turned back towards Winterbourne. I hoped he would at least forebear from shooting again until I'd had time to get back to the house. But I didn't have much faith in him, so I hurried back along the track, though the cold had stiffened my leg.

Somewhere out in the mist, I heard the harsh caw of the cormorant, and I caught a whiff of a rotten, fishy smell. The bird must be close at hand. My eyes searched the grey miasma for its black silhouette, but I could see nothing. Something behind me made an answering call. Robert Cooper and his familiar. It was a sobering thought, knowing he was somewhere behind me in the mist with his gun.

They called to each other a few more times, and I'd never felt more thankful when the dark outline of Winterbourne came into view. I almost broke out into a run to get through the arch and into the courtyard, and though fog persisted for another week, I didn't go outside in it again.

15

I SHUT MYSELF IN THE LIBRARY and avoided looking out of the windows at the swirling bank of fog. It seemed like it would never lift, and the house became claustrophobic and dark due to its constant presence. Sounds were muted and the air seemed damp and thick, even in the library with its underfloor heating. I worked longer hours than I was contracted to as I felt an urge to get the job done. What had seemed such a magical world when I first arrived no longer enchanted me. I don't know if it was because of the fog, or because Lucien had left, or because of Robert Cooper and the way he talked to that damn bird.

But I felt unnerved and uncomfortable. As if I was always looking over my shoulder and peering into shadows. Unexpected noises made me jump. And though I'd tried to put the episode with the moths out of my mind, every now and again I would brush my hand against one of the bookshelves and it would come away marked by the dust from a moth's wing. I'd tried to tell myself I'd imagined the hundreds of death's-head moths that had infested the library that day, but here was evidence to the contrary. They had been real.

When I wasn't working, I immersed myself in reading. I reread old favourites for comfort and discovered new writers that took me to unknown worlds. I chose stories set in faraway places, under hot suns and cloudless skies, where there was no chance of suffocating fogs. And I often thought of my old job, and Marisa, and the bright, modern library at home which seemed a million miles from this one.

One afternoon, in an idle moment, I decided to explore the plan chest. The top drawer was empty. It was where, following Lucien's instructions, I'd found the laptop that I was using to do the cataloguing. But I'd never looked in any of the other drawers, as I assumed the contents wouldn't be relevant to my work.

I pulled on the small brass handles of the second drawer with no expectations. At first it wouldn't open. Then the right side gave a bit, making the drawer crooked. I shoved it back in, trying to straighten it, jiggling it a little from side to side. It took a few attempts, but finally I got it open. My reward was a pile of sketchbooks, thick and heavy, with clothbound board covers. I carried them over to one of the big round tables and took the first from the pile.

When I opened it and saw the name 'Lucien Broussard' handwritten in an ornate calligraphic script, I must admit my heart fluttered. But this book was too old to have belonged to the current Lucien Broussard. It must have been his father's, or perhaps his grandfather's.

I turned the pages slowly. Every sheet was filled with sketches. Some were landscapes I recognised from the island, and seascapes which must have been drawn from the top of the cliffs. The lighthouse featured in one of them, Winterbourne in another and the old Michael Kirk, already missing its roof. There were pictures of birds, seabirds and garden varieties, including an ominous-looking cormorant which could easily have been the bird that plagued me now, but almost certainly wasn't. There were dogs on the pages, and deer, sheep and goats, as well as studies of plants and flowers. Whoever had drawn them was clearly a skilled artist, filling in details where necessary, but also able to represent what he saw in a few bold strokes of his pencil. I was more than a little impressed.

There were four sketchbooks altogether. The other three were from further afield and didn't include drawings of Craigsea Rock. One was filled with pictures of London, and looking at the street scenes, with a mixture of horse-drawn vehicles and early motor cars, it must have dated from the turn of the last century. Towards the end of the book, there were pictures that were recognisable as Paris as well, interiors and street scenes, and one tantalising sketch of a beautiful young woman. There was no name, no captions or titles to any of the drawings, but could she possibly have been Lucien's grandmother? I was intrigued.

There were pictures of Egypt and the pyramids, and scenes of India and Turkey in the other two sketchbooks, extensive travels in the Alps, as well as a few that appeared to have been drawn from onboard a ship in the Norwegian fjords. Whichever Lucien Broussard was responsible for them was very well travelled.

I piled them up and put them back into their drawer. I wondered whether to ask Lucien about them if he returned, but perhaps that would be intrusive.

The third drawer opened easily and was filled with something more expected, a large stack of architectural drawings and floorplans. I took them out to study them and saw immediately that these were the blueprints for Winterbourne. It was such a glorious house, and the architect's drawings had set it in a series of formal gardens, which must have been part of the original plans. Perhaps he'd not realised how inhospitable the setting was to everything but the hardiest of flora. There were elegant pen and ink drawings from every elevation, and it refuelled some of the wonder I'd felt when I first arrived. The floorplans fascinated me even more. The ground floor was such a warren. The grand reception rooms for the householders were supported by dozens of corridors and smaller rooms and offices that were the domain of the servants. There were plenty of rooms I'd never even been into, to which locked doors barred the way. I assumed this was because they were simply not used anymore, rather than to hide any secrets, but I thought it might be fun to have a nose around, if I could locate the keys. Also worthy of investigation, I saw that there were stairs leading down from behind the butler's pantry. A plan of the basement showed a series of rooms labelled 'Turkish bath', complete with the outline of what was either a giant tub or a small plunge pool. I wondered if it was still there.

Comparing the ground floor and first floor plans, I could see that indeed the library was easily as big as the ballroom, if not bigger. There were scores of bedrooms. I suppose these were needed when the Broussards threw a ball. There could be no 'carriages at one' on Craigsea.

I pondered over how clever the architect had been in creating a house that was at once beautiful and also functional for the way people lived at the time it was built. Of course, nothing like this would ever be built again, because even the super-wealthy don't have such huge armies of servants. Simple, labour-saving household devices have seen to that.

It was when I was working out how the second floor related to the first, or more specifically whether my bedroom was above Lucien's bedroom or the far end of the library, that I noticed something strange on the blueprint.

There was a void. At one end of the library, between it and the next labelled bedroom, there was a gap. It was a small rectangle that had no label and showed no features. There wasn't a window or a fireplace, or even a door, marked on the blueprint. Just a white, rectangular void. I thought perhaps it could be some sort of area of structural support for the tower. But checking it against the second-floor plan, it seemed to be directly below my bedroom.

I stood up and went over to the end wall of the library. It was completely obscured by shelves of books, of course. I went out of the library and along the corridor. The next door I came to was unlocked. It was for the bedroom shown on the blueprint. There was no door corresponding to the gap between it and the end of the library. I went into the corridor and inspected the wall closely, full expecting there to be a secret door, or signs that a door had existed but had been walled across. There was nothing. The wall was pristine.

I went back into the empty bedroom. There was a wardrobe positioned against the wall that it shared with the void. I opened the wardrobe but there was no Narnia moment. It was empty and the back of it was solid, even as I banged my fist on it and felt all around the edges for hinges or a hidden door handle. It seemed a silly idea, as I shut the wardrobe and went back to the library. But could it be there was a door which was now hidden by the wardrobe?

I decided I would go back to the bedroom once the Coopers had gone, and see if I was able to shift the wardrobe enough to inspect the wall behind it. I knew that old houses sometimes had secret rooms. There had to be a way of getting into this one.

I went back to the library and looked out of the window. Amazingly, the fog seemed less dense than it had done for days. Good. I would go and look from the outside. I went quietly down the grand staircase and out of the front door, as I didn't want to go through the kitchen and face Mrs Cooper's questions. Outside, it was as damp and clammy as ever but now at least I could make out the balustrade along the far edge of the terrace. I walked along the side of the house until I was standing underneath the row of library windows. I counted up to the last one. I knew the bedroom on the far side of the void was a corner room, so its window would be the last one on that side of the house. But when I looked, there were two dark windows beyond the lit windows of the library. So, the secret room did have a window after all.

I stared up at it, wondering what was behind the glass. Solid black as far as I could see. The room looked much darker than the bedroom next to it, and I realised that either the panes of glass had been painted black on the inside or that it was a fake window, one of those architectural tricks to keep the outside of a building looking symmetrical, regardless of what was going on inside.

As I turned to go back around the corner of the house to the front door, something fluttering down through the mist caught my eye. A long white feather landed on the flagstones in front of me. I peered upwards, but there was no sign of any bird, either flying past or roosting on the roof, as I'd occasionally seen gulls do.

I picked up the feather. It was pure white, in pristine condition. All the barbs held together with no splits, and at the base of the quill, there was a frill of soft white down. I twisted it in my fingers, then took it inside. Back in my room, I placed it on the mantelpiece. It looked to me like a swan's feather, though there were no swans on the island. It must have come from a gull. I would consult one of the bird books in the library and see if I could work out what sort of gull it came from. And I wondered if its owner would miss it, or did birds shed feathers just as casually as humans shed hair?

After supper, I dragged out the washing up and tidying up so I could be sure that the Coopers had left the house. Then, as soon as the outer door slammed behind them, I went back up to the bedroom at the end of the library corridor. The wardrobe that stood against the wall adjoining the void was wide, and even though it was empty, it proved to be too heavy for me to move. There was a drawer at the bottom and when I opened it, I found it was full of folded blankets. I took them out and piled them on the bed, then removed the drawer as well, hoping this would be enough to make a difference.

Taking a deep breath and pressing my shoulder against the wardrobe's side, I shoved as hard as I could. With a screeching of its feet against the wooden floorboards, it moved slightly. Enough for me to get my hands round the corner of its side and back, and then lever it out a few more inches. That would be enough. Panting with the exertion, I pulled my mobile from my pocket and shone the torch into the narrow gap behind it.

I gasped.

Where I was expecting to see a door, there was nothing. Flat, plain wall. I let my eyes wander slowly over its smooth surface. There were no miniscule cracks, no secret keyhole or recessed handle. No button that might be pressed to reveal an Aladdin's cave. Those were the stuff of stories, not real life.

I had to face it. The void was just a void, with no way in, and no secret treasures for me to discover.

Outside, the shearwaters erupted an ugly chorus of agreement.

16

THE FOG FINALLY BLEW THROUGH, leaving Craigsea Rock a winter wonderland of frost that glimmered in the pallid winter sunshine. I was able to get outside again, and the fresh air was a welcome treat after days and days in the fusty library. I found myself drawn to Beacon Hill, though I wouldn't always climb all the way to the top.

I'd done this several times before I realised exactly what I was up to.

I always made my way to the southern shoulder of the hill, to a point where I was high enough to see the cove and the jetty at the south end of the island. Then I would look for the RIB. If it was there, tied up in its usual place, I would feel a slight slump of disappointment. But if it was missing, that meant that Cooper had gone to the mainland. I would watch for a while in case I could spot it returning. It was only when I saw it coming into the harbour that I understood what I was looking for. But, no, Lucien Broussard wasn't on the RIB with Cooper.

I think my cheeks flamed red, even though I was alone on the hill and nobody knew what I was thinking. The man barely spoke to me when he was here, so why was I pining for his return? I stomped down the hill and along the track back to Winterbourne, but I couldn't keep myself from thinking about him. I kept reliving that moment on the beach when he'd peeled off his sweater, and the way his warmth transferred from the fabric to my skin. I remembered staring at his hand as he'd refilled my wine glass in the dining room the following evening. And how reassuring his voice had sounded when he'd spoken to me in the kitchen after my encounter with the stag. 'Are you all right, Anne? You look like you've seen a ghost.' I hadn't experienced feelings like this for anyone before, and it unsettled me.

The next time I went out, I turned north towards the Halfpoint Wall. I'd seen the old lighthouse from the top of Beacon Hill, but I'd never been there. It would be a long walk, almost the entire length of the island, but the days were getting shorter and the fine weather rarer, so I decided it was now or never. I packed a flask of tea and made a couple of cheese sandwiches out of the end of the previous day's loaf. Mrs Cooper watched my preparations, but she didn't say anything. That was fine by me. I didn't need another lecture about how I might put Robert Cooper out if he had to come searching for me. And I could hardly get lost. There was a track that led up the spine of the island from the Halfpoint all the way to the lighthouse at its northern tip.

I guessed it would take me about two hours to walk there, then I could have my lunch and walk back, hopefully reaching Winterbourne before dusk fell. I packed a large torch in my backpack, just in case it took longer and I arrived home after sundown. I didn't feel bad about taking the day off as I'd done way more than my hours while I was stuck in the library during the fog.

'See you later,' I called to Mrs Cooper as I left the kitchen.

'No doubt,' she said. There was a sour tone to her voice, but I put it out of my mind as I strode out along the path that led up to the Halfpoint gate. The sun was playing hide and seek with clouds that were bubbling up over the sea to the west, but they were white and puffy. I didn't see a threat of rain.

The walk was a pleasure. I was getting better at identifying the birds I spotted, and north of the Halfpoint Wall there were also the sheep and deer to look out for. For all the lack of exercise over the past couple of weeks, I was surprised at how energised and fit I felt. I was the only human for miles around, and such was my mood that I started singing as I walked. My voice isn't particularly tuneful, and I'd never sing in public or do karaoke, but there were only the birds to hear me missing the high notes and they didn't seem to mind.

The sound of a twig cracking somewhere behind me gave me cause to stop mid-chorus. I looked round sharply, but the path behind me was completely empty. There weren't even any trees nearby that would shed branches onto the track. A movement in a stand of dead bracken caught my eye. That must have been it. Some small animal, or a bird maybe, breaking the stem of a dried fern. I walked on, but I didn't resume my singing.

My mind wandered back to the void between the library and the next-door bedroom. What secrets were contained in that space? And why was the door that led to the floor above always locked? What had Mrs Cooper been doing that night, when I'd seen her with blood on her hand? I had started to doubt what I thought I saw. It wasn't blood, just some trick of the torchlight, reflecting off the red corridor walls. Or she'd been using a red rag to clean something and that's why it looked like blood. She shouldn't have been there at that hour of the night, but perhaps I misremembered the time. Whatever the explanation, I didn't feel I could question her. The whole episode left me feeling unsettled. Winterbourne left me feeling unsettled. I should work faster and start to think about what I'd do and where I'd go once the cataloguing was finished.

As I crested the top of the domed moorland that comprised the northern third of the island, the lighthouse came into view. It stood on a short spit that stuck out into the sea, at the top of the highest of all Craigsea's cliffs. It was a round tower that once had been painted white, but now much of the paint had been scoured away, leaving it a dirty, mottled grey colour. At the top, there was a band of faded red paint, above which the glass lantern room glinted in the sun.

The sight of it renewed my vigour, and as I was now walking downhill, I sped up without really thinking about it. From a distance, the tower didn't look very high, but the nearer I came the taller it seemed to be. Thirty feet, fifty feet, seventy feet ... my estimate changed by the minute as I got closer.

I heard a clatter of gravel on the track behind me. There was someone following me. I whipped my head round over my shoulder and Loki barked a cheerful greeting.

'Oh no, Loki. Not again?' I put out a hand and he rushed to me, tail wagging. 'What are you doing all the way up here? Is Cooper with you?'

He barked in answer but told me nothing.

I straightened up and looked back along the track. There was no sign of Robert Cooper up on the moor. I felt relieved. I hated the way he was always appearing when I was out and about, as if he was spying on me. Though Lord knows why he would do that. I didn't exactly go anywhere interesting.

'Come on, stay with me.' I carried on walking and Loki fell into step by my side.

Ten minutes later, I was at the base of the lighthouse. With cliffs and sea on three sides, the narrow spit of land on which it stood was bleak and windy. I could easily imagine how isolated it must have felt as a working lighthouse, with an endless vista of grey water stretching to the horizon, and a succession of storms rolling in. The waves crashed relentlessly on the rocks below, and every minute or so a great plume of spray would rise over the cliff edge before falling away tumultuously. Each time it happened, Loki danced around me, barking with furious excitement.

I walked up to the door. The paint was faded and peeling. The wood was weather-beaten and warped. The place must have needed year-round maintenance and obviously hadn't had any for a considerable time. I tried the door handle. It moved stiffly and when I pressed my shoulder against the door, it pushed open with a creak of protest.

'Stay here,' I said to the dog. Then I squeezed through the gap, into the base of the lighthouse.

It was dark at the bottom. There didn't seem to be any windows on the ground floor level, or for some way up the tower. I supposed they would have been constantly drubbed with seawater. I dug the torch out of my backpack and shone it around. I was in some sort of engine room. There was a rusty machine that I guessed was a generator to power the lamp, and along one wall there were rows of barrels. A strong smell of oil pervaded the air. The light must have run on diesel.

Opposite the barrels of oil, a stone staircase clung to the curving wall as it made its assent up the tower. I swung the torch beam up and saw its spiral form snaking up to the top. At intervals weak daylight bled in through the lighthouse windows, but even on the sunniest of days the place must have been overwhelmingly dull and gloomy. I looked around for a light switch, but of course, if the generator hadn't run in years, there'd be no power left.

I desperately wanted to climb the staircase and see the view from the top. There was no banister, just a rusted chain attached to the tower wall. Something to grab hold of, but possibly not reliable. I could see that the lower steps were worn, some of them sloping, and there was water dripping from higher up the staircase, probably spray from the waves coming in through a broken window. That meant they might be slippery. I flexed my weak leg. If I'd been a sensible person, a logical person, I wouldn't have been so foolhardy, but I leant my thumb stick against the wall by the door, took the torch in my left hand and tested the tension in the chain handrail with my right. It held fast. I tugged on it hard. It seemed strong enough. I looked up. The stairs spiralled away forever, but I didn't need to climb all the way to the top.

It was easy going at first, but the tower narrowed as it got higher, and that meant the steps became steeper the higher I climbed. I was pulling myself up using the chain, and I wished I had gloves, because its surface was rough and bits of rust flaked off in my hand each time I grabbed it. At regular intervals, there were wooden joists stretching across the tower. There must have floors, dividing the tower into rooms, but there was no sign of that now. At the second-floor level, there was a rectangular opening, but any window frame or glass was long missing. This was where the spray was blowing in, and I took particular care on the wet steps. Although I was nowhere near the top yet, it would still be a long fall if I slipped.

Once I'd passed that empty window, the steps were dry again. There was more daylight further up and I passed a succession of windows that still had their glass, albeit the frames looked rotten and in need of repair. I kept going, breathing harder with the exertion of the climb. The smell of diesel oil had fallen away and now the air smelt of a mixture of rotting wood and the breath of the sea. Gradually, I became aware of a sweeter note, as if there was something rancid, slowing mouldering away. Some of the window frames had blooms of fungus on them. Maybe these accounted for the strange aroma.

As the stench became stronger, I also became aware of a low buzzing sound coming from somewhere above me. Was some part of the machinery for the light at the top still live? Maybe some water had leaked in, causing it to short circuit. The pitch of this droning rose and fell in intensity and as it became louder, the sound became more piercing.

As I reached the top of the staircase, both the noise and the smell became more acute. At this point, I could see that steel joists had been used to support the top floor, presumably because of the weight of the huge lamp in the lantern room. It meant that the floor was mainly intact, through there were a few chinks in it where individual floorboards had rotted away. I didn't need my torch up here, so I switched it off and craned my neck to look upwards as I emerged into the lantern room.

A black speck buzzed into my line of vision, then another, and I realised immediately that the droning wasn't a machine. It was flies. Great big, black blowflies. Thousands. Hundreds of thousands. They were swarming on the floor, the walls, the ceiling and even on the glass panes of the windows and the lantern itself. But most of all they formed a writhing black and blue mass on the floor just at the top of the staircase, right in front of my face as I emerged into the lantern room. This was the cause of the stench. I was overcome with a violent urge to throw up.

I needed to get away, but I couldn't tear my eyes from what was in front of me.

Emerging from the swarming mound was something small, wrinkled, the colour of human flesh. A hand. A tiny, tiny human hand. It must have been the hand of a newborn.

As I watched, it disappeared under the tide of the angry black horde, intent on devouring it.

17

I GASPED AND MY LEGS CRUMPLED under me. I fell backwards, and if I hadn't managed to get a hand up to the chain and grab it, I would have undoubtedly fallen to my death. As it was, I smashed back against the tower wall, one hip crushed on the edge of a step and my shoulder wrenched back painfully as my arm took my weight.

My scream echoed down the interior of the lighthouse.

My head banged against the wall and I saw stars. The torch rattled down the stairs and rolled over the edge. A fraction of a second later, I heard it smash on the floor at the base of the tower.

I was violently sick.

Still panting, I wiped my mouth with my arm. I was mouth breathing to minimise the stink of the carcass, and I couldn't process what I'd just seen. A baby? Who would leave a dead baby up here? Where had it come from?

Slowly, clutching at the heavy chain with trembling hands to keep myself steady, I clambered to my feet. I was torn. I had an overwhelming urge to hurry down the staircase as fast as I could, to get out of this godforsaken tower. Adrenalin surged through me, urging me to get away. But part of me needed to confirm what I'd just seen. I needed to know that I hadn't imagined it.

The droning buzz of the blowflies vibrated through my skull like a warning. An omen of something unpleasant to come. Climbing the stairs had made me sweat. Now it turned ice cold on my skin.

I took a deep breath and gritted my teeth. Could I face my fears? I went back up a few steps so I could once again see into the lantern room. My whole body shook as I slowly raised my head. The sight that met my eyes was just as repulsive. A million swarming flies, greedy with bloodlust, feasting on the small body that lay on the floor in front of me. But this time I could see it more clearly. It wasn't a human baby. It was a bird, some sort of gull perhaps. What I had seen as a tiny, pink, crumpled fist was the poor creature's pink, scaly foot. I'd seen it for a flash of a second and my brain had filled in the gaps, creating a little hand in my mind's eye.

I swore softly under my breath, disgusted with what I saw and disgusted with my own imagination for making it into something so much worse.

The flies finally noticed my presence, and a phalanx of them started buzzing round my head angrily.

'It's all right. You can keep it,' I said. I felt furious with them, even though they were only behaving as nature dictated. They followed me down the first few steps, then landed gleefully on the spattering of vomit as I stepped carefully over it.

I made my way back down the stairs on shaking legs, clutching the chain handrail at every step. I moved as quickly as I was able, given my weak leg and the more recent bumps from the fall I'd just taken. My need to get out eclipsed the pain in my shoulder and my hip. As I got further down into the darkness, I had to feel my way, keeping close to the wall as I placed each foot carefully on the step below. Descending into the unseen, my imagination started playing tricks on me again. Was there something waiting for me in the gloom at the base of the lighthouse? A malevolent presence that would block my way? A hand that would grab at me in the dark? At the bottom, I ran blindly across the uneven floor, stumbling onto my knees and getting up even more quickly. I wrenched the warped door but it wouldn't open. I was trapped and I panicked. I screamed. I spun round, making myself dizzy. I was losing control.

What would Malcolm have done? I stopped and bent forwards placing my hands on my knees, head dropped low. I mustn't faint.

I leant against the wall, pressing my cheek against the cold stone. Breathe in. Breathe out. Breathe in. Breathe out. It was a struggle, but I managed to calm myself down. When the pounding of my heart had receded, I went back to the door and grasped the handle with both hands. This time, it opened and a second later I took a great gulp of the fresh sea air. I staggered out onto the short grass in front of the lighthouse, and lay panting, fighting to regain my equilibrium.

It hadn't been a baby. Just a bird.

Just a bird. It must have flown in through one of the missing windows and failed to find its way out again.

I repeated this to myself, over and over, as I calmed down. After a few minutes I was able to sit up, then eventually stand up. I felt weak, drained of energy. But I was okay, just about.

Then I realised that I'd left my stick in the bottom of the tower. Panic threatened again until I clamped my teeth on the inside of my cheek. Deep breath. The door was still open, and I should be able to reach in for it without having to go inside. I went back to the foot of the lighthouse and, clutching the door frame for security, reached inside. It took several attempts, but then my outstretched fingers encountered it where I'd left it leaning up against the wall. It clattered to the floor and I swore at myself. But my anger helped me overcome my fear and I lunged into the darkness, grabbed it and got out fast.

It felt reassuring to have it in my hand, but I was still shaken as I set off as quickly as I could back along the spit. There was no sign of Loki, but maybe he'd become bored, or maybe the clatter when I dropped the torch had scared him off. I hoped he'd reappear for the walk back with me.

At the point where the lighthouse spit widened out onto the mainland, I checked my watch. I needed to make it back before dark, as I no longer had the torch. I had my phone torch, but that was a much tinier beam to walk by. Still, I'd be on the track and hopefully not much of my journey would fall after dusk.

The clatter of a stone falling down the cliff face to one side of me made me jump, and I quickly turned to where the sound had come from. I was shocked to see a woman, standing at the cliff's edge some thirty or so metres away. It wasn't Mrs Cooper, and I didn't recognise her. She was young, with long brown hair whipping around her head in the wind. A long, dark coat shrouded her almost to her ankles and, beneath it, I could just see pair of black Dr. Martens. She was staring out to sea, unaware of my presence. Her pallid face, huge dark eyes and drawn expression exposed grief and regret so vividly I could almost feel her pain.

Who was she?

She took a step closer to the edge, leaning forward to peer down at the rocks below.

I was about to call out to her when, from behind me, I heard a deep, throaty growl.

'Loki!' I turned. He was crouched low, his ears back and his teeth bared. He had his tail tucked down low between his hind legs. The growl rolled on. I stepped towards him, holding out a hand. 'Steady, boy.' He feigned snapping at me, warning me to back off. For some reason, he felt threatened by the woman. His hackles rose and he pushed up on his paws as if he was about to spring.

'Loki!' This time I was more commanding. 'Stay.'

I turned back to the woman, but she wasn't there. There was no sign of her, nowhere she could be. The ground rose away from the cliff edge at a gentle slope for several hundred yards, barren of trees or rocks where she might have hidden from the dog. There was only one place she could be. I hobbled as fast as I could to where I'd seen her standing, dreading what I might see when I looked over the edge.

Loki charged past me, barking wildly. He seemed as confused as I was.

Surely she wouldn't have jumped out of fear of Loki? Perhaps there was a path down, hidden from view.

But there wasn't. I went as close to the edge of the cliff as I dared, but there was no track leading down to the shore. I became more and more scared. She must have thrown herself over the edge. She must be dead.

When I came to the precise spot where she'd been standing, I gingerly slid my feet forward until I was standing right at the edge. I was out of breath and starting to feel lightheaded with fear. I could barely bring myself to look over. My imagination had already shown me her broken, battered body on the rocks below. I stared out to sea, willing myself to be wrong. But how could I be?

I closed my eyes, lowered my head, then opened them again, dizzy with expectation.

There was no body.

A tumble of jagged rocks and a roiling sea. The waves ploughed forward, then retreated even faster, again and again and again, scouring the granite, making it sparkle. Could her body have been washed away? Or was she never here at all? I was right on the edge. I was leaning forward, craning to see if she was clinging to the cliff face. Was that her there? No. Just bracken, brown and wet, tossed by the wind, that I'd mistaken for her hair.

I thought I heard a woman's voice crying out, carried towards me, then snatched away again. But it must have been a bird. The wind howled around me, scouring my cheeks and hands with icy rain. I was alone.

Who was she? Was she real or was she a ghost? Had I really seen her at all? The blind terror that I'd felt at the bottom of the lighthouse swept through me once again. What had brought me here? I felt certain that it had been her malevolent presence I'd felt in the darkness, and now she'd led me to the cliff's edge? Why?

Wasn't that obvious?

The cliff suddenly seemed higher. The churning cauldron and razor-edged rocks at its base appeared further away. The dark water exercised a magnetic draw over me and I couldn't tear my eyes away from the sea's chaotic ebb and flow. The whirling eddies invited me in. Invisible rips were waiting to suck me under. The freezing cold would sap my will to live with the promise of a dreamless sleep.

Somewhere above me, a gull shrieked with demonic laughter. It knew what the island wanted of me.

I was ready to launch myself off the edge.

I was ready to fly.

To swim.

To sleep.

I took a deep breath and stretched my arms wide.

The smallest shift in my centre of gravity would send me toppling over the edge. But then, as I made the first move, I felt a sharp pain in my calf. Teeth sinking into my flesh.

I fell hard on the rocky edge and was dragged back.

Loki saved me from certain death.

18

I COVERED THE GROUND between the lighthouse and Winterbourne as fast as I possibly could, but it still seemed to take twice as long as it had to get there. Fear had exhausted me, and the biting cold drained me further. Walking almost the full length of the island and then climbing the lighthouse would have been too much for me anyway, without the shock of the dead bird and the flies, and then the fall on the stairs, followed by the vision of the woman on the cliffs ... That Loki had saved my life I had no doubt, and now he trotted glued to my side the whole way back.

Dusk swooped on me before I was halfway to Halfpoint Wall. To the west, the sky turned a dirty orange, streaked with dark, jagged clouds. The air temperature dropped further, and I felt cold to the bone despite the body heat I was generating with my movement. The sun slipped away quickly, taking with it any sense of my position on the island. Within a few minutes, it seemed as if Loki and I were walking in a blackout. There was no moon, and the smudgy clouds obliterated the stars. I used the torch on my mobile to light the track ahead of us. It was rutted and stony, and the last thing I wanted was to twist an ankle with a misstep.

My hand trembled and quickly became numb as I held out the phone in front of me. I wanted nothing more than to be back in the library, where I would be warm and where the lights were bright. My thoughts were a jumble. Who was the woman on the cliffs and where had she gone? I felt sure I would have seen her body at the bottom if she'd fallen over the edge where she'd been standing. She would have landed on a strip of sharp, treacherous rocks, a little too high for her body to have been washed out to sea. But she hadn't been on the rocks, and she hadn't been at the top of the cliffs or anywhere beyond. Had I really just imagined her? I'd been unnerved by what I'd seen in the lighthouse. There was so much on Craigsea Rock that was strange, and which defied explanation. Maybe my mind had started playing tricks on me.

By the time we reached the gate in the Halfpoint Wall, I could tell Loki was bored with my slow pace. I let him through, then shooed him on.

'Go find Robert Cooper,' I said.

He lolloped off down the track with a happy bark, his duty to shepherd me home accomplished. I limped down the track, only marginally cheered by seeing the lights of Winterbourne before me at last.

Once I'd winced my way out of my coat and boots, the warmth of the kitchen was a panacea. It enveloped me and I felt immediately better. Somehow, I was able to put everything that had happened aside. There was the smell of something savoury in the oven and Mrs Cooper was clattering pans on the range.

Clattering them for a reason, it became quickly apparent.

'I don't suppose you remember what I said to you when you left this morning?' There was a hiss of anger in her voice.

I sighed, sitting down at the table. 'I had a fall. I couldn't walk back as quickly as I would have liked.'

'That so?'

'I'm sorry. Is there a problem?' I hadn't inconvenienced her by missing supper as she was still cooking it, and my time was my own.

'Robert Cooper's out looking for you.'

'That's hardly necessary.'

'You just said you took a fall. What if you'd broken a bone, couldn't walk back? There was a white feather on your mantelpiece today. I don't know who put it there, but that's the foretelling of a death. Scared me half to death when I saw it.'

I didn't care for the revelation that she'd been in my room, but I was aware that she sometimes cleaned in there. 'I put it there. I found it out on the terrace yesterday. And I don't believe in old wives' tales.' This was very pointed, but I was fed up with being treated like a child.

She glared at me. 'Doesn't change the fact that Robert Cooper is out there now, in the cold and the dark, looking for you.'

She had a point. 'I'm sorry.' I meant it. But it wasn't my fault the island didn't have a phone signal or Wi-Fi, or any other reasonable form of communication.

We both fell silent. I refused to believe her nonsense about the white feather. After a while, her anger seemed to abate. 'You could lay the table and slice some bread,' she said.

'Of course.' I went to the drawer to fetch the cutlery. 'Can I ask you something, Mrs Cooper?'

She nodded.

'Are there visitors on the island?' Perhaps someone had arrived without me knowing.

'Visitors?' She shook her head, frowning. 'Why do you ask that?'

'I saw a woman today, up near the lighthouse. I'd never seen her before. Is there someone else living here?'

Her eyes widened for a fraction of a second, but I couldn't miss her shock. Or her annoyance.

'There's no one else here. Perhaps it was Robert Cooper, from a distance?'

Of course it wasn't Cooper. He was over six feet tall, broad and muscular. 'She had long hair, blowing in the wind.'

'Maybe your own reflection. The land can play tricks on you that way, like a mirage.'

'It wasn't me.'

She shrugged and turned back to the range. I think the implication was that I'd imagined it. I wasn't entirely sure that she was wrong. A question sprang into my mind.

'What happened to the librarian who worked here before me? Why did he or she leave?'

'Frances Sparrow?' she said. Her expression softened for a moment, then changed. She looked as if she regretted saying the name out loud.

I committed the name to memory. 'Tell me about her.'

'Nothing to tell. She wasn't suited to such an isolated life. She was lonely and went back the mainland, back to her family.'

Although I'd never caught Mrs Cooper in a lie before, the way her hands fluttered as she said this made me think that she was lying now. The story seemed contrived and lacking in detail, the two sentences rehearsed. Not that I could blame anyone for being lonely at Winterbourne. But something in the way Mrs Cooper spoke had seemed off.

At that moment the kitchen door opened and Robert Cooper came in. His cheeks were flush from the cold, and he was rubbing his hands together to bring the life back into them.

'Mrs Cooper was just telling me about Frances Sparrow,' I said quickly, studying his face for his reaction. He didn't seem the least bit surprised to see me, and I wondered if he'd really been out looking for me.

'Poor dead girl,' he said, pulling out a chair and reaching for a slice of the bread I'd just cut.

'Dead?' I said. I looked at Mrs Cooper, but she was bent down at the range, checking on something in the oven.

Robert Cooper ignored me. He wasn't one for idle gossip.

Mrs Cooper brought a steaming casserole to the table and placed it on an iron trivet.

'Dead?' I said again, very much addressing her.

'Took her own life, they say,' said Cooper.

'Robert Cooper, you know she went back to her family. That stuff about her being dead was just a silly rumour in Craigross.'

'Who would start a rumour like that?' I said.

Mrs Cooper put a dish of boiled cabbage on the table. 'Oh, there are plenty of folk in Craigross who fancy they know what goes on out here. Imagine all sorts of things. But she left the island of her own free will and went back to her family. End of. If she did something stupid after that, it was nothing to do with Craigsea Rock.'

Now, I was part horrified, part intrigued. I felt as if I already knew something of Frances Sparrow from the evidence of her work in the library. Her small, neat handwriting and the choices she'd made in the way she catalogued had given rise to an idea of what sort of person she was. Neat. Fastidious. Contained. Was I typecasting her because, like me, she was a librarian? The profession has a certain reputation for being quiet and sensible which may or may not be based in reality. I was quiet and sensible to a degree. My former colleagues had been quiet and sensible to a degree. But there was danger in generalising.

I wanted to know more about Frances Sparrow, but I didn't think she was the woman who vanished from the cliff top. I was starting to think I'd imagined the whole episode. After the shock of the blowflies and the gull carcass ... I was uncertain exactly what it could have been, but some kind of hallucination seemed the easiest answer. I'd had some similar strange experiences in the first few weeks after the accident. I thought I was seeing my brother, alive and well, or for a split second I'd feel as if I was in the car careening out of control. Trauma can make the mind do all manner of strange flips.

The meal passed in silence, and I got the sense that neither of the Coopers would be willing to answer any more questions about Frances Sparrow. Perhaps I could ask Lucien about her if he ever returned. I cleared the dishes and did the washing up. Mrs Cooper was tidying stuff away, while Robert Cooper stared morosely into the fireplace at the side of the range. For once he seemed to be waiting for Mrs Cooper before setting off home.

I excused myself and headed up to the library. It was my intention to put in a couple of hours work at least, given that I hadn't done any during the day. But the sound of voices outside drew me to the window before I'd settled down at my desk. A man and a woman arguing. It had to be the Coopers, clearly, so I kept myself to one side of the window frame and peered at an angle at the terrace below. They were standing by the balustrade. Cooper was smoking a cigarette, a habit which I knew Mrs Cooper disapproved of. She appeared to be berating him about something and he was scowling at her words.

I deftly raised the latch and opened the window a crack to hear them.

Mrs Cooper was in full flow. '... you were a bloody fool to say that, Robert Cooper. Now she'll be nosing around to try and find out what happened to Sparrow.'

'Don't mean she'll be successful.'

'You need to shut your yap and stop crowing.'

'There's nothing for her to find out.' Cooper sounded furious. 'Just leave it be now.'

'If you did your job properly, I could leave things be. But you make that very difficult.'

As I watched, Robert Cooper ground the end of his cigarette under his heel and stormed off in the direction of the front of the house. Mrs Cooper swore softly under her breath and picked up the crushed cigarette butt. A flash of intuition told me she'd look up at the house before she went back inside, so I melted away from the window. I waited a couple of minutes, then looked down at the terrace again. She was gone and it was safe for me to close the window.

But hearing this made me more determined than ever to find out why Frances Sparrow had left Winterbourne when she'd barely started work on the catalogue. Had she had a disagreement with Lucien Broussard about the work? It didn't seem likely, given his utter lack of interest in the minutiae of what I was doing.

Downstairs, I heard the kitchen door slam as the Coopers left for the night.

I was alone in the house.

'Who are you, Frances Sparrow and what happened to you?' I said out loud.

The shearwaters answered me with their chorus of discontent.

I should have read it as a warning to mind my own business.

I didn't believe in ghosts, but I did believe in mysteries, and in my own ability to solve them. If the Coopers were going to obfuscate what happened to Frances Sparrow, I'd conduct my own research.

I waited for a week to pass, then I mentioned to Mrs Cooper that I wanted to make a trip to the mainland with Cooper next time he went. Hopefully, she would have forgotten about my questions about Frances Sparrow, or at the very least she wouldn't join the dots between them and my desire to go to Craigross. As it happened, she didn't even ask why I needed to go there, but simply said that Robert Cooper would be going across for the supplies the following day.

I got up early and went down to the jetty as instructed. Robert Cooper was already waiting for me on the RIB. His face fell slightly as he saw me approaching. He must have been hoping that I would be late, so he could set off without me, and it made me wonder what he might want to get up to in Craigross that he would rather I didn't know about. Not that I cared. I had my own agenda for the few hours I would get to spend on the mainland.

This time he didn't help me down the ladder, and I only just managed to set foot in the boat before he tugged in the mooring line and revved the engine. I had to grab the back of one of the seats to stop myself being toppled over as we sped out of the harbour. The cormorant was sitting on the end of the jetty, and as we passed it by it croaked and took flight. Robert Cooper grunted back at it, then looked at me with a wide grin. But I wasn't in on the joke, and I didn't know how to react. I stared at him blankly and his smile turned to a grimace.

Relatively speaking, the sea was calm as we left the shelter of the harbour wall, but there was still a swell on it. My stomach somersaulted as we were lifted, then dropped over and over, and though I kept my eyes firmly on the far horizon, it only took five minutes to make me feel addled and sick.

I added seasickness pills to my small shopping list. It was also bitterly cold. The wind cut through my thin jacket and made my eyes stream. Winter was setting in and it would become more difficult to cross to the mainland over the coming months.

This crossing didn't seem nearly as long as when I'd first arrived at Craigsea Rock. However this time Robert Cooper appeared to be simmering with resentment for the entire journey. Did he blame me for getting the rough side of his sister's tongue when he blurted out that Frances Sparrow was dead? I couldn't think what else might have piqued him. I hadn't seen him in more than a week. I might have believed he was just in a sour mood, had it not been for the cheery wave and smile with which he greeted one of the old fishermen as we came into Craigross's tiny harbour.

'Tom-boy!' he called out in greeting.

'Cooper!' the man shouted back.

I suspected he'd found himself a drinking companion and that lifted his mood.

As he tied up the RIB, I clambered up the ladder onto the harbour wall.

'What time will we set off back?' I said, turning to look down at him from the top.

'When the tide's ready.'

'And what time will that be?'

He made a performance of looking at sea, and looking at his watch, and then squinting up at the bright spot where the sun was fighting to cut through the clouds. As if that would tell him anything about the tides.

I waited.

He looked at his watch again. 'Three o'clock. Not a minute later.'

'Thank you,' I said. I walked away along the stone breakwater, then turned in the direction of the shop. I didn't need to buy much, but I didn't want Cooper to see me going into the library. From within the shop, I would be able to see when he went into the pub, and then I could head towards the library without giving away what I was up to.

He followed me into the shop. I pretended to be choosing a postcard that I had no one to send to.

'There's the lists, Mrs Unwin,' he said, putting a couple of crumpled sheets of paper onto the shop counter. I recognised Mrs Cooper's loopy handwriting on them.

I waited until he'd gone, then took my purchases to the counter. Mrs Unwin snatched the shopping lists out of the way.

'Are you all right, love?' said Mrs Unwin, as I used my mobile to make a cardless payment.

'All right? How do you mean?'

'Not too lonely out there with just them two ghouls for company?'

Genuine concern or digging for gossip? Both, I supposed. 'I'm fine. There's a lot to do in the library, so I stay busy.'

'You should come back here more often. That solitude isn't good for a person.'

'But I don't know anyone here either.' I thought about Frances Sparrow. 'Did you know the woman who worked on Craigsea before me?'

'Pale wee thing?'

I nodded, though I had no idea what she looked like.

'She used to come in here, once in a blue moon. Then she stopped and I heard she'd gone home to her family. Some personal problems, someone said.'

I wondered who, and how they'd known about Frances Sparrow's personal problems. 'Did you see her when she left?'

Mrs Unwin shrugged. 'No. I'm not rightly sure when that was. She wasn't a regular customer. I barely knew her.'

She seemed to be backtracking, and I wondered why.

As we'd been talking, the shopkeeper had been wrapping my purchases in brown paper, sealing them up with tape. She pushed the packages across the counter to me. I stuffed them into my backpack and left the shop. There was no sign of Robert Cooper, so I guessed he must have gone into the pub. I couldn't imagine what else he might do until it was time to go back to Craigsea.

I turned up the high street, away from the front, heading towards the library. As I walked, I checked my phone. I would be able to get a signal here for the first time in weeks. But it wasn't worth getting excited about. There were no voice messages, no texts and only a handful of emails. All but one of these were marketing junk, promising me ten per cent off my order, extolling the delights of a mixed wine case, reminding me that I had Audible credits. The one personal email was from Marisa, a brief couple of lines checking in how I was and whether I would consider coming back to work in the new year.

I went into the tiny Craigross library, and as soon as I'd worked out how to get onto the internet on the public PCs, I wrote a quick answer to her, explaining that I would be working at Winterbourne for the foreseeable future, and that I'd get in touch with her as soon as I finished there. Some people couldn't exist a day without internet access, but it was a couple of months since I'd been online, and that was my business taken care of. There was no message from my parents, but this didn't surprise me and I felt relief rather than sorrow.

I checked my watch. I still had a couple of hours until the tide was right for our return to Craigsea, though I intended to arrive at the jetty extra early. For some reason, I didn't quite trust Cooper and his timings. In the meantime, I had research to do.

I typed 'Frances Sparrow' into the Google search bar. The results told me nothing. Initially, Google suggested that I had meant to search for Francis Sparrow, who it turned out was a moderately successful American football player. But my Frances Sparrow didn't appear to have a life online. No Facebook page, no other social media accounts. I added the word 'librarian' to the search, but that drew a blank as well. Then I tried 'Frances Sparrow death'. Robert Cooper had said she was dead, but surely if she'd died, there would be some sort of record of it, somewhere. An accident would have been reported. There had been no mention of any illness, and this made me realise I had no idea how old she was, or what part of the country she would have gone back home to, if what Mrs Cooper had said was true.

Perhaps Frances Sparrow wasn't her real name. But why would they have lied to me about her name?

Maybe she was alive and well, back with her family somewhere. Some people just don't have much of an online presence. If you googled 'Anne Adams', you wouldn't find very much at all relating to me. Just a couple of local paper stories about how I'd killed my brother.

It certainly fed my suspicion that she'd never left the island at all. Perhaps she was dead after all. There was the fresh grave in the churchyard, and to me it had looked bigger than the hole needed for even a dog the size of Loki.

I couldn't shake this thought, no matter how reasonable the other possibilities might be.

It was gone two, so I made my way back to the harbour in a hurry. I wouldn't put it past Robert Cooper to set off back without me.

He was loading the supplies onto the RIB when I walked out along the jetty. I could see his eyes narrow as he clocked my arrival, but he didn't make any comment as I climbed slowly down the ladder and lowered myself into the boat. We set off at half past two.

'Would you have waited until three for me?' I asked, as we cleared the protection of the harbour.

'Mrs Cooper would send me back for you if I didn't.'

Low clouds made it seem as if it would soon be dark. The sea was the colour of wet slate. And I thought about the fresh grave on Craigsea Rock as I watched Robert Cooper steer the boat through the troughs and peaks of the waves. It was colder now than on the journey out and I was shivering.

I didn't want to believe what I was thinking. But I did.

19

OVER THE NEXT FEW DAYS following my visit to the mainland, I wondered if I'd been wise to return. Something was going on here, something wasn't right. I hadn't imagined that woman on the cliffs and I felt sure that the Coopers had lied to me about Frances Sparrow and about the grave in the Michael Kirk. If anything, I was starting to understand why Frances's tenure in the library had been short. Winterbourne and Craigsea Rock shared a capacity to disturb. The bumps and creaks I heard when I was alone in the house, which I'd previously put down to 'old building syndrome', now seemed sinister. I didn't feel comfortable here on my own anymore, but I felt even less comfortable when the Coopers were around.

My time in Craigross hadn't gained me any concrete information and had only heightened my anxiety over the situation in which I found myself. To stop myself from brooding about that moment on the cliff edge and what could have happened, I threw myself into my work with even more diligence. Rearranging the shelves in line with the new catalogue meant moving entire stacks of books from one end of the library to the other, and by working hard at it, I could ensure that I went up to my bed every evening exhausted enough to sleep, no matter how loudly the shearwaters shrieked.

Or so I optimistically thought. However, it didn't take much to prove me wrong. One evening about a week later, Mrs Cooper served up roast seabird of some kind, that Robert had shot a couple of weeks before. Since then, it had hung in one of the outbuildings, and when he brought it into the kitchen for butchering, it stank. It didn't taste good to me. The tough meat was oily and fishy, though the Coopers relished it. Within a couple of hours of eating, I was racked with griping stomach pains.

I lay curled on my bed in a foetal position, wondering whether making myself throw up would be a good idea. I felt hot and cold by turns, and I was unable to galvanise myself to go down to the kitchen to make a cup of mint tea to soothe my gut. Vowing I would never eat such meat again didn't help my predicament.

The pain came and went in waves, and eventually I dozed off during a longer hiatus. When I woke up, in the grip of a new onslaught, my blanket had fallen to the floor and I was shivering. But I was distracted from my own predicament by a sound. From somewhere downstairs, I could hear a woman singing. Not Mrs Cooper. She only ever managed a tuneless whistle. This person was singing the aria from *Rusalka*. I could only just hear it, and wanting to hear more, I swung my legs off the bed and sat up. A stab of pain in my gut made me pause. I sat for a moment, breathing deeply. Then I had to rush to my bathroom as the rancid bolus of half-digested meat finally forced its way up my throat.

It tasted even worse on the way out, and I retched and retched, long after my stomach was void of contents. I felt weak but relieved, pulling myself up to lean over the sink and rinsing my mouth out with ice-cold water from the tap.

I hadn't imagined the singing. I could still hear it, though the aria was no longer familiar. I opened my bedroom door and walked slowly along the corridor, listening for where the sound was coming from. I don't know why, but I wanted to remain unseen, so rather than taking the grand staircase, I crept down the servants' stairs. At the bottom, I could hear it more clearly and when I emerged into the butler's corridor, it became obvious to me that it was coming from the drawing room. Now I could also hear the music of an accompanying orchestra. It wasn't a person singing here in the house. That meant it was a recording being played. But by whom? The Coopers had left together as I, already feeling queasy, had tackled the washing up.

Was Lucien back?

Barefoot, I crept right up to the drawing room door without making a sound. I rested my ear against one of its panels. Beneath the swell of the aria I could hear the clink of cutlery against china. Someone was eating, and it sounded like more than one person. As the music ebbed away, a man spoke, though I couldn't make out the words. Lucien?

A woman answered him.

She had a clipped English accent that I recognised. It was the woman whom I'd spoken to when I applied for the job. That strange five-minute phone interview, the result of which was my being here.

I stepped back, scared of betraying my presence with an accidental sound. I slumped heavily against the wall opposite. What was she doing here? When had they both arrived? A clattering sound from the kitchen made my heart thunder. Mrs Cooper must still be here. I panicked and slipped through the door at the end of the butler's corridor. I stood panting at the bottom of the grand staircase and listened as Mrs Cooper came along the corridor towards the drawing room.

I checked my watch. It was gone midnight. Robert Cooper must have gone across to the mainland to fetch them right after our revolting dinner.

I should have gone back to my bed, but my curiosity got the better of me. I needed to see what the woman with the upper-class voice looked like. I would never have admitted it, but I was jealous. She was dining with Lucien Broussard, to the accompaniment of opera. I pictured them sitting opposite each other by the fireplace, warming up after the rigours of the crossing, and in my mind's eye, the woman was beautiful, with translucent, alabaster skin and bright, intelligent eyes. Long, slender legs crossed at the ankles, elegant hands sparkling with diamonds. Dining with Lucien, just as I'd dined with him once when I'd first arrived on the island. I still had such clear memories of that evening and I often replayed them in my mind. I was happy that evening, and I'd hoped to repeat it. But now Lucien was repeating it with someone else.

It was stupid and childish, but I had to see if I was right about her looks. A sharp cramping in my gut made me gasp, but it didn't deter me. I went to the front door and let myself out, closing it carefully but not all the way, so I would be able to get back inside easily. The drawing room windows were just around the corner, overlooking the terrace.

The flagstones were icy under my bare feet, so I covered the distance as quickly as I could. The windows were dark as the curtains had been drawn. I looked for a gap I would be able to squint through. I was in luck. A sharp strip of soft light showed between the edge of the far curtain and the window frame. I pressed the side of my face against the glass to see as much of the room as the gap would allow.

Lucien was sitting at a small table by the fireplace with his back to me. Opposite him sat the woman whose voice I heard. But she was nothing like the woman I'd imagined. There were no diamonds on her fingers, just a simple wedding band on her left hand. She was smartly dressed in a bouclé skirt suit, but her legs weren't long and her figure wasn't willowy. She had thick ankles and flat shoes. Her face was flushed and her brown hair was messy and windswept, no doubt because of the crossing. Her dark eyes were small and sharp like a rodent's, peering out from a fleshy face.

She couldn't be Broussard's wife, I decided. After all, she looked quite a bit older than him. She must be an employee. His secretary or business associate.

She took a sip of wine, then said something, but I could hear even less through the window than I could through the door. As I watched, Mrs Cooper came in and cleared two empty plates from in front of them. I guessed they hadn't been offered oily, rancid-tasting seabird for their dinner. Lucien waved her away and the woman spoke again. I think what she said made Lucien laugh, as I saw his shoulders shake.

My feet burnt with the ferocious cold and my teeth were chattering so loudly that I feared they would hear me inside. I ran back to the front door and scurried up the grand staircase. Once I was back in my room, I rubbed my feet roughly with my bath towel to bring the circulation back to them. Then I put on a pair of warm socks, wrapped myself in my bathrobe and got back into bed. If I'd been alone in the house, I would have gone down to the kitchen to make hot tea, but not tonight.

In the morning, I stared in the mirror above the bathroom sink. The ravages of the night before were written plainly on my face. My complexion was washed out and the only colour was in the dark rings under my eyes. What's more, I felt as bad as I looked. I'd slept badly after I came back to bed. I hadn't been able to get warm and even now, after a hot shower,

I was still shivery, and I felt depleted of energy for the day ahead.

Down in the kitchen, Robert Cooper was already eating his breakfast, and my place was laid at the table as usual. Mrs Cooper, however, was busily assembling breakfast for two on the butler's trolley she used for delivering meals to the dining room. Two plates of cooked food hidden under silver domes, a silver toast rack, fully loaded, butter, marmalade, a pot of coffee and small jugs of milk and cream.

'You'll be okay to sort your own eggs, won't you, dear?'

She rarely called me dear. Only when I'd been brought back to the house, wet and cold, after being caught in the rip.

I nodded and went across to the range.

She looked me up and down. 'You look like you've seen a ghost. Pale as whey.'

'I'm fine,' I said. 'Is Mr Broussard back?'

Her expression became tight-lipped.

I nodded at the trolley. 'With someone else?'

'Mr Broussard is back, and Mrs Allard is here.' It sounded as if the words had to be dragged out of her.

'She be his lawyer,' said Robert Cooper, earning himself a filthy look from his sister.

'I think she's the lady I spoke to on the phone when I applied for the job,' I said.

Both the Coopers ignored my comment. Robert pushed back his chair and headed out, while Mrs Cooper trundled her trolley away down the butler's corridor. I was left alone to fry my own eggs, feeling slighted that I hadn't been invited to share breakfast in the dining room.

By the time Mrs Cooper returned, I was picking at two fried eggs on toast. But the rancid stench of the previous evening's meal hung in the air, and I couldn't face them. I still felt sick, and I went from feeling too hot by the range to shivering at the table. When Mrs Cooper had her back turned, I scraped the remains into the bin and quickly washed up my plate. Then I headed smartly for the door. I didn't see why I should hang around and wash up Lucien and his lawyer's breakfast plates. I had plenty to get on with up in the library.

'Sulking doesn't suit you,' Mrs Cooper called after me.

It made me annoyed that she could so clearly see through me. Was my jealousy so obvious? I would sulk if I wanted to. I paused outside the dining room door. The woman was talking.

'How much you can raise will depend on how many you sell and where you sell them. You could send a few of the more valuable first editions to auction in London, or we could offload a quantity of less valuable titles to dealers across the country. Whichever route you choose, of course, will affect the value of the remaining collection.'

'It's not so much about the money,' Lucien said. 'It's more—'

A sound from the kitchen alerted me that Mrs Cooper was heading in this direction. I couldn't afford to be caught listening, so I had to forego the rest of Lucien's reply. I ran up the grand staircase, thankful of the thick carpet that dulled my footfall, and slipped into the library. Is that why he wanted the whole collection catalogued, so he could start selling it off book by book? Did he need the money? From the start of his answer, it seemed not. But then why else would he break up the collection? However, it was none of my business what he did with his books. Once I'd finished my task, I'd leave Craigsea Rock and probably never see him again.

With this sour thought in mind, I settled down to work. The more I did each day, the sooner I'd be able to go. I started out okay, but my mind wasn't on it and my concentration soon lapsed. I folded my arms on my desk and rested my head on them. The world spun when I closed my eyes, so I had to open them. It wasn't much better. I took a few deep breaths and thought about what needed doing.

I don't know how long I'd been asleep when the library door opened. I sat up sharply and was hit by a wave of dizziness. I rubbed my eyes with my hands and sighed.

'Are you okay, Anne?'

It wasn't Lucien's voice. It was Mrs Allard's. I opened my eyes to see the lawyer walking towards my desk.

I straightened up. 'I'm fine. Can I help you?'

'I'm Janice Allard. We spoke on the phone when you applied for the job.'

'I remember.' I wasn't likely to forget. A five-minute interview with only a couple of questions, then the job was mine. At the time, I was too elated and excited to realise how strange it had been. Now, it seemed entirely in keeping with the way things were done at Winterbourne.

'I just thought I'd introduce myself and take a look at Lucien's magnificent collection.' She looked around at the shelves, wide-eyed.

'It's a bit muddled at the moment,' I said. 'I'm moving things around gradually as I catalogue them.' I gestured at the shelves with my arm, and the movement caused my head to spin and my stomach to lurch.

'You're doing amazing work, according to Lucien. I was sorry when he said you weren't feeling well enough to join us for breakfast. Are you feeling better now?'

'He said ... Yes, thank you. I didn't sleep very well, but I'm fine now.' A feeling of deep unease settled low in my gut. Why would Lucien have said that? There was no way of him knowing that I wasn't feeling well. Didn't he trust me to talk to Janice Allard? I didn't have secrets of his to share.

Presumably she did, but if she was his lawyer, she wouldn't blurt them out.

'It's an extraordinary collection, isn't it?' She wandered across to the shelf where I'd started cataloguing the fiction, then ran her finger along the spines of the books. After a couple of moments, she pulled one out and flicked through the opening pages.

'It is.' I went to join her at the shelf, and she quickly pushed the book back into its space and moved away. 'Can I ask you something?' I said.

'Ask away.' She was browsing poetry.

'What happened to Frances Sparrow?'

She spun round to face me. 'Frances Sparrow? Oh, that was such a sad thing. She came here because she was running away from family problems, but she didn't find the peace that she sought.' She turned back to the shelf. 'Such a pity. Such a beautiful girl, but fragile.'

'She wasn't here long, was she? What happened?'

'No. Just a couple of weeks before ... tragedy struck.'

I waited for her to continue speaking, gripping the edge of the nearest table to steady myself on increasingly shaky legs.

'Don't listen to what people in Craigross say. It was certainly an accident, nothing more than that.'

'An accident?'

'She slipped and fell on the cliffs at the far end of the island.'

'Near the lighthouse?'

'I believe so.'

My mind was racing. So was my heart.

'Is she buried here?'

'No, of course not. She was returned to her family.'

Her voice sounded as if it was coming to me from the distant end of a long tunnel. As my vision blurred, I heard the click of the door opening again. A man's voice, warped, the words distorted.

I was falling. Spinning. Tumbling down. I should have hit the floor by now, but I carried on twisting and turning, over and over and over, and everything went black.

20

My chest was burning. My legs were on fire. I was running, as hard as I could, as fast as I could. But I couldn't see where I was going because on either side of me tall hedges hemmed the path. In front of me a rolling cloud of mist shrouded the way ahead, and when I looked back the mist was closing off the path behind me. There were twists and turns, ninety-degree corners suddenly looming out of the fog, but always, the view ahead was identical to the view behind.

I was in a maze.

As I looked up, the hedges towered even higher above me. The path divided. Left or right? I seemed to remember that the way to solve a maze was to always take the left fork. Or the right? Which had I taken at the last junction? I couldn't stop running, so the decision was made by my feet. I ran on and on, never reaching the centre, never reaching the exit. The hedges grew taller, and the mist became more dense and my muscles started to stiffen in the cold.

There was no escape.

I was above the maze, looking down. I could see myself running through the tight, sharp hedges and the swirling mist. I was going around and around the same few paths over and over again. The maze covered the whole island. Winterbourne stood at its centre and the paths spiralled out from the house, ending abruptly at the edges of the cliffs on every side. If I didn't keep to the groove I was running, I could end up plummeting over the edge and being smashed to pieces on the rocks below.

There was no one else in the maze and no sign of the sheep or the deer. My eyes scanned the paths from above, looking for Loki or Robert Cooper, but I couldn't see them. The only living being I saw, apart from myself, was the cormorant. It was perched on top of a hedge, its wings outstretched, and having seen it, I could hear its grunts of dissatisfaction cutting through the fog.

I was flying.

Then I was falling.

Then, with a thud, I was back in my own body, in my own bed in the yellow bedroom at Winterbourne. My head ached as if it were made from wood. My eyes prickled as if they'd been rolled in sand. My mouth was dead. Every bone felt splintered, every muscle cracked and perished like ageing rubber bands. The covers were drawn up tight to my neck, and wrapped round me at the sides like a shroud.

I felt as hot and dry as a plank in a sauna, until a cooling hand swept across my brow. I sighed. Such relief.

'Hush now, the fever's breaking.' It was Lucien's voice.

I struggled to open my eyes. They were glued shut, and my arms were trapped in the winding sheet so I couldn't rub them.

'Have some water.'

A glass was pressed against my lips. Cold water seeped between them and ran down my chin. I forced my mouth to open a crack so I could take more, and my parched tongue softened. It felt good.

'Medicine.'

The curved bowl of spoon pushed against my lower lip and a bitter syrup dripped into my mouth, followed by more water to wash away the taste.

'Sleep now,' said the voice, and I did.

I woke up shivering. The room was dark, the bedcovers were on the floor. It was night-time and I was alone. My head spun as I tried to sit up and I gasped, limbs creaking as I tried to move.

A small light flickered on in the corner of the room. A shadowy form was silhouetted in an armchair. So, I wasn't alone.

'Stay where you are. I'll get them.' It was Mrs Cooper.

She shuffled to side of the bed where the duvet lay, and bent to lift it. It felt cold as it touched my bare legs and I winced.

'How are you feeling, dear?'

'I ...' I put a hand to my forehead, too weak to speak and too confused to formulate a coherent answer.

'I'll make you some tea.'

While she was gone, I stumbled to the bathroom, my legs behaving like those of a new born foal. I had to hold onto the furniture to keep my balance, stopping several times to catch my breath before I reached the lavatory. I sat shivering for longer than I needed, trying to regather my strength to return to bed. Eventually, I was able to pull myself up by gripping the edge of the basin. A stranger stared back at me from the mirror. Greasy, sweaty hair stuck out at all angles. My eyes were dull, with red rims and dark circles spreading to my cheeks. My whole face looked hollowed out, as if I hadn't eaten in weeks, and the taut drum of my belly suggested it had been some time since I'd had a decent meal. My lips were chapped and, as if I needed confirmation that I was ill, I stuck out my tongue. It was white and cracked.

How long had I been like this?

Mrs Cooper came back into the room just as I slumped back down on the bed. She put down her tray and tsked at me as she pulled up the duvet and straightened the blanket on top of it.

'You'd do better to stay in bed as much as you can,' she said, placing the tray on the covers next to my legs. 'Here's hot, sweet tea, and some toast if you think you can manage it.'

My stomach roiled at the smell of the burnt crusts, and the sight of the thickly spread butter and great chunks of marmalade made me feel sick. But the tea was welcome. I picked up the mug using both hands, hardly able to trust myself to take its weight. My hands shook, splashing tea on the blanket, but I got it to my mouth, and never has tea tasted so good. I practically drained the mug in one long gulp.

Mrs Cooper watched me appreciatively. 'I'd say you're on the mend.'

I put down the cup. 'Is Lucien around?'

'Lucien?' Her eyebrows shot up. 'He's not here. He left the island the day you fell ill.'

'When was that?'

She counted silently on her fingers. 'Six days ago. You fainted in the library, and you've had a high fever ever since. Robert Cooper fetched Dr Aspley over from Craigross, you were that ill. She confirmed what we thought. You had pneumonia.'

'But Lucien was here. He gave me some medicine.'

Mrs Cooper shook her head. 'He's not been here. When you fainted, Robert Cooper carried you up to your room, and then straightaway took Lucien and Mrs Allard back to the mainland. It's just been me looking after you.' She gave me a quizzical look.

I said nothing.

'For the first couple of days you were hallucinating, talking all sorts of gibberish about sparrows and lighthouses and secrets. You must have imagined he was here.'

But I knew I hadn't imagined it. I was certain that Lucien had been in the room with me at some point during my illness.

'Eat your toast,' she said abruptly. 'I've got to get on and make the dinner. I'll bring you some in a while.'

I hoped to God it wasn't going to be another bloody seabird.

The sweetness of the tea had revived me, and after a while I fell on the toast ravenously. Like the tea, nothing had ever tasted so good.

But why was Mrs Cooper lying to me about Lucien being here?

21

It took a couple of weeks before I was well enough to get back to working in the library. The doctor visited again, the day after I woke up. She was a young woman, with white-blonde hair pulled up in a ponytail and friendly smile. She seemed relieved to find me conscious.

'You had a bad bout of pneumonia,' she said. 'Hypoxia in the initial stage probably caused you to faint, and you were coughing up blood and suffering a dangerously high fever by the time I saw you. The Coopers were right to send for me. We were able to get you onto antibiotics straightaway.' She tilted her head to one side. 'They probably saved your life.'

The Coopers saving my life wasn't something I'd had on my bingo card, but then there was nothing predictable about living at Winterbourne.

Dr Aspley suggested that I remain in bed for at least another week, and she gave me more antibiotics.

'I'm fine, really,' I said. 'I'm sorry you felt the need to come all the way out here. It must be such a waste of your time.'

'Seeing patients is never a waste of time,' she said, 'and Mr Broussard has been very generous to the Craigross practice over the years, so it's the least I can do.'

She was pretty and I felt a slight stab of jealousy at the mention of his name. That made me cross with myself. 'Well, you won't need to come again. Like I said, I'm fine.'

I used my enforced bed rest to catch up on reading. There were literally hundreds of books in the library that had caught my attention, so I could at least work through a few of them. Mrs Cooper made sure I had extra blankets and a plug-in oil radiator to keep my room warm, bringing up and clearing away my meals without a grumble.

By the end of the week, I had cabin fever in a big way. I stared out of my bedroom window towards the cliffs, wishing I had the strength to stride out across the island and get some fresh air. But a steady rain was falling, with never a break in the clouds or a moment's let up as it puttered against the glass. I knew I'd be risking my recovery to go out in it and anyway, I barely had the strength to go down one floor to sit in the library.

But that's what I did, and the change of scene lifted my little librarian heart and brightened my mood. I felt an urge to get back to work, but I curled up tight in one of the armchairs until it passed, revelling in the luxury of being surrounded by thousands of books. The noise of the rain was louder in the library as it had so many windows, but it was somehow soothing, and bathed in the amber arc of a reading lamp at my shoulder, I was content to let my recovery take its own pace.

Mrs Cooper brought vegetable soup and a brace of freshly baked cheese scones for my lunch, and I felt my strength returning. When I finished eating, I felt energised enough to take a turn around the room. Amazingly, there were still alcoves I had yet to explore and shelves I had yet to catalogue. I'd taken a cursory look around when I'd first arrived, but every day spent in the vast room was a journey of discovery. What treasure would I find now, my mind hungry for stimulation, on the lookout for something bizarre, or brilliant, or both?

Be careful what you wish for, isn't that what they say?

But that thought was a million miles away as I browsed the shelves with a fresh eye. I wanted to be distracted by unfamiliar literary treasures. I started at the furthest corner from the door, at the shelf closest to the last of the library's long row of windows. The ancient books shelved here had caught the sun over many years, and their spines were faded to the palest pinks, blues and greens. The tooled gold lettering had been rubbed away by time and uncountable hands. They'd been neglected, and for that reason I'd always assumed there was nothing of any real value on this shelf. I'd already noted that once the cataloguing was done, I would suggest to Lucien that he might fit blinds to the library windows to protect the books from the bleaching effect of the sun.

I ran a finger along one of the middle shelves, which was eye level for me. I would need to bring a ladder stool across to look at the higher shelves, and I wasn't sure I had the strength to do that yet. It was a jumble of fiction and non-fiction, some of which were in very poor condition, with frayed bindings and buckled spines. They were old, that much was easy to see, and as I pulled a few out to inspect them, I found they were mostly from the early to mid 1800s. There were authors I'd heard of, such as Trollope, Melville and Balzac, but plenty more that I hadn't. *The Queen of the West Wind* by Martha Elizabeth Moston caught my eye for the churning, swirling winds embossed on its spine. I pulled it from the shelf, expecting high romance or tales of derring-do, but instead I discovered a volume of exquisite poetry portraying a world of luscious beauty and gut-wrenching sorrow.

Come Death, and be my queen,
Lie down by my side,
Quench the dreams that have driven me,
Come Death, and be my bride.

... and pages more.

When molten gold runs through my veins,
And diamonds glister in my eyes,
When watchmen bow to a crooked moon,
I'll sprinkle rubies in your path,
And lead you to the emerald court where she,
The Queen of the West Wind, reigns.

How could I resist? I took the book back to my armchair and escaped into Martha Elizabeth Moston's secret world of laudanum-addled princesses, wicked princes, ingenues betrayed, and men as handsome as the devil himself, if not more so. I enveloped myself in her purple haze, slipped away, only to wake abruptly when Mrs Cooper arrived with a tray of tea and biscuits.

I pulled myself up in the chair and the book thudded face down onto the library's thick carpet, falling open at the page I'd been reading when I'd drifted off. Mrs Cooper deposited her load and retreated without saying a word. It was a little odd, but I was used to her now. We didn't have much in common, so there was no small talk between us, and she didn't need to ask how I was feeling several times a day.

As I bent from the chair to retrieve the book, a scrap of folded paper slipped from between its pages. It was lined, probably torn from a notebook, and unlike the pages it came from, it wasn't yellowed with age. I could see the dark shadow of something handwritten on the other side. I unfolded it as I went across to the table where Mrs Cooper had deposited the tea.

Mythical Monsters by Charles Gould

That was all it said. Just the title of a book and its author. But I recognised the handwriting from notes I'd found in the librarian's desk. It was Frances Sparrow's hand.

I studied it while I drank my tea, as if by staring at the words on the paper I might divine some additional meaning from them. Of course, I didn't. I went to the desk and found Frances Sparrow's notebook in the drawer. It was the same size as the piece of paper and the printed lines were the same. I flicked through it, looking for where the page had been torn out and found a jagged edge right at the back. Frances Sparrow had torn a page from her notebook, jotted down the title and author of a book, and had left it tucked between the pages of *The Queen of the West Wind*. I wished I knew where it had fluttered out from. Was she using it as a bookmark to mark a particular poem she wanted to go back to? I snatched up the book of poetry and leafed through it, looking for a sign. But there was nothing, so there was no way of knowing her intent.

I turned my attention to the digestives Mrs Cooper had brought with the tea and crunched my way through them. Chocolate biscuits in the library! Marisa would be horrified. But my appetite had returned, and I didn't leave a crumb.

It was only much later, after the Coopers had left for the night and I was alone in the house, tucked up under my duvet with extra blankets and a hot water bottle, that the thought came to me. Maybe the slip of paper had nothing to with *The Queen of the West Wind* and everything to do with *Mythical Monsters*. The more I thought about it, the more logical it seemed. For whatever reason, Frances Sparrow had taken note of the title. Perhaps as an aide-mémoire, perhaps because it was something she intended to read. And then she'd unintentionally left it in the book of poetry and had never had the chance to go back to it.

It made sense. Sort of.

I pulled my dressing gown tightly around myself and slipped my feet into a pair of trainers. I had to see what there was in *Mythical Monsters* that might have attracted Frances' attention. It was still several hours until midnight, so the power was on, but I'd learnt my lesson early and I took a large torch from the dressing table, despite knowing there were torches in the library.

The house was silent and the library window showed nothing but a black velvet cloak outside. However, as I peered out into the formless middle distance, I could hear the shearwaters' harsh and tuneless singing carried on the wind, above the rhythmic symphony of the waves. It was warmer in the library than in my bedroom, but I still shivered.

There was no listing in the catalogue for *Mythical Monsters*, but that didn't surprise me. I'm sure I would have remembered that title if I had already included it. That meant I would have to search the jumbled shelves of books that I hadn't got to yet. In other words, about two-thirds of the library.

I checked out a couple of obvious places where I remembered seeing odd groupings of books on mythology and folklore. When these turned up nothing, I realised I was in for the long haul. I was going to have to start at one end of the room and just keep going until I came across the book. Assuming of course it was a book that existed and that there was a copy of it here. I parked that thought. I had to at least try to find it. Frances Sparrow had recorded the title for a reason, and I was intrigued.

However, I was still convalescing, and shifting the ladder stool from shelf to shelf and climbing up and down it to check the top rows of books took its toll. As I reached the lower shelves, I sank down gratefully onto the stool and then crouched down on the floor to read the titles at the bottom, appreciating the rest it afforded. I made slow progress. A lot of the spines were damaged or faded, and I had to twist my head from one side to the other to read titles and authors facing in different directions. Respite came every now and again when I came to a stack that comprised entirely of encyclopaedias or magazine editions.

After an hour there had been no sign of the elusive beasts. I was exhausted and my mouth and throat felt like parchment. Running a finger along the shelves disturbed a fine layer of paper dust into air that was already dry. I went down to the kitchen and made myself some tea. I wolfed down a couple of cheese scones with butter to give me the energy to continue and returned to my task with renewed vigour.

Back in the library, I surveyed my progress. It was decent, but there were still plenty of shelves to go. I congratulated myself on not getting sidetracked by several interesting-looking books I'd laid eyes on for the first time, contenting myself instead by pulling them out of the shelves by an inch or two, so I could easily come back to them.

On and on I went, up and down the small ladder stool, stooping lower to the bottom shelves, moving on to the next stack. It had to be here.

And it was, at the end of the bottom shelf of one the very last stacks left to check. I spotted it moments before I was ready to give up in despondence. *Mythical Monsters* by Charles Gould. My, what an object of beauty it was. The book was bound in dark-brown cloth, which had been heavily embossed to appear like crocodile skin. The title and author were blocked in gold letters in a medieval-style typeface. On the centre of the front cover, a gilded dragon marched across the ground, ridden by a tiny creature that looked part human child, part bird. I squinted at it. It certainly seemed to have a beak. At the very top and bottom of the front cover were two rows of Chinese pictograms also blocked in gold.

I stared at the cover for several minutes, puzzling over the meaning of the symbols. The spine told me it had been published by W. H. Allen and Co. I went back to my chair and opened it. The title page gave the publication date as 1886 and proclaimed ninety-three illustrations. The first one of these lay opposite, protected by a layer of tissue paper. I gasped as I gently lifted it. A vast sea serpent, with blue and green iridescent scales, writhed in a tumultuous sea, dwarfing a small whaling boat, at the prow of which a muscular seaman was taking aim with his harpoon. The creature was spectacular, with a maw of dragon's teeth, feathery silver gills, red spines down its back and a tail that split into two sinuous ropes with sharp barbs on the ends.

The caption identified it as Jörmungandr, the great sea worm from Norse mythology. I was transfixed. The illustration was as beautiful as the creature was horrifying. I turned the pages and was confronted with griffins, unicorns, dragons, mermaids, flying horses, phoenixes and all sorts of monsters I'd never previously encountered. I was enraptured, gazing at the illustrations and getting caught up as I read snippets about manticores and Jorogumo, a Japanese woman with the body of a giant spider.

But what did any of this mean to Frances Sparrow?

Illness is a cruel mistress and I felt exhausted. My eyes were falling shut and I needed my bed. I would have to carry on my investigations in the morning. Reluctantly, I closed the book and bent to slide it back into its space on the bottom shelf of the stack, but as I did, the edge of the cover caught on something protruding from the side of the shelf. I pressed *Mythical Monsters* up against the next book to try to get past the bump, but it wouldn't go further into the shelf.

I pulled it out and pushed my hand into the narrow space. My fingers glided against the varnished wood until I felt a bump, a small, hard protrusion. I explored it with the tip of my index finger. It was completely smooth and seemed to be circular in shape, about the same diameter as a penny. It certainly wasn't a knot in the wood, as that would have been planed away. I kept feeling it. I'd never come across anything like this in any of the other shelves. It didn't seem to be part of the construction, but maybe it was a covering for a screw head?

I picked up the book from where I'd placed it on the floor and examined the cover on the side of the bump. There was a small dent in the edge, testament to where the book hit the protrusion whenever it was pushed back into the shelf.

I felt it again, pressing against the side of the disc with my nail to see if I could flick it off. I couldn't.

I pressed it and, to my surprise, it moved under the pressure. It was a button.

Somewhere from behind the shelf, there was a creak, and then the low screech of wood moving against wood. The entire shelf started to move backwards, away from me, swinging into what should have been a solid wall.

And I ... I was no longer sleepy.

I was very wide awake indeed.

22

I KNEW IN AN INSTANT THAT I'd stumbled upon the void that had so puzzled me in the plan of Winterbourne's first floor. Stumbled upon? I'd been cleverly led here by Frances Sparrow, as clearly as if she'd left me a trail of breadcrumbs. But her intentions were the furthest thing from my mind as I stood up and peered into the black space directly in front of me.

My heart beat like fury. I'd discovered a hidden room, and now Winterbourne was going to spill her secrets for me.

Taking a deep breath, I stepped over the threshold into the darkness, using my left hand to gently push the shelf further open and feeling with my right hand for a light switch. The air was stale with the dust of old books, so I knew even before I found the light that this was an extension of the library. Then my finger hit an old-fashioned toggle switch and a second later the room was bathed in the amber glow from a Victorian brass light fitting. The electrics in here obviously hadn't been modernised along with the main part of the library, and were probably original.

I looked around. The void was larger than I would have expected from the floorplan, an irregular wedge shape some twenty feet long and maybe twelve feet wide at the widest point, which would correspond to the outside wall, tapering to just four feet at the opposite end. It was entirely lined with bookshelves, which explained why the window looked blocked from the outside, and all of them were fully laden. But there was something different here to the main library. Lots of the books had been arranged face out, so one could see the entirety of the front cover, rather than just the spine.

I stepped further into the room and started to slowly walk the shelves, taking in a title here, a cover image there. First, I spotted *Thalia* by Arius, a book banned by the Catholic Church for more than a thousand years. Then a book with a glossy black cover and plain white text, *Lord Horror* by David Britton, a depraved Nazi-themed horror title which became the last book to be banned in the UK. Seeing this took my breath away as it had been my understanding that every single copy had been pulped. Nearby, *The Anarchist Cookbook*, for recipes on how to make bombs. And there were other titles that I had never heard of: *Thoughts of a Corpse*, *The Pivot of Civilisation*, *Darwin's Black Box* and so many more.

On the other side of the room, one of the shelves seemed filled with grimoires, ancient books with weird runes and occult symbols on blood red or black or ivory covers. They were dog-eared and grimy from use, and one or two had small amulets hanging from the spines, attached by threadbare ribbons or fraying string. Prominent on this shelf were several copies of *Malleus Maleficarum*. This was *The Hammer of Witches*, a text from the late 1400s that had inflamed the brutal witch hunts which set Europe and Britain alight for the next two hundred years. And on the shelf above, *The Lesser Key of Solomon*, the most famous and celebrated grimoire of all.

I saw *Mein Kampf* side by side with *The Prince*, next to *The Protocols of the Elders of Zion*. *The Satanic Bible* by Anton LaVey was shelved alongside a score of titles by Aleister Crowley. Books on the occult, books on satanism, books on torture, murder, rape, incest, unimaginable violence. The memoirs of murderers and serial killers.

Books that were evil.

I moved faster and faster between the shelves, feeling more and more repulsed with every successive title I read or recognised. My stomach churned, my breath became short. A wave of anxiety made me rush for the door, but I caught my elbow on the shelf that had swung in, and it swung back suddenly, hard and fast. I gripped the edge of small table in the centre of the room to steady myself as my legs turned to water.

So far, I hadn't touched a single volume, but my left hand came to rest on a book that was already lying out on the table. It was bound in soft, buff-coloured calfskin. There was no title on the cover, no author. With little forethought, I lifted the front cover to see what the title page said. No writing, just a symbol. A swastika, in the heaviest and blackest ink, so bold it almost leapt from the paper on which it was printed. I pulled my hand back as if I'd been burnt. Because I knew.

The jacket wasn't calfskin.

And at that moment, the lights went out.

I was thrown into a state of panic, and it was a couple of seconds before I logged the fact that it was just the midnight curfew. But my addled brain had also registered a soft click as the bookcase had locked back into place. Irrational fear blossomed in my chest. The darkness in the void was one hundred per cent. No chink of light penetrated from the outside.

I reached my hand out to find the edge of the table. I couldn't afford to lose the sense of where I was. But instead of feeling the curved wooden edge I sought, my fingers touched soft leather. The book bound in skin. I shrieked and lashed out at it, dashing it to the floor, repulsed. Panicky and nauseous at the same time.

I needed to calm myself down.

Breathe slowly while you wait for your eyes to become accustomed to the dark.

I listened to the soft hiss of my own breath, mapping the shape of the room in my mind. My heart was still running too fast. My hands were shaking, even though I was pressing them, palms down, onto the cold surface of the table. I knew, of course I knew, that the books in this room were like any others, inanimate objects that recorded knowledge and stories and thoughts. But these books ... they felt like they had a presence. There was a sentience in the void. I could feel it in my bones. I could sense it in the air, a shimmering.

An invisible mirage in a place devoid of light.

Fear isn't an emotion. It's an ice-cold physical response that takes control of the body. The lizard brain takes charge.

I had to get out. The bookshelf-door had slammed shut somewhere behind me. I turned round and faced where I thought it was. I could still see nothing, even though by now my eyes should have accustomised. But you can't see light that isn't there. I took a deep breath and, holding my hands out in front of me, I took two steps forward, sliding my feet flat along the carpet in case of obstacles. My hands felt nothing.

I had to find the right shelf, and then find the button on this side that would open the door.

I inched forward some more. The air around me thrummed. I could hear the roar of my own blood in my ears. I wasn't alone in the room. The feeling that there was a malevolent presence in there with me grew with each passing second. Was that a slight movement of the floor I just felt? As if someone heavier than me was moving on the same floorboards?

I held my breath and listened.

A rustle of clothing. No, that was just me, just my arm moving across my body.

I took a step and . . .

'Ooof!'

I'd hit something. Not a hard bookcase. Not the table. Someone. There was someone in the room with me. I screamed. My head was spinning and in the total darkness I became disorientated. I lost all sense of space, lost my balance, stumbled, and then the world spun out of control. One blackout was replaced by another as my face hit the floor.

23

I was being carried through the dark house, up a flight of stairs, along a corridor. As I opened my eyes, the sense of panic I'd felt in the secret chamber hadn't left me, and I twisted my body to get away.

'Shhhhh . . .'

Was it Robert Cooper? I breathed in. The man smelt of a musky, spicy cologne. Not Robert Cooper, who smelt of engine oil and rotting fish. A pool of light preceded us along the floor. Whoever it was had a torch in one hand. But glancing up towards his face, all I could see was a dark silhouette.

'Who . . .'

'Shhhhh . . .'

'Please put me down.' I struggled again and the man finally relinquished his hold on me, dropping the torch as he did so. I stumbled. My legs weren't ready, and I dropped to my knees. As I did, I saw the man's hand reaching for the light, and in that moment I saw a familiar tattoo on his left forearm. The black circle with the arrows pointing out from it like that points of a compass.

'Lucien?'

'Who else did you expect?'

'But . . .' I felt dizzy as I tried to stand.

He was on his feet again and he bent to place an arm around my waist and pull me up.

'I'm sorry,' I said, though I don't know why I was apologising. 'I didn't know you were back.'

'I arrived this evening.'

He guided me along the corridor towards my bedroom door. As we reached it, he used his free hand to push down the handle.

'Thank you,' I said, panicking again. 'I'm fine now. Honestly, I am.'

He propelled me into the room and towards the bed.

'Clearly you're not, Anne. You've been ill, and you've had a shock.'

He pushed me to a sitting position on the edge of the bed, then shone his torch around the room. The light caught my own torch on the bedside table, but I realised now that my larger torch was still down in the library. He flicked on the second torch, then stood both lights so their beams pointed at the white ceiling, reflecting the light back down into the room.

I expected him to take his leave then, but he came and sat by my side on the bed.

A minute's silence grew to three, but I didn't have anything to say, and I didn't understand why he was still here, in my room.

Eventually, he spoke. 'How did you find the way in?'

I explained about finding the note in *The Queen of the West Wind*.

'Ah, Frances loved that book. I often saw her reading it.'

'I'm sorry. I shouldn't have gone in there,' I said.

'You're right. You shouldn't have.'

I was taken aback by the undercurrent of anger in his voice.

'I had no idea what sort of books they were . . .'

'But you can see that's why I keep them shut away? Those books are dangerous and distasteful. Frances discovered them and they terrified her.'

This hardly surprised me. After all, why was he keeping such a cabinet of horrors?

'My plan was to tell you about them before you saw them. To prepare you for them.'

'If they were mine, I'd dispose of them. I'd burn them or toss them in the ocean.'

'Of course you wouldn't,' he said with a dry laugh. 'You understand the importance of books as the records of human endeavour, and even the evil must be catalogued, lest we forget what men are capable of.'

Sitting next to each other on the bed, neither of us had so far had to meet the other's eye. But what had he meant when he said he would have prepared me for them?

'I won't catalogue them. Please tell me you don't expect that of me.'

Now Lucien twisted his body towards mine, and I looked at him. His expression was serious, but it didn't make him any less handsome in the soft reflected glow from the torches.

'Frances was fragile, and before I realised what was happening, she'd got caught up reading some of the books which are kept in the annexe. She took them to heart and became detached from reality, disturbed by them.' He took one of my hands and turned it to face upwards. He studied my palm for a moment. 'You're stronger than her. You're intelligent. You understand the importance of such books, for academic study and to serve as a warning from history. But you can see that I have to be careful. They can't fall into just anyone's hands.'

'Then perhaps you should donate them to the British Library. That way, genuine scholars would gain access to them.'

His brows lowered into a frown. I seem to have said something stupid. I looked away from him, wishing he would go. But he still held my hand in his, and his hand was deliciously warm. I became aware, once again, of the smell of his cologne. I could hear him breathing, could almost feel the warmth of his breath on my face. How long had it been since I'd sat this close to someone else, or felt the touch of a hand, or a breath of scent?

The realisation of how insular my life had become caused a sudden constriction in my chest, and I didn't want him to leave after all. But what did I want? In the silent room, our breathing became synchronised.

'The books are special. Gifting them to the British Library would be a waste.' He spoke quickly, dismissing my suggestion.

I tried to pull my hand from his, but his grip was firm.

Our eyes met.

'I won't catalogue them,' I said.

'It's part of your job. Were you able to pick and choose what books you shelved in your previous job?'

I couldn't tear my eyes from his face. 'No.'

He reached up to my face with his free hand, running his index finger down my jaw. My head tilted towards his palm as I took a sharp intake of breath. His hand dropped to my breast, sending a jolt of electric current down my spine. Without a second's thought, I leant forward to kiss him. As his mouth met mine, he let go of my hand and clasped the back of my neck, gathering me in as our kiss became more intense.

I opened myself up to him. And at that moment, there was nowhere I would rather have been. Or anyone else I'd rather have had as my first lover.

He left almost immediately. I was still drunk on his ardour, bruised lips parted, eyes half-shut, muscles molten. He didn't say a word, just pulled on his clothes in silence, his eyes never leaving my face.

'I . . .' But I didn't know what I meant to say.

He picked up one of the torches and was gone.

I drifted into a dreamless sleep. Or had I dreamt all of it? The secret room, the forbidden books, the rapturous moments as our bodies moved together until desire was slaked? When I woke up, I didn't believe my memory. It couldn't have been. But my clothes were still strewn on the floor, dropped as he'd peeled them off me, and my bed still smelt of his cologne and his sweat.

It had happened, and I didn't know what to think.

I didn't know how I'd behave when I next saw him, or how he would expect me to behave. Would we pretend nothing had happened between us, although every cell of my body told me it had? Or was it the start of something? Would he return to my room?

I was desperate to see him, and to talk to him. In my own foolish way, I imagined that I was in love with him, and he with me. I knew this was childish. I knew we'd just come together in the heat of the moment, satisfying a carnal urge which we both felt. My fear and heightened emotions. His adrenalin rush from rescuing a damsel in distress.

I checked my watch. The morning was half gone. He would have breakfasted by now and would be out and about somewhere on the island with Robert Cooper, Loki at their heels. I dressed in a hurry and ran down to the kitchen. Mrs Cooper was watching over a pot of something indescribable. I quickly sawed off a hunk of bread and slathered it in butter, balancing it on the corner of the table as I pulled on my outdoor clothes.

Mrs Cooper gave me a knowing look. 'If you're well enough to galivant out of doors, you're well enough to get back to your chores in here.'

She was right, but I scooted out of the door, pretending not to hear her.

The day was sharp and clear, the air cutting the back of my throat like glass. I took deep breaths and swung my arms as I strode down the track towards Beacon Hill. The landscape was rimed and brittle. Even the pebbles under my feet snapped with ice, and my breath formed great swirling clouds that drifted upwards and away over my shoulder as I marched. Once I got to the top of the hill, I'd be able to see most of the island, and hopefully that would include Lucien.

And then what?

I could maybe stroll in that direction for my walk. Maybe accidentally bump into him. Or meet him as he returned to Winterbourne.

I skidded on the path up the hill. It was icy and the frosty grass was slippery. As it got steeper, I found it more taxing. I hadn't been out of the house for more than a week, and like most people recovering from illness, I'd overestimated my stamina. I was soon out of breath, and I had to slow down. I paused, about a third of the way up, to see what I could see so far. Nothing to the north but the Halfpoint Wall. All the gates were shut. Winterbourne looked resplendent, with all its roofs encrusted with frost and plumes of smoke shunting out of its chimneys. I spun round slowly, one arm raised to shield my eyes from the sun. No sign of Lucien, or of Robert Cooper and his dog, but to see the full extent in either direction, I needed to climb higher.

I struggled on, feeling far less ebullient than when I'd left the house. At least most of the way back would be downhill.

I'd have to abandon the idea of accidentally meeting Lucien out on a walk, unless he was very close to the house. It had exhausted me getting this far already.

When I was nearly at the top, I stopped again, resting against a flat boulder for a few minutes, until its cold cut through the seat of my jeans, forcing me to stand up. I was squinting in the direction of the wall and now I could see beyond it. Once again, no sighting of humans or animals, not even the sheep and goats. The wind was stronger up here, grazing my cheeks with ice and finding its way into the layers between my clothes. I shivered and walked around the hill to the south to find shelter from it.

Now I could see the cottages by the harbour, and there was Loki, running back and forth along the sea wall, looking so much smaller than he really was at this distance. What was he barking at? Ah, there was the damned cormorant, sitting on one of Robert Cooper's lobster pots at the near end of the jetty. As I squinted to see what Loki would do next, the RIB came into view from behind the sea wall, pulling away towards the mouth of the harbour. Robert Cooper was standing at the wheel, but there was another figure on the seat next to him.

I didn't need to see him close, or even from the front, to know who it was. There was only one person it could be.

Lucien was leaving.

Getting away from me as fast as he possibly could. It told me all I needed to know.

24

As Lucien left, the snow came. The ground was white by the time I got back to Winterbourne, bedraggled and exhausted. There was no sign of Mrs Cooper, but she'd left one of the vast Belfast sinks piled high with washing up for me. My convalescence was over as far as she was concerned, and what had started as an offer of help on my part now appeared to have become an entitlement on her side.

I hung up my dripping coat and kicked off my snowy boots. The thin blanket of snow was already starting to absorb the sounds of the island. I could barely hear the sea, and the birds were all quiet. None of them would be flying in the rapidly deteriorating conditions.

The wind had continued to strengthen as I'd walked back and now the snow, which had been falling vertically as I came down Beacon Hill, was blowing past the kitchen windows almost horizontally. Heavy clouds had blotted out the sun. The day's sparkle had gone, and I felt deflated and anxious. Had Lucien played me for a fool? Was it just some *droit de seigneur* opportunity, a chance to entertain himself?

I was too worn out to make a start on the washing up straightaway, so I sat at the kitchen table and nursed a cup of tea. My mind wandered back to the events of the previous evening. Not with Lucien, but before he'd appeared. I heartily wished I'd never discovered the secret room. All the books it contained were dubious and some of them had shaken me to the core. Of course, I'd heard of the abominations committed by the Nazis in the concentration camps, but I'd had no idea that I'd have such a visceral reaction to seeing one of those books. I'd practically thrown up. It was only the jolt of the lights going out that had shocked me out of it. And then Lucien had appeared from nowhere. How had he got into the room when the door was shut? I guessed he had arrived just as the lights went out and the door was closing. He was the presence I'd sensed in the room. But why hadn't he said something to announce himself? Maybe it hadn't been him. Perhaps he'd discovered me some time later, still passed out on the floor. I had no idea what had happened or how long had elapsed between when I fainted and when I woke up in Lucien's arms.

I finished my tea and started Mrs Cooper's huge pile of washing up, formulating a letter of resignation in my mind as I did it. How could I stay here after what had happened? I knew I wouldn't be able to face him again without wanting to curl up and die. And what if the Coopers realised? It would be excruciating. My position here at Winterbourne would become untenable.

But there was no sign of either of them at lunchtime. I was not surprised by Robert Cooper's absence. Maybe the snowstorm would keep him stranded on the mainland. At the very least it would make for a singularly unpleasant return crossing. But peering out of a first-floor window down the track that led back towards the harbour, all I could see was a blank white canvas. A slight, curving indent marked out the sweep of the road, but it was covered in snow. I could understand why Mrs Cooper wasn't likely to come back. She might end up snowed in at Winterbourne by nightfall. It was certainly more sensible for her to remain in her cottage, down in its sheltered spot on the bay.

This meant I had the house to myself, and I suspected it would be the case until it stopped snowing and the Coopers could get back up here on foot or on the quad bike. That was fine by me. I'd rather wallow in my shame and embarrassment on my own than in the company of others. The house was well-provisioned and warm. At least the library was warm, and I could sink myself into my work as a distraction. The sooner I finished the job, the sooner I could get off the island for good.

Apart from the hours when I was sleeping, I took to dividing my time between the kitchen and the library, leaning against the range sipping hot tea or lying on my front on the library carpet to make the most of the underfloor heating. I read and I worked, and I stared out of the window trying not to think about Lucien and what had happened between us. For more than a week, the snow hid the even the faintest outline of the tracks leading away from the house and barraged the doors so I couldn't even have left the building if I wanted to. The sky remained dark, the low clouds relentless in unburdening themselves upon us. From outside, I could hear the low patter of a million snowflakes falling on the frozen surface of the previous night's dump. Drifts creaked on Winterbourne's roofs and icicles formed like glittering stilettos hanging from the chins of the frozen gargoyles.

Once, I saw a pair of magpies skittering across the terrace in search of something to eat and, after that, I put out breadcrumbs and dripping for them on a windowsill, and a bowl of water which would freeze solid every couple of hours unless I opened the window and smashed the ice with a wooden spoon.

They became regular visitors, along with some tits and a lone blackbird. I was glad the gulls didn't come. They would have taken all the food in a couple of swoops, and I didn't care for them so much. One morning, I saw the cormorant watching from a distance, and I'm afraid I scared it away with snowballs. I suspected that Robert Cooper had sent it to spy on me.

Inside the house, the structure creaked with the weight of the snow. Doors popped open unexpectedly, pipes shuddered, and more than once I heard the scraping of tiny claws between the walls. Mice, who had come inside to shelter from the cold. Nothing more than that.

In all this time – and I quickly lost track of how many days it had been – I didn't feel tempted even once to go back into the secret library. I'd seen enough and I never wanted to go back in there again. I got on with my work in the main part of the library, hoping only to hasten my departure from the island.

I decided to draft my letter of resignation, so I would have it ready to hand to Lucien, should he suddenly reappear. I didn't want the opportunity to weaken in his presence, to hope for something that couldn't be. If I had the letter on me, I could give it to him straightaway, no matter how tongue-tied and embarrassed I might be. There wouldn't even be any need for a conversation. A brief note would do. He would know why I was leaving, whatever I wrote in the letter.

The library was equipped with stationery, but only in as much as it related to my work cataloguing the books. I wanted a sheet of writing paper and an envelope. I didn't dare go into Lucien's study for it, so I pinned my hopes on the bureau in the morning room. It was on the south side of the house, its windows facing the track that led to Beacon Hill and on to the harbour. I hadn't been into the room since Mrs Cooper had shown me around the house on my first day at Winterbourne. It seemed such an archaic idea to me, a room in which the lady of the manor would sit and attend to her correspondence after breakfast every morning. But maybe there was still some writing paper in the little Georgian writing desk by the window.

The door hinges moaned as I opened the door. Clearly no one else used this room either. It was cold, the air damp and clammy, and although a fire was set in the fireplace, it hadn't been lit for so long that a layer of dust coated the logs and the front of the grate. The mirror above the mantelpiece showed traces of damp where the silvering on the reverse of the glass had begun to sheer off. No one took care of this room the way the rest of the house was maintained, and I had to wonder why.

I sat down at the bureau. The chair's upholstery felt cold and lumpy through my jeans, perhaps a little damp. The sloping desk flap was locked, but the key was in place and, once I'd pulled out the desk supports on either side, I was able to open it. The wood was a little warped, so it didn't rest entirely true on the wooden supports, but it was still a beautiful piece of furniture. The writing surface was inlaid with green leather, tooled with a gold border, while inside there were enough drawers and pigeonholes to satisfy the most ardent of letter writers.

I pulled open one of the little drawers to reveal two fat brass fountainpens, their surfaces a little tarnished, and a silver propelling pencil. I picked up the pencil and turned the mechanism, but there was no lead in it. A drawer on the opposite side contained a small brass seal and some broken sticks of red sealing wax. There was a small cupboard in the centre. Inside it I found a pair of crystal inkwells and several dried-out bottles of black and blue ink. And in the pigeonholes, I found what

I was looking for—reams of writing paper. Thick, heavy cartridge paper, embossed with the initials L.B. in a deep, claret red. I couldn't write to Lucien on his own headed paper, but thankfully I found a wad of plain continuation sheets. I helped myself to half a dozen or so sheets and closed the desk. I would retreat to the warmth of the library to write the actual letter.

As I pushed the chair back to stand up, my curiosity got the better of me and I pulled open the top drawer of the lower section of the desk, beneath the writing flap. It didn't want to come at first, but I took both the small brass handles and manipulated it a bit until it sat straight, and then, with a good tug, it opened. Unlike the neat upper portion of the desk, the contents of the drawer were a mess. There were pens and pencils, a couple of dog-eared notebooks and a large, folded sheet that turned out to be a hand-drawn map of the island. Bulldog clips, treasury tags, a dusty box of drawing charcoals, and a stale packet of cigarettes. Business cards. Elastic bands. An old stamp, too old to be of use now. All the sort of ephemera that people shove into drawers when they don't know what else to do with them. Someone had used this desk regularly, but I had a strong feeling it wasn't Lucien. And, anyway, he had his own study at the other end of the house. This, I suspected, had been a woman's desk.

In the very back corner, behind all the gubbins, beyond where I could see, my fingers felt something solid. Smooth, hard covers, with the edges of pages between. A book. I pulled it out, not caring that I scattered pencils, scissors and a stapler out of the drawer and onto the floor. It was a Moleskine notebook, A5 in size, with a navy cover. It looked quite new, which was at odds with most of the contents of the desk. As dusk seemed to fall earlier under the heavy cover of snow clouds, I looked round for a light. There was a standard lamp next to the desk, and when I pressed my toe on the floor switch near its base, it lit up. I opened the notebook and flicked through the pages.

I saw straightaway that it was a diary. Not bought as such, with the days and dates printed in it, but a blank notebook someone had used as a diary, writing the dates in by hand.

A hand I recognised.

Frances Sparrow's.

The entries, all written in blue ink, varied in length from a couple of paragraphs to several pages long. The first entry was made in February 2023. The final entry, just over halfway through the notebook, had been made in May 2023, so just four months before I'd arrived at Winterbourne. After that final entry, the rest of the diary was blank.

I read the final entry first, and when I started to read, I stopped breathing until I reached the end. My eyes raced across the pages and I could hear Frances Sparrow's voice in my head, though I'd never heard her speak. By the time I finished, I felt dizzy and my hands were shaking.

Outside, the cormorant cackled. Robert Cooper must be nearby. Had he managed to make his way here through the snow? I flicked out the light and ran back up the stairs to the sanctuary of the library, taking the diary with me.

Why was Frances Sparrow's diary shoved to the back of a drawer in a desk that nobody ever used? Had she put it there? Or had it been found by someone else and hidden? I couldn't think clearly. Surely, when Frances left the island she would have taken it with her. A personal diary wasn't the sort of thing to be left lying around. But having read her final entry, I wasn't convinced she'd left the island at all. My mind went back to the fresh grave in the Michael Kirk. If someone were to dig it up, I doubt very much it would be dog's bones that they would find.

I hid the diary in the plan chest and went down to the kitchen to make some tea. I wanted to check whether there was any sign of Robert Cooper having made it through to Winterbourne. My suspicions were well-founded. On the kitchen table, there was a box of fresh supplies, including milk, eggs, bacon and a paper bag containing root vegetables that were very much past their sell-by date. Puddles of water on the floor showed his passage from the back door to the table, but he didn't seem to have ventured anywhere else. I went through the rear vestibule and opened the door. In the half-light, I could see the tracks of the quad bike in the snow. He'd come and gone without bothering to check how I was or if there was anything else I needed. Maybe the cormorant had told him I was alive and well, having seen me through the window.

I quickly made my tea and went back to the library. As darkness fell, it started to snow again. I fetched the diary from the plan chest and curled up in the armchair by the fireplace. With no small measure of trepidation, I opened it and started reading from the beginning.

25

FRANCES SPARROW HAD NEAT, ROUNDED handwriting, with well-formed letters and a slight slant to the right, suggesting she was right-handed. The early pages were pleasant enough to read. She detailed her arrival at Winterbourne, full of enthusiasm and excitement for her new job, and a thrilling first crossing. She didn't suffer from seasickness. Either that, or the sea was exceptionally calm that day.

She did, however, seem to have some early reservations about Robert Cooper and his familiar.

The man who collected me in the boat, Robert Cooper he told me his name was, seems a most unsavoury character. Gruff. Didn't respond to any attempts at conversation on my part, and seemed to take no pleasure at being out on the water on such a bright, cold day. But I wasn't going to let his taciturn presence, or the smell of fish that seemed to waft around him, spoil my enjoyment. As we neared the island, I got out my binoculars, the better to see the birds and I was rewarded with sightings of gulls, oystercatchers, fulmars, kittiwakes, razorbills and best of all – puffins! That's one to tick off the bucket list!

There was also a beetle-browed cormorant, with stunning turquoise eyes, waiting to greet us on the jetty. It opened its wings like a great bat, raised its cruelly hooked beak and gobbled at us. And the strange little man in the boat gobbled right back at it. Like they were the best of friends. Then the man looked at me in a way I can only describe as leering. I hope I don't have to have much to do with him while I'm here.

She wrote in her diary nearly every day for the first couple of weeks, describing the library and documenting her roamings around the island. She covered far more ground than I had, far more quickly, but then I don't suppose she was recovering from injuries when she arrived here. I realised that I had no idea how old she was, but she seemed fit, and her voice sounded young. She explored the lighthouse without incident, and most tellingly described the Michael Kirk's graveyard without mentioning the fresh grave that had loomed so large on my visit there. This sent a shiver up my spine.

After this initial period of exploration, the entries became less frequent. She didn't write about her work in the library, and the initial joie de vivre of her words quickly drained away. The tone became more sombre and reading between the lines I surmised that Mrs Cooper was the cause.

I'm sure if washing dishes had been in the job description I might have thought twice about coming here.

I'm far happier when Mrs C. leaves me to sort my own lunch. Her sandwiches are coarse, and even when she's baked a fresh loaf, the bread she uses for my lunch always seems stale.

Someone has been snooping in my room. No medal for guessing who it might have been.

After a while, I became a little impatient with her moaning. Some of the entries made her sound like a spoilt child. She also wasn't a dog person. She disliked Loki intensely and the feeling seemed to be mutual.

But then Lucien arrived on the island, and everything changed. For Frances Sparrow it was love at first sight. Her infatuation with her employer was far more intense than my own, but it still made uncomfortable reading and I think my cheeks burnt red as she recounted how she would climb Beacon Hill to spy out where he was and what he was up to, and then manufacture ways of bumping into him, within the house or grounds, and engaging him in conversation.

Lucien is just the sort of man I would choose for a husband. It goes without saying he's a handsome brute, but that's not the most important thing. His manners are impeccable, he's kind and generous, and we share the same ribald sense of humour.

I hadn't seen any evidence in the pages so far of her 'ribald sense of humour', and nor had I detected such a thing in Lucien. But then I supposed a serial seducer, as I began to suspect Lucien was, would cut his coat to suit his cloth. I remembered how passionately he'd talked about books and reading, which were my own passions, on the evening when we'd had dinner together. And how dazzled I'd been.

It became increasingly clear that Frances Sparrow assumed that Lucien felt the same way about her. From what she wrote, I could see that he was leading her on, that he wanted her to believe that. He was lining her up for seduction as easily as he'd lined me up, but as I read I felt more and more disturbed by the little worm of jealousy that was twisting itself around in my gut. I could see through Lucien now, but still I wanted him. My mind wandered to those few precious hours that he'd spent in my bed. They were hazy, dream-like. Then I came to my senses with a jolt.

I was scared. Scared of Lucien Broussard and his intentions. Scared of Robert Cooper and Mrs Cooper, who were certainly not my allies. I felt trapped. Sequestered by the weather, isolated in an empty house, alone on an island with no way of communicating with the outside world. I would need to find a way off the island, an excuse to go to the Craigross that wouldn't arouse suspicion. But I could do nothing until the snow stopped so, despite knowing what was coming, I carried on reading. Another person's secrets make a compelling narrative.

He was clever enough to make her think that she'd seduced him.

We kissed, then he pushed me away. 'No, we shouldn't,' he said. I could hardly breathe. My heart has never beat so loud or so fast in my chest. I knew he was right, but when I kissed him again, he was lost. Overwhelmed by his feelings for me, he carried me to his bed and made love to me . . .

There was a lengthy description. Frances Sparrow was living out her own Regency romance, with Lucien Broussard cast as Darcy. And what had my story been? Part *Rebecca*, part *Jane Eyre*? Is that what we do? Cast ourselves in our own favourite novels?

Of course, he disappeared the following morning. Working off the same script, no doubt. She was beside herself with worry for the first couple of days, and then when it dawned on her that she was being ignored, she sunk into the darkest of places. It would be easy to dismiss Frances Sparrow as a foolish woman who should have known better. But since when is naivety a crime? Especially in the face of Lucien Broussard's behaviour? My heart broke for her, and for the ways in which we were alike.

It was at this point that she discovered the library's secret. And it was at this point when I think she began to unhinge. Her writing changed. It was subtle at first, but over the next few pages it became larger and wilder. There were ink splatters where she'd pressed too hard on her nib, and small tears where she'd gouged the paper. Some of the words were smudged by what I assumed to have been tears that had fallen as she'd been writing. She was repulsed by what she found in the hidden room. She took what she considered to be the worst of the books it contained out onto the terrace and tried to set light to them. Lucien suddenly appeared, alerted, she believed, by Robert Cooper.

His rage burnt more intensely than the fire I'd started. His eyes became as black as anthracite and he bared his teeth. He grabbed at the books I was holding, forcing me to drop then. He slapped me hard across the face, and the force of his blow caused me to fall against the balustrade and down onto the flagstones. Then, as I watched, he plunged his hands into the flames and drew out the first few books I'd thrown onto the pyre. They came out virtually undamaged and he held them like cherished children in his arms. After that, he kicked over the brazier, spreading burning coals out across the lawn, cursing in a language I didn't understand. From the wreckage of the fire, he plucked the largest of the books I'd tried to burn, that unspeakable ledger of the dead. He carefully brushed the soot from its red cover. When he opened it, a small flame sprung to life from its pages. He smiled and extinguished it with a kiss.

I remembered seeing the scorch marks on the Nazi book that lay on the table in the secret chamber, but I had no idea what she was referring to when she mentioned the 'ledger of the dead'. I didn't know what to make of what she'd written about Lucien's behaviour. How much of it was true and how much of it was the distorted reality in which she appeared to be living?

After that, I wept over every word she wrote. I already knew the end of the story and reading the entries that led up to it was like watching a car crash in slow motion. She discovered she was pregnant. When she told Lucien, at first he was overjoyed, but then inexplicably changed his mind and demanded that she terminate. She asked Robert Cooper to take her across to the mainland, but he refused. Lucien had forbidden it. They were at an impasse, then she miscarried. Alone, in the library, in the middle of the night after all the lights had gone out. She mentioned the spot where she'd lain in agony for hours, and when I looked across at it, I saw a faint stain on the carpet I'd never noticed before. Her blood? I shivered and felt deeply uncomfortable. Her distress was almost palpable in the room.

In the next entry she wrote of scrubbing the carpet, and taking the tiny scrap of flesh that would have grown into her child and burying it near the lighthouse in a tiny, secret grave. My blood ran cold and I shivered. Someone had just walked over my grave, and that someone was Frances Sparrow.

Then came her final entry.

I know what happened. Mrs C. poisoned my food to kill my baby, at Lucien's command. I will never forgive them and if I could think of a way to kill them all, I would. I've locked myself in my room, but I'm planning my escape from the island. I'll take the RIB and make the crossing in the small hours. And after that, I'll have to fade from view, to literally disappear. Because the devil will come after me, for what I know of him.

If that plan fails, I'll set my spirit free. My body might lie here forever more, but I'll be gone.

I will be free.

And I will have revenge on Lucien Broussard, even if it takes a hundred lifetimes.

She didn't get away. Whatever happened that night, I felt certain that Frances Sparrow's body now lies in the Michael Kirk. I suspect she was caught trying to take the RIB. I suspect Robert Cooper was ordered to deal with her. She had discovered things about Broussard that he didn't want the outside world to know. It had put her in mortal danger, and when she tried to escape it had cost her her life.

Was there a space in the graveyard earmarked for me as well?

26

I PUT THE DIARY BACK where I'd taken it from. I didn't know if she'd placed it there, or if Lucien had discovered it and hidden it. If this was the case, I didn't want him to know that I'd found it. I never wrote the letter of resignation I'd been planning. It would be akin to signing my own death warrant. In my room, I could see the marks around the window frame where Robert Cooper had put up bars to stop Frances from jumping out. That, and the stain on the library carpet, bore testament to the veracity of her words.

But what did it mean for me?

Lucien knew that I knew about the secret collection. He'd even demanded that I catalogue it. If I did that, would he let me leave the island when I finished? I doubted it, and I could see no way out. The fact that it would still take me months to finish cataloguing the main part of the library brought me scant comfort. Yes, I had time to make a plan, but for the life of me, I couldn't see what that plan would be. After Frances's escape attempt, I felt quite sure that Robert Cooper would now secure the RIB to the jetty with a padlock and chain, or disable the engine or something. Anything to be sure that I couldn't sneak away in it. And without access to the RIB, I was stuck here, no matter how many months I had left.

The clouds lifted, the sun shone and the Coopers returned to the daily routine. Everywhere, I could hear the drip-drip-dripping of meltwater as the snow vanished from the roofs and window ledges. Small streams ran down through the rocks beside the terrace, and the kitchen courtyard became a sea of brown slush under the tyres of the quad bike.

Mrs Cooper seemed relieved to get back to the Winterbourne kitchen. 'Believe me, you don't want to be snowed in with Robert Cooper for a couple of weeks,' she said, stirring a vast cauldron of soup which looked as if it could last us for the rest of the winter.

I tried to behave as normally as possible around them. I didn't dare let on that I knew what had happened to Frances Sparrow, that Robert Cooper was a murderer and that Mrs Cooper an accessory to murder. I tried to stay out of their way, but at mealtimes I had to act as if nothing was wrong. I found it harder and harder to trust Mrs Cooper's cooking, watching carefully to see that my portions were served from the same pot as hers and Robert Cooper's. If she left me a sandwich out for lunch, I would hide it carefully at the bottom of the bin, then make my own from scratch. If she ever noticed that extra food was being eaten, she never said anything. Perhaps she thought it was Robert Cooper helping himself to extras.

It was stressful, and the strength and good health that had been so hard-earned at the start of my time on Craigsea began to slip away. I lost weight, and the face that stared back at me from the mirror was pale and hollow-cheeked. With the return of the sunshine, I started walking again to build up my strength, but I always felt watched, and followed. Loki came with me wherever I went, and even when I made sure to shut him on his side of the Halfpoint Wall, he'd turn up, dogging my footsteps within a few short minutes. Robert Cooper's cormorant was also much in evidence, sunning its wings on walls and rocks, making its horrid little screeching noises whenever I passed by. Sometimes, even though I couldn't see him, I heard Robert Cooper reply from somewhere in the vicinity.

I became obsessed with what I'd read in Frances Sparrow's diary. More than once, late at night, I sneaked down the grand staircase to the morning room. I would sit shivering in the lumpy chair in front of the bureau, reading and rereading all that she'd written by the light of my torch. My imagination began to fill in gaps in what she said, and I looked at the evidence of her work in the library with fresh eyes, trying to understand what she'd been through. Some nights, when I sat alone, reading in the dark, it was as if she was speaking directly to me. Warning me of what lay ahead, but not showing me any way to escape my predicament.

There was one thing in the diary that puzzled me, a mention that I returned to again and again. The 'unspeakable ledger'. What was she referring to? Obviously, it was one of the books in the hidden room, but I hadn't seen anything that resembled a ledger. And what could make her describe such a book as 'unspeakable'. I kept pushing these questions out of my mind. I didn't want to go back into that room and revisit those horrors. The whole collection was unspeakable and I wanted nothing more to do with it.

But Frances spoke to me. Her words echoed through me, even when I wasn't reading the diary. In the end I gave in. I had to know.

I waited until the Coopers had gone for the night, and I waited some more just in case one of them came back for something forgotten. When they'd been gone several hours, I put down the book I'd been reading and went to the bookcase where *Mythical Monsters* was shelved. I drew it out and pushed the wooden button that opened the door. It creaked again like the first time, and then I was in. I switched on the lights and propped the door open. I didn't want to risk it closing on me like last time. Lucien had carried me out that time after I'd fainted, and I hadn't seen how he'd opened the door from the inside. I placed my torch on the table in the centre of the room, noticing that the repellent flesh-coloured skin-bound book was no longer there. I glanced around and saw that it had been shelved next to several similar volumes. So, Lucien had been in here since that evening. At least, I assumed it was Lucien, rather than one of the Coopers.

Frances Sparrow had mentioned that the ledger was a large book with a red cover, so surely I'd be able to find it. I started checking out the bottom shelves of all the bookcases, as these were the deepest shelves where the largest books tended to be stored. A lot of them were illustrated books, featuring art or photography. One might have termed them coffee table books, though the content of these books wasn't fit to grace any respectable living rooms. The titles told me all I needed to know, with references to erotica, fetishism, sadism, satanism and war. It really was the private library for the four horsemen of the apocalypse. There was no temptation to linger over these volumes and within a few minutes, I'd spotted a heavy-looking tome bound in red leather. There was nothing written on its spine, so I pulled it out of the shelf and placed it on the table in the middle of the room. A couple of black singe marks on the soft Moroccan leather told me I'd found the right book. It still smelt faintly of smoke.

This was the 'unspeakable ledger'.

I stared at it. Now it was in front of me, I was unwilling to open it. A sense of trepidation gave way to deep-rooted anxiety.

I didn't need to see this. I wasn't going to catalogue this part of the library, so what was I doing here? But curiosity scratched at me like a cat. This was the first book Frances had thrown onto her fire, the book she considered the worst of all. I felt compelled to bear witness to what had driven her to take her own life.

Taking a deep breath, I raised the cover. The pages were heavy, yellow parchment, the first of which was blank. Having taken the plunge, I became impatient and turned to the second page. It was covered in small, neat script, the ink faded to light brown. It took me a moment to recognise what it was, but studying it, I realised it was in ancient Aramaic, which meant I had no chance of understanding any of it. I flicked over the next few pages. They were also in Aramaic, but then there were some written in Arabic and after that I recognised Latin, Sanskrit, Greek and a clutch of European languages in gothic fonts. The early pages were fragile and ragged, but towards the end of the book, the parchment seemed newer, as if pages had been added in later. I inspected the binding. Apart from the burns, the leather cover was in good condition and not at all ancient.

I turned back to the first page, wanting to compare the quality of the parchment to the later pages, and my breath caught in my throat. The page that had been blank before, and I would have sworn on my life that it had been blank, was blank no longer. In the centre there was a symbol, hand drawn in red ink, that I recognised immediately. It was the symbol of Lucien Broussard and Robert Cooper's tattoos, and now I saw it for what it was.

It was the satanic symbol for chaos.

I was plunged into ice-cold fear. My heart clenched, my lungs stopped breathing, my muscles were paralysed. As I stared at the symbol, the solid circle with its eight arrows pointing outwards, it started to slowly rotate on the page, and my fear grew stronger. With a shaking hand, I stretched out my forefinger to touch it. It burnt my skin and, snatching my hand away, I took a sudden gulp of air, like a drowning man reaching the surface.

I turned to the next page and, in front of my eyes, the Aramaic script morphed to become copperplate. Now I could read it.

> *Golgotha. Three deaths, including the King of the Jews. My crowning success, my most important achievement. I watched from a distance, and I took great pleasure in the consternation of his followers. It can't be denied that he put on a brave show, but it's hard to be sad about the death of a man certain of his own immortality . . .*

What the hell was I reading? An eyewitness account of the Crucifixion? But as I read on, the words started to dissolve from the page. They faded away, as if they were being 'unwritten', and I couldn't read quickly enough to stay ahead. I turned back to the first page. The chaos symbol was spinning faster than before.

I thumbed frantically through the pages, trying to read what I could as the text turned to copperplate, but mostly I could only catch the first few sentences before it faded to illegibility. Sometimes there was a place name I recognised, or a date.

> *I have joined the crusaders in Languedoc to spread Pope Innocent's call for the persecution of the Cathars. Only I can rouse them to such acts of wanton cruelty . . .*

Currently in Van Diemen's Land, where I'm encouraging the stalwarts of the British Empire to commit their time-honoured pursuit of hunting and killing the local population. It's hardly sporting, given that the Englishmen have guns and the Aborigines don't, but then I place little value on the Brits' much-vaunted sportsman-like behaviour...

The death toll in Circassia has reached two million now, and still I whisper in General Zass's ear...

Though hundreds of years apart, all the entries seemed to be written in the same hand, spoken in the one voice.

... the bloodbath of Anatolia, largely unnoticed as Europe implodes with its own bloody conflict. I've stalked 35,000 miles of trenches, to send men from both sides over the top to certain death...

... the Osage, murdered for their land rights. They are a peace-loving tribe, but what they have is too valuable...

Holodomor, Ukraine, 1932, 3.5 million starved to death. Hollowed-out faces, dead eyes, crying children, the pain of the world distilled...

I reached the World War II entries and hardly dared to turn the pages. I couldn't bear to read the place names and the numbers of the dead, the smug glorification of all the Nazis had done. Who could have the imagination to have written such a book? Why would anyone else want to read it? But as much as I wanted to follow Frances's lead and burn this book, I couldn't tear my eyes from the pages.

Bangladesh, 1971, three million . . .
Uganda, 1972–78, 300,000 murdered . . .
Cambodia, 1975–79, three million dead in four years . . .
Rwanda, 1994, 800,000 Tutsis met their end . . .
Darfur, 2003, ongoing – 500,000 dead and counting . . .
Myanmar, 2016, ongoing – 43,000 Rohingya wiped out . . .

It was never-ending. Humanity was where evolution had taken a wrong turn. I was wearied and disgusted, but now the words disappeared faster than I could read them. A litany of death, murder on an industrial scale. Here was every major war and genocide, celebrated by an observer who was on the wrong side of history every time, glorifying in any small part he'd been able to play. Whose words were these? My eyes bled tears as my heart was torn to shreds. Of course, I knew these things had happened, but to be confronted with them, written out large in a ledger that seemed to celebrate them as achievements, was more repugnant than anything I could ever have imagined.

This was the book, according to Frances Sparrow, that Lucien had been desperate to save. This was the glittering jewel of his monstrous collection.

27

I COULD BEAR IT NO MORE. I slammed the book shut, ignoring the hissing noise that emanated from its pages, and pushed it back into its space on the shelf. I ran out of the secret chamber, pulling the bookcase shut behind me. I would never, never go back in there, and no matter what Lucien Broussard threatened me with, I would never catalogue the world's depravity as represented in that room.

I left the library and ran to my bedroom. I hoped that I would wake up in the morning to discover that this had all been a terrible dream. A nightmare of epic proportions. A book with writing that transfigured in front of your eyes? It couldn't be real, could it? A horrible figment of an imagination that had run amok, spooked by Frances Sparrow's diary and now seeing things that weren't there. Things that weren't real.

But how could I wake up from it, if I couldn't get to sleep?

At some point during the night, I must have become delirious, because it's the only way I can explain what happened next. I know I got myself ready for bed. My hands were shaking and I was shivering as I changed into my pyjamas, not from cold, but from shock. I still couldn't comprehend what I'd just seen, so I think my mind switched to some sort of autopilot, trying to steer me through my usual night-time routine.

I cleaned my teeth. I got into bed. I turned out the light. But then I tossed and turned. My mind was racing, going over and over what I'd seen. Letters in Sanskrit and Arabic morphed into Greek and Chinese in front of my eyes. Words danced in my peripheral vision, just too far out of sight or too distorted for me to read. But I knew what they said already. They told of death and incomparable cruelty.

I awoke with a start. There was a noise outside. It was still night. My room was frigid, and an arctic blast made me realise that my window was open. How could that be? I threw back the duvet and went across the room. A flurry of snowflakes drifted across the floor and there was enough light from an almost-full moon for me to see that the curtain, dancing in the breeze, was sopping wet. The window was flapping wide open, not secured on the stay, which would have been the case if I'd opened it. And anyway, I hadn't. It was the middle of winter. Snow lay on the ground outside. It was barely warm enough in my room with the windows shut, the curtains drawn and the radiator on. I wasn't mad enough to have gone to bed with the window open.

I had to lean quite far out to reach its handle to pull it shut. As I did so, I glanced down. The snow-covered terrace shone bright white in the moon's glare, and I was shocked to see a figure standing at the balustrade. It was a woman, and she was leaning forward slightly over the stone railing, staring intently out at the sea beyond. I knew immediately it was the young woman I'd seen at the lighthouse. I'd come to accept in my mind that she'd been a ghost or a figment of my imagination, but this iteration of her looked as real as real could be. I could see regular clouds of her breath billowing up and away where she was standing. Ghosts don't breathe, do they?

At first I thought she must be Frances Sparrow. But I knew Frances Sparrow was dead. Perhaps the Coopers had a relative who occasionally visited. But what would she be doing here at Winterbourne in the middle of the night rather than tucked up in the Coopers' cottage?

'Hello,' I called down to her. My teeth were chattering, so the word came out as more of a huff.

The woman jerked as if she'd been hit by lightning, and looked around. At first she couldn't place the sound. Then she looked up and saw me. With a soft gasp, she ran down the steps and onto the short stretch of grass that sloped to the cliff edge.

'No,' I shouted after her. 'Wait.' My heart cried out to her at the same time, but she ran and skidded through the snow, veering off into the rock garden at the side of the terrace and disappearing.

I shoved my bare feet into trainers and snatched my dressing gown, tying the belt as I ran down the corridor to the top of the grand stairs. I took them two at time, swinging around the first-floor landing on the banister, not caring how thunderous my footsteps sounded. I burst out of the front door and ran around the side of the house to the terrace.

There was no sign of her, just the jagged footprints she'd left in the snow. Ghosts don't leave footprints. I ran after her, down into the rock garden, but the footsteps petered out on the bare rocks, from which the snow had been blown away, and I couldn't work out where she'd gone.

I didn't know what to do. It was too cold for her to be outside for more than a few minutes. Despite running around, I was already shivering. Should I get dressed properly and go after her? Or run down to the cottage and send Robert Cooper out on the quad bike to find her? Something told me I wasn't supposed to have seen her, whoever she was, and I was loath to divulge this to the Coopers.

A sound above me made me turn and look up at the tower. I caught a movement, a flash of light on glass, a window being opened. For a fleeting second I saw a face. The woman I'd seen at the lighthouse again. The woman who'd just run away from me into the rock garden. How could she have reached the top of the tower without passing me on the way?

'Hey,' I called. 'Who are you?'

But the window clicked shut and with the moonlight reflecting off the panes, the tower's windows created a blank face. There was no one there. I was seeing things. The distress I'd suffered earlier in the library had robbed me of sleep and now I was experiencing some sort of lucid dream. There was no woman and never had been. I'd imagined her on the terrace and in the tower. I was the only person at Winterbourne, at least until the Coopers came back in the morning.

But then . . . another movement at the top of the tower caught my eye. It was the woman again. There was a ledge at the top of the tower, with a low balustrade. She was standing on the ledge, staring down with unseeing eyes. She was going to jump. I started running again, around to the front door, up the grand staircase to the second floor, along the corridor to the door which led up to the tower.

Like always, it was locked.

I banged on it with my fist and shouted, 'Please, let me in. Let me help you.'

Of course, there was no answer. Only the guttural shrieks of the shearwaters, carried on the wind that was blowing this way from the cliffs.

There had to be a key somewhere in the house. I ran down to the kitchen as fast as my damaged leg could manage. The butler's pantry was right next to it, just off the butler's corridor, and I knew there was a large, rolltop desk in there where Mrs Cooper did her accounts. That might be the place where spare sets of keys were kept. Of course, the desk was locked, but the drawers opened. I rifled through them. There were notebooks and pencils, tins that once held mint cake which were now full of coppers, packs of cards, boxes of matches, a penknife, a travel sewing kit, all manner of whatnots and thingamajigs but not a single set of keys. Not even to open the top of the desk itself.

I thought about finding a crowbar to prise it open, but I didn't have time.

Half crying with fear for what I would find, I ran back out to the terrace. If I spoke to her from there, perhaps I could persuade her not to do it. That was, if she hadn't already jumped. My heart was in my mouth as I rounded the corner of the house, expecting to see a smashed and twisted body lying on the flagstones. But there was nothing, apart from my own footprints in the snow. I looked up. There was no one on the ledge, and no lights in the tower's windows.

It was as if she'd never existed.

It must have been the ghost of Frances Sparrow, tormenting me in my addled, sleep-deprived state.

I felt dizzy. I had to get away from Winterbourne. I couldn't bear to stay in the house for a minute longer. I threw a few things into a small backpack and dressed in my warmest clothes. Down at the kitchen door, I put on my walking boots and my warm jacket. I was going to leave the island. By the time the Coopers came up here in the morning, I'd be long gone.

I jogged slowly down the icy track towards the harbour, not letting the stiffness in my bad leg hold me back. The night air was freezing, and it felt as if every breath was ripping my lungs to shreds. At some point I slowed to a walk, skidding and slipping on the frosty ground, stumbling through wide drifts of snow, falling more than once.

The frozen island glittered all around me, bathed in moonlight and, far above, stars twinkled in a sky clear enough to see the Milky Way. The bitter cold enveloped me, holding me tighter and tighter in its embrace, until my teeth nearly cracked from chattering and my bones could have splintered as easily as glass. My hands and feet were numb. They were burning. My eyes watered and my tears froze on my lashes.

And still I walked, pushing hard into the wind. I was almost there. As I rounded a bend in the track, the dark outline of the cottages came into sight. There were no lights shining in the Coopers' windows, no smoke emitting from their chimney. They must be asleep. To avoid the crunch of my feet on the gravel being heard, I shifted to walking on the grass verge at the side of the track. Frost crackled under my boots, but they wouldn't hear that. I skirted round the far side of the empty cottage and then, walking as quickly and quietly as I was able, I approached the jetty.

I could see the RIB, bobbing gently by the harbour wall, and was overcome by a wave of panic. What if I couldn't get it to start? Or if, rather than being tied up, it was moored with a chain and padlock?

As I climbed the couple of steps onto the breakwater, I heard a movement behind me. I spun round to see Loki creeping towards me, legs bent and low to the ground. Our eyes met and he bared his teeth, growling low and deep in his throat.

'Shhhhh, Loki. It's me.'

He snapped his jaws and let out a single bark.

'No,' I said, holding out one hand, palm down. 'Go home, Loki.'

I turned away from him and started along the jetty. I had to get to the RIB and get away before the dog roused Robert

Cooper. But I heard him coming after me. He growled louder. I turned back and walked towards him, and he stopped growling, watching me with wide black eyes. As I came level with him, he came at me, nipping at my calves to drive me off the jetty as if he were herding sheep.

He was guarding the RIB.

I squatted down. 'Stop it, Loki,' I hissed. 'You have to let me go.' I looked back towards the end of the harbour wall and he growled again.

As I stood up and made my move, he started to bark, over and over, as loud as he could. There was no chance that Cooper wouldn't wake up and come outside to investigate. I'd thought of Loki as my friend, but he was faithful to his master and he knew his job as a guard dog.

I turned back towards the track and started to run.

Behind me, he stayed where he was, barking and howling.

I heard the cottage door opening and flung myself down in the snowy bracken.

'Loki, shut yer trap,' yelled Cooper. Footsteps, more shouting, the sound of Loki yelping in pain. Cooper must have hit him.

The cottage door slammed shut and I lay panting amid the prickly stems. I waited until everything was quiet once more, then looked down towards the jetty. Loki was sitting sentinel at the land end, blocking my way to the boat. I cursed myself for not thinking to bring a bit of bacon or something to keep him quiet, though I couldn't be sure even that would work. I turned and headed back up the track to Winterbourne.

My attempt to escape the island might have failed, but one battle doesn't make a war. I was determined. I would find a way to escape if it killed me.

28

I STRUGGLED BACK ALONG THE TRACK towards the house. What had I been thinking? Even if Loki hadn't been there, how would I have navigated the RIB across to Craigross? I had no idea how to start the motor or negotiate a choppy sea. I'd failed to make a plan and acted on impulse. Next time, I'd be more prepared.

The house felt positively tropical after more than an hour outside. A lukewarm shower burnt my skin. I rubbed myself vigorously with a rough towel and my skin glowed lobster red in the torchlight. But I was exhausted and dejected. It was close to dawn and all I wanted to do was escape into sleep.

It was a troubled sleep, when it finally came. Memories from the previous evening churned through my mind. The woman in the tower. What had happened to her? Had I seen Frances Sparrow's ghost? Then I remembered the book, with the symbol of chaos on the title page, and chunks of text swam before my eyes. A litany of genocide, recorded by who? And why? I didn't understand any of it.

Long after the sun had risen, I finally got up and went down to the kitchen. I needed hot tea and hot food.

'You missed breakfast,' said Mrs Cooper when I appeared. Her tone was accusing.

'I overslept,' I said. I hoped the lie was convincing. I filled the kettle at the sink without meeting her eye.

'You weren't the only one. Loki woke us in the night with a hell of a racket.' She scanned my face as she said this.

'Oh?' I said. 'Is that something he does often?'

I earnt myself a look of disbelief. 'Robert Cooper won't have it, and Loki knows better.'

I decided not to comment further. I made my tea, and a fried egg on toast, and sat down. Mrs Cooper was kneading bread dough at the other end of the table.

'Can I ask you something?' I said.

She raised her eyes to study my face, but she didn't say no.

'Did Frances Sparrow and Lucien Broussard have some kind of relationship?'

Her expression told me this was the last question she was expecting me to ask. But she covered her surprise quickly, working the dough harder and faster.

'He was her employer. That was the relationship.'

'Nothing more intimate?'

She didn't speak, but slammed the dough on the table a couple of times before cutting it in two with a large knife and placing each piece into a bread tin. She covered each one with a damp tea towel and put them both into the warming oven to let them rise. Then she came back to the table and stood opposite me, leaning forward with her knuckles on the wooden surface.

'Don't be getting any ideas like that. About Frances Sparrow or about your own chances with him. He wouldn't look at the likes of her or you. Just get your work here done, then you can go home.'

I took my plate and mug to the sink and washed them up. Mrs Cooper didn't move.

'I'll get back to work then.' What else could I say? It had been stupid to ask her. Even if she knew about what had happened between Frances and Lucien, she wasn't likely to share it with me. But I needed to know what had happened here. Without a doubt, Frances Sparrow had taken her own life. Lucien Broussard and his sick book collection had driven her to it. What in God's name was that book with the vanishing script and the spinning symbol of chaos at the front?

When I got to the library, I went straight to the secret chamber, determined to prove to myself that the whole thing had been my imagination. It had to have been. Writing can't transfigure or disappear from a page. It had been a dream.

I felt feverish as I pressed the button and pushed the shelf back to enter the room. I flicked on the lights and turned straight to the bookcase where the ledger was shelved. But it wasn't there. I could have sworn I'd put it back on the shelf before I'd fled the library the previous evening. I stared at the place where it had been. There was a large book with a black cover in its place. There was no title or author on its spine, so I pulled it out and flipped it open. It was a book of erotic photos, weird pictures of unsavoury fetishes. I slammed it shut quickly and put it back on the shelf. It was vile, but at least it proved to me that the book with the chaos symbol had just been a fever dream.

I felt my forehead as I straightened up. It was hot. I was coming down with something. I must have been delirious when I came in here last night. That was the explanation, and I was satisfied with it. I could shut this place up and put it out of my mind. Just get back to the mundane work of cataloguing the main library and pretend this place didn't even exist. I wanted to get off the island, and it looked like finishing the job would offer the best chance of it.

As I turned to leave, a flash of red on the table snagged my retinas.

No . . . Please, no.

But there it was, lying on the table. I hadn't looked that way as I'd rushed in, but now I saw it. There was no mistaking it.

I covered my face with my hands. It did exist. I hadn't imagined it, and the realisation shook my core, setting off a wave of fear that threatened to engulf me. But I'd put it back on the shelf, so what was it doing out here on the table? I tried to turn away from it, I tried to leave the chamber. But I could do neither. The book exerted some kind of hold over me. It drew me to it, and I was powerless to resist. I stumbled like a sleepwalker towards the table. I reached for the ledger and drew it across the shining mahogany surface. As if in a dream, I opened it.

The circle of chaos was still but then, before my eyes, it started to slowly turn. I was mesmerised and with no intent on my part, my fingers began to turn the pages. I went to the last entry, to the last page I'd looked at. Only now, it wasn't the last entry. Where the next page had been blank, I saw writing. Overnight, three more pages had been filled with the same bold copperplate handwriting as the rest. It was a hand I was familiar with. I'd been too shocked the day before to make the connection, but I knew this handwriting from notes I'd received about books in the library.

It was Lucien's hand.

I gripped the edge of the table as the realisation hit me like a punch in the chest. The implications robbed me of breath, and I put a hand to my throat, wheezing. If he'd written this new entry, he'd written the entire book. All the first-hand accounts of the worst moments in human history. The early entries written in Aramaic and Sanskrit, in Chinese and Latin and Cyrillic, all those terrifying testimonies of human barbarianism that had transfigured into English. He'd written them.

Who the hell was he?

Weak with shock, I started to read the new entry.

It told of a massacre of innocent women and children in a place I'd never heard of. It told of brutal acts of vengeance and war that blossomed, spreading across the world as country after country was sucked into the conflagration. It told of missiles wiping out cities, of untold misery. Millions of deaths, lives and homes destroyed. Vast legions of casualties and refugees with no help and nowhere to go. It told of Armageddon as all the world's nuclear arsenals were detonated over two desperate days. It told of the end of humanity, in every sense of the word.

None of it made sense, until I looked for the date at the top of the page.

This hadn't happened. Of course it hadn't. This was the future. A vision of the future or an inevitability?

Only one man could answer that question.

29

WHATEVER THE HORRIFYING FUTURE for mankind, the implications for my own present situation were more pressing. If Lucien had written those pages, it meant he was back on the island. He must have arrived while I was out on the moor during the night. Could he know that I'd discovered his infernal ledger? No, I'd replaced it on the shelf when I'd left the previous evening. I was certain of that. But could he tell from the book itself that someone had read it? Did the script revert to its original languages when the cover was closed, or would Lucien have seen that it had presented itself in English for me to read?

With shaking hands, I slowly closed the book. It hissed as its pages settled. I didn't want to touch it again, but I gently slid it back across the table to where it had originally lain. Lucien mustn't know that I'd read this most recent entry. I slipped out of the room and closed the secret door, and only then did I feel able to breathe again.

I sat at my desk. I was too shaken to work, so I closed my eyes and counted my breathing. Eventually I felt calm enough to open them again. Everything in the library was the same as before, even though everything in my life had changed. How could I have fancied that I was in love with Lucien Broussard?

I'd let him seduce me but now I think I'd be repulsed if I saw him. Seeing what I'd just seen made me even more desperate to escape from the island.

As it was beginning to get dark, I heard Loki barking down on the terrace. I went to the window to see why. As I looked down, I heard male voices. Then I saw three shadowy figures, standing outside the ballroom windows, looking down towards the sea. I instinctively moved back from the window, then looked down from the side, where the curtain would hide me from view. Not that the men were looking up at the house, but I wasn't taking any chances.

One of them was Broussard.

'Scat, Loki,' he said to the dog, shooing him away with a one hand.

Loki let out a low growl and bared his teeth, making one of the other men laugh.

'That's some hellhound you have there,' the man said.

'He's not mine. He belongs to my man,' said Lucien. He squatted down and whispered something in Loki's ear. Loki galloped away around the side of the house and Lucien straightened up.

The other man said something in a low tone and pointed down towards the sea. I couldn't hear the rest of the conversation, but I stayed where I was, watching. Who were these men and what were they doing on the island?

After a few minutes they went back inside, and I returned to my desk.

Half an hour later, the library door opened and Lucien came in.

I took a deep breath and steadied myself. I had to act as if everything was normal. How was one supposed to act with a man you'd slept with, who'd then disappeared for weeks without a word? I looked up and waited for him to speak.

'Anne,' he said, with a nod.

'Hello, Lucien.'

'I hear from Mrs Cooper that you're fully recovered from your illness.'

'I'm much better, thank you.'

'Good.' He looked around the library briefly before his gaze settled back on my face. 'I have two associates with me, book buyers who've come to view some of my collection. I wonder if you'd care to join us for dinner?'

In all the world, it was the last thing I wanted to do, but I found myself saying yes. 'Thank you, of course I'll come.'

'Come to my study at seven for drinks. They'll probably have questions about the books.' With that, he left.

At five past seven, I knocked, then opened the door of Lucien's study. I'd made an effort to look presentable, putting on black trousers rather than my habitual jeans and a freshly laundered shirt. It was the best I could do. I hadn't brought dresses or heels with me, or for that matter makeup.

All three of the men stood up when I came into the room, and Lucien did the round of introductions.

'Gentlemen, this is Anne Adams, who's currently hard at work cataloguing my collection.'

'Hello,' I said, though my voice was barely audible with nerves.

'Anne, this is Thomas de Groot,' said Lucien, nodding towards the man on his left, 'and this is Sherman Kennedy.' The man to his right inclined his head.

Each of them held out a hand in turn, and we shook hands. Thomas de Groot was a tall, blond man with an accent that I guessed was Dutch. He was in a pale grey wool suit with navy silk shirt and matching tie. His highly polished black leather lace-ups were barely suitable for trip to Craigsea, but he probably had no idea in advance of what the island was like. Kennedy was an American, and I knew this from the cut of his suit before he even opened his mouth and said, 'Charmed to make your acquaintance, ma'am,' in a strong southern accent. He wore cowboy boots under his suit which, to me, looked very odd.

Lucien handed me a full glass of sherry without asking what I wanted, but I needed all the Dutch courage the alcohol would give me, so I accepted it gratefully. It was a couple of months since I'd had any liquor and it tasted good. Of course it would. Lucien was hardly going to serve anything cheap and nasty.

They'd obviously been in the middle of some discussion before I came into the room and, with the introductions completed, they returned to it.

Sherman Kennedy was telling a long, involved story about striking a deal for a very coveted title by offering access to another collector's library in addition to the asking price, in exchange for which he had to locate a particular title for the collector in question. I didn't really follow the ins and outs of it, having missed the start, but de Groot found parts of it highly entertaining and laughed loudly and often. I snuck a glance at Lucien. He was smiling, but not with his eyes, and I got the impression he found Kennedy's tale rather preposterous.

By the time the story had run its course, I'd finished my sherry and Mrs Cooper appeared in the doorway to tell us dinner was served. I hadn't contributed anything to the conversation so far, and this suited me fine.

We went through to the dining room. The table was laid for four, with silver candelabras, and at each place setting a battalion of crystal glasses sparkled in the light of the chandelier above. Naturally, Lucien sat at the head of the table and he indicated to me to sit opposite him, with the two visitors on either side. Mrs Cooper served the food in stony silence. I got the feeling that she was put out that I was being included in the party, particularly given our exchange of words earlier in the day. It was the first three course meal I'd had at Winterbourne, with a first course of smoked venison, followed by roast gigot of lamb and then treacle tart with custard. It was a step up from our usual kitchen meals and the two guests tucked in heartily. Their talk was all of book dealing, with lots of name-dropping of people I couldn't possibly have heard of and discussions of prices that had been paid at book auctions. It seemed that they always managed a steal, while their rivals constantly paid well over the odds.

As the meal progressed, Lucien was the assiduous host, making sure everyone's glass was topped up, including mine. Ordinarily, it was a conversation I would have found fascinating, but the events of the previous twenty-four hours had put me on edge. Or, more truthfully, had absolutely terrified me. I couldn't concentrate on what the men were saying, and I could barely get a mouthful of food down. I knew Lucien was watching me, because I was watching him. Although he chipped into the conversation often enough, I could tell he wasn't engaged by it. He didn't see the two men as his colleagues or equals in any way, making me wonder how straight his dealings with them would be. When he saw that I was watching him, he gave me a sly grin. It wasn't friendly. It was lupine and predatory, and made me shift uncomfortably in my chair. I was beginning to wonder how I'd ever found him attractive.

Once the plates were cleared by an increasingly belligerent Mrs Cooper, Lucien took our wine glasses and replaced them with port glasses. He cleared his throat.

'Right, gentlemen, let's get on to business. What's on your wish lists? We can check with Anne to see if any of them can be accommodated.'

I was exhausted and had been about to make my excuses and go to bed, but now, suddenly, we'd reached the point of my having been invited in the first place. Kennedy, on my right, passed me the port decanter. I was about to pass it straight to de Groot when Lucien caught my eye. He inclined his head towards the glass in front of me. His meaning was clear, so I poured myself half a glass, though I had no intention of drinking it.

Once de Groot had filled his glass, Sherman Kennedy raised his in a toast.

'To books, and to the treasures we might find in the Winterbourne library.' He raised his glass to his lips and drank almost half of it down in one go.

We followed suit, though I took only the tiniest sip.

'I'll go first,' said de Groot. 'I've heard, Lucien, that you have an entire set of signed first editions of Dickens. I don't suppose you'd be willing to part with them.'

'I don't suppose you could afford them,' said Lucien.

'My client certainly could, but if you don't want to part with them, fair enough.'

'I have a customer who's after first editions of Churchill's *History of the English-Speaking Peoples*.'

Lucien nodded at me.

'We've three complete sets,' I said. 'All of them signed.' I felt relieved that I could answer him. It wasn't as if I had the entire library catalogue in my head.

'Perhaps I could look at them?' said Kennedy.

'Anne will pull out the books you're interested in for you to look at in the morning,' said Lucien.

I pushed my chair back. 'I'll just run and fetch a bit a paper to make a note of the titles,' I said.

Lucien stood up. 'I'll get some from my study.'

While he was gone, the two men continued to reel off books they'd be interested in buying. Some were familiar, and I knew we had, but there were a lot I'd never heard of. After sherry, wine and port, I couldn't possibly keep the list in my head, so I'd have to ask them to repeat them when Lucien returned.

He was only gone a couple of minutes. He came to my end of the table and presented me with a sheaf of lined paper and a heavy mother-of-pearl fountain pen that I'd seen lying on his desk in his study. Was this the pen he'd used to write the new entries in the red ledger? I didn't want to touch it, but I had no choice. My hand shook as I picked up the pen, and there was a tremor in my voice as I asked Kennedy and de Groot to go over their wishes again.

Lucien gave me a quizzical look, but I avoided his eye and concentrated on writing down the details of the books.

Over the next hour, I filled three sheets of paper with the books the two dealers were looking for. I confirmed that we had some of them and promised to check the catalogue for the others. All the while, Lucien was watching, barely contributing to the conversation. The port went round again, and I added more to my glass. It was nearly empty, and I realised I'd been repeatedly sipping the ruby liquid to steady my nerves. My head was swimming. God, how I wanted this evening to end.

Both book dealers were quite drunk now. I could see that de Groot was running out of steam, but Sherman Kennedy was ploughing on, elaborating his requests with unnecessary details and anecdotes of other deals he'd struck.

'There is just one last thing I want to add to your list,' said de Groot, talking directly to me and interrupting Kennedy in full flow.

I nodded, pen poised.

'Have you got any pre-Victorian erotica in your library?'

Victorian erotica was easy to find, especially with the advent of photography, but earlier works relied on illustrations and were not so plentiful.

'We have,' I said. 'Lucien has some excellent examples in his secret library, and I'm sure I could find some for you.'

'What?' shouted Kennedy, eyes aglow. 'Lucien, you have a secret library? Why haven't we heard about this? What ya got in there? This I need to see.'

'You won't believe what he's got,' I said recklessly, too drunk to register Lucien's warning look. 'All sorts of erotica, books on sadism and black magic. Grimoires. Even . . .'

'Anne!' Lucien stood up. His face had turned dark, his eyes malevolent.

'This is interesting,' said de Groot.

Lucien marched the length of the table, grabbed my upper arm and yanked me out of my chair. I staggered against him, unsteady on my feet.

'How dare you,' he hissed in my ear.

I opened my mouth, but I had no words. I'd realised immediately what I'd done, and then I'd compounded it. Maybe I'd done it on purpose. I glanced from de Groot to Kennedy, looking to them for a way out. But de Groot was staring into his lap, his face flushed with embarrassment. Kennedy was laughing, the sort of man that enjoyed a spectacle.

Lucien marched me from the room.

'You're hurting me,' I gasped as he pushed me through the door into the corridor.

He let go of my arm, propelling me away from him. I tripped on the edge of a Persian rug and crashed into the wood panelling opposite. The breath was knocked out of me and I fell to the floor. Lucien carefully closed the door behind us, then stood glaring down at me.

'Damn you,' he snarled. His fists were clenched by his side.

I cowered, certain he was about to strike me.

But he turned away and went back into the dining room. From within, I could hear Kennedy speaking, his voice high-pitched with excitement. He stopped speaking abruptly as Lucien entered.

I struggled to my feet and ran up to my room, tears of anger streaming down my cheeks, while deep within my chest, my heartbeat was a drumroll of terror.

30

I THREW MYSELF DOWN ON MY BED, then immediately stood up and paced my room. Panic had brought on a surge of adrenalin and I couldn't keep still. I tore at a fingernail with my teeth, but even the slash of pain and taste of blood in my mouth didn't jolt me back to my senses.

What had I done? What was I to do now?

I went to the bathroom and splashed cold water on my face. As I rubbed my eyes with the towel, I heard a wretched moaning and spun round, before realising that the noise was coming from my own throat. Lucien might have to smooth things over with his guests now, but what would he do when they were gone. I thought about the fate of Frances Sparrow. She'd never left the island. Was that what was in store for me? Was my fate at Winterbourne now sealed?

The only way off Craigsea Rock was on the RIB and that was guarded. It was too far to swim, and the water was too cold besides. I was trapped here with a man who apparently knew the future fate of mankind, and I couldn't look to the Coopers for help of any kind.

But maybe one of the two visitors would help me. My mind settled on de Groot. He was the more measured of the pair, and he certainly hadn't been amused by what he'd just seen.

Perhaps I could slip him a note somehow, maybe when we met in the library to go over the books they'd expressed an interest in. I'd have to somehow manage it without either Lucien or Kennedy seeing. I didn't trust Kennedy. He'd given me several leering looks over the course of the evening, and he'd laughed unashamedly as Lucien had dragged me out of the room.

What to say? Telling him I was being held here against my will would sound overdramatic, and what help would I ask for? What could he do for me?

As I pondered this question, I heard Loki barking down on the terrace. I went to the window and opened it quietly. The three men were back out on the terrace, smoking cigars now. I leant out and could hear the murmur of their voices, but they were talking too quietly for me to catch the gist of their conversation. I closed the window and slipped quietly down the stairs to the library, the windows of which would be directly above where they were standing. Without switching on the lights, I went to the middle of the three bay windows and, staying beneath the level of the windowsill, opened one of them just a crack. I still couldn't hear.

Beneath the windows there was a narrow ledge with a low parapet. Hardly daring to breathe, I climbed out onto it and lay down, so I would be hidden from view, should one of them chance to look up.

De Groot was speaking. 'But come on, Lucien. There's a robust market for grimoires, the older the better. You could make a fine profit on just one or two.'

'I have plenty of clients who'd be interested,' said Kennedy.

'They're not for sale.' Lucien's voice carried an undertow of displeasure. 'I'll consider your offers on books in the library, but the collection Anne alluded to is private and will never come to auction. She spoke out of turn.'

'She'd be passably pretty if it wasn't for that awful scar on her face.' Kennedy was slurring his words now.

'I find it quite attractive,' said de Groot. There was something deeply disturbing about the way he said it. I felt a sudden urge to be sick.

A barely perceptible click from somewhere above me made me look up at the tower, but I couldn't see anything.

'Do you think she would . . .' The Dutchman left the rest of the sentence hanging in the air. What? What did he want from me?

'Stay away from her.'

'Sure, sure. My apologies, but you can't . . .'

A rustle of clothing above made me twist my body to look up again. It was followed by a soft sigh. Was there someone on the floor above? Forgetting the men on the terrace below, I stood up on the ledge to see better, gripping the balustrade to keep my balance. A woman was silhouetted against a dim light in the tower window behind her. I recognised the woman I'd seen at the lighthouse, her long hair hanging forward, virtually covering her face. A cold tremor rose up my back. There was someone walking on my grave.

'Who are you?' I whispered. I didn't want the men below to hear me.

The lights went out. It was midnight.

The woman vanished, but the sigh and the rustle of her clothes had sounded as real as she'd looked on the day I'd seen her at the lighthouse. Could she really be an apparition? I didn't believe in ghosts. Did I?

I glanced down at the terrace. It was empty. The men must have gone back inside, and I was alone in darkness. Alone on the island. And more afraid than I'd ever been in my life.

The creak of the library door opening behind me made me start. I clutched the balustrade, unwilling to go back inside and make myself known. I turned and peered in through the window as a shadowy figure crossed the floor towards me. Something, perhaps the softness of the tread, perhaps its form, told me it was a woman.

A dead woman. A visitation from beyond the grave.

'Frances?'

She had almost reached the window.

'You should never have come here. You're not right for Winterbourne.' It was Mrs Cooper's rasping whisper.

I must have gasped in surprise. I almost lost my balance. I clung to the windowsill for support, and felt a cold hand settle on my own.

'You should have stayed in your cosy little life back on the mainland.'

Suddenly enraged, I bit back. 'You know nothing about my life.'

'But of course we do. Why do you think Mr Broussard selected you for the job? Because of your superior librarian skills?' She let out a dry laugh. 'You were chosen because nobody would miss you when things went bad. And they have, haven't they?'

'What do you mean?' Her grip was hurting my hand, but I couldn't bring myself to pull away.

'You're nothing compared to Frances. She was everything you're not.' The venom in her voice made me shiver.

'I'm not trying to be Frances. I came here to do a job and I'll leave when I've finished. My being here has nothing to do with you. I work for Lucien.'

'You don't understand Lucien Broussard – you know nothing about him. I've known him for years. He's earnt our loyalty, me and Robert Cooper. He's been good to us. So don't think you can just walk in here and try to turn him against us, and dig up what happened with Frances Sparrow.'

She was silent for a few moments, and in the moonlight I could see her face. Her eyes were vacant. She was somewhere else in time. Somewhere in her memories.

'Whatever happened to Frances makes no difference to me,' I said, trying to take control of the narrative.

She ignored me and now I tried to pull my hand away. She loosened her grip, but then suddenly tightened it again. 'You know you mean nothing to Lucien. His heart will always belong to her, his little sparrow.'

'And he means nothing to me. He disgusts me and the sooner I'm finished here, the better.'

She turned her head away from me, as if she didn't want to hear.

'What do you want, Mrs Cooper? Why did you come to me?'

'To warn you off. You've seen things here you shouldn't have seen. You need to forget them. You need to leave the island.'

'Frances never left the island, did she?'

'You have no idea what happened to Frances.'

'Tell me about it.'

'You wouldn't understand. And it's none of your business.'

I'd had enough. I wanted her gone. I made a move to climb back in through the window, but she barred my way with her arm.

'She's been watching you and you've made her angry, trying to usurp her place at Winterbourne, trying to worm your way into his affections. Prying and digging where you're not wanted.'

'She's dead. She doesn't even know of my existence.' A blast of cold wind hit me in the back as I said this. I shivered. 'Get out of my way.'

'You shouldn't be here.'

Mrs Cooper was stronger than I would have imagined. She put her hands on my shoulders to try and keep me from coming back into the room. She pushed against me with all the force she could muster, and I belatedly realised she was doing worse than just keeping me out. She was trying to force me back over the balustrade. If I went backwards over the edge, I would land on the terrace on my head.

I fought back, trying to draw upon every ounce of inner strength. But alcohol in my veins and the lack of food in my stomach made me weak.

'Please . . .' I said, and instantly despised myself.

Her claw-like hands were biting into my flesh through my thin blouse, and I could see that her jaw was set with grim determination. We wrestled in silence, just rasping breaths and gasps of pain. The tussle seemed like it would never end. My hands were on her upper arms, but I just didn't have the strength to dislodge her grip. I was dizzy and in my mind's eye I was already spinning away over the parapet. My head would split like a ripe melon on the flagstones and there'd be another fresh grave at the Michael Kirk.

'Let go,' I shrieked.

With one final, gargantuan effort, I thrust her sideways and, losing her balance, she finally gave up her grip on my shoulders. She skidded to the floor with the sound of bones cracking. I scrambled in through the window, breathing heavily, my heart beating wildly in my chest as I could still feel the imprint of her nails in the flesh above my collarbones.

'Get away from me.'

With a moan of pain, she attempted to stand up, but crashed back onto her knees as one ankle gave way under her. I heard the breath expelled from her body with the impact. Impassive,

I stood over her, watching her struggles. I didn't help her. It was all I could do to suppress the urge to kick her while she was down.

She crawled towards the door, and when she was finally over the threshold, I slammed it shut with satisfaction.

What had I become?

And what would become of me in the morning, once the book dealers had left, and Lucien could deal with my transgression without an audience?

31

I SAT IN THE DARKENED LIBRARY for over an hour. There was no way I could return to my room yet. I'd heard Mrs Cooper make her way slowly along the corridor to the top of the stairs with grunts and moans. What would Lucien do when he saw her? And Robert Cooper? She would almost certainly spin the story to blame me. But I was already in trouble, and I was terrified of what the morning would bring.

Perhaps I should flee from the house. Only where could I go? Loki would find me for them. I couldn't get off the island and I wouldn't be able to survive very long on my own in the open. The snow had virtually disappeared, but it was still bitingly cold out there. All I could do was wait for the inevitable.

I was sober now. The cold air and the adrenalin had cleared the fuzziness.

A thought crept into the corner of my mind and stood alone in the shadows. I pushed it away. I didn't want to consider it. But it snuck back and skirted the outer edges of my consciousness. I resisted, refusing to give it space to grow, pushing my thoughts in other directions. But I kept circling back. It was the only option I had.

Eventually, I tiptoed back to my room and made myself look presentable again. When I checked in the bathroom mirror, there were deep bruises blossoming on both my shoulders, so I buttoned my shirt up to the neck. I couldn't do anything to hide Mrs Cooper's claw mark on the back of my hand, but I brushed my hair and washed my face. I needed to look rational, not like a wild woman who was seeing ghosts and getting into brawls.

I picked up a torch and tiptoed down the servants' stairs to the first floor, where I assumed the two book dealers had been given rooms. My plan was to throw myself on their mercy and beg them to insist on taking me back to the mainland with them. They'd seen how Lucien had manhandled me earlier, so how could they refuse? I didn't know which room either of them was in, but if I appealed to one, I was sure the other would also cooperate.

The two biggest guest bedrooms were opposite each other at the far end of the corridor that I emerged into. I switched off my torch and made my way silently along the wooden floor, praying that I wouldn't hit a creaky board. I wanted to listen at their doors first for any slight hint of which man was in which room. I'd already decided that, if I had the choice, I would approach Kennedy first. There had been something disturbing about de Groot's comment on my scar. The American, I decided, was cast from the what-you-see-is-what-you-get mould, and if he took pity on me I was sure that he would help me.

There was a line of soft light at the bottom of one of the two doors. The other one was dark. Someone was reading in bed with a torch, while the other was probably fast asleep. This was confirmed as I listened at the keyhole of the room without the light. The soft rumble of somebody snoring met my ears.

Taking a deep breath and feeling a tightening across the back of my shoulders, I tapped gently on the other door and then opened it a crack. There was a panicked fumbling sound and a gasp from the direction of the bed.

'Who is there?' It was de Groot's voice.

Damn!

A torch was standing upended on the bedside table, reflecting a soft amber glow down from the ceiling. It meant I couldn't properly read de Groot's face, but I could see that his hair was tousled, and he was clutching the bedcovers up to his chest. Above the covers, his pale shoulders were bare and bony.

'It's Anne Adams,' I said, stepping into the room and closing the door softly behind me. I stood with my back pressed against the wood, not wanting to move closer to the bed.

'This is unexpected.' He pushed himself up the bed into a sitting position. He seemed slightly out of breath.

'I need help. I want to leave the island. Please take me with you when you leave tomorrow.' The words tumbled out of my mouth at speed.

'Come closer,' was all he said.

I moved to stand at the end of his bed. I could see his face more clearly now he was sitting up. The ghost of a smile, his head cocked slightly to one side as he appraised me in the dim light.

'Please,' I said.

'Why do you just not ask Lucien's man to take you to the mainland?'

'It's ... Bad things have happened here in the past. I'm scared.'

'Afraid of Lucien? He's a pussycat.'

'It would be better for me if I could leave with you and Mr Kennedy tomorrow.'

He shook his head in puzzlement. He still wasn't getting it.

'He's got a book with a spinning wheel. The words change and disappear. He's writing the future. He's evil ...' I stopped talking. It sounded mad, even to me, and de Groot's eyes were now wide with disbelief.

'I need your help.'

De Groot's mouth turned down at the corners. 'I wouldn't want to do anything that would offend Broussard. He's potentially one of my biggest clients.'

I remained silent, as he considered my request. *Risk alienating your best customer to aid a madwoman.* I was wasting my time.

'If I help you off the island, what would I get in return?'

His eyes swept my body and I felt sickened. His meaning was quite clear. He took my hesitancy to mean that I was considering his suggestion and the next thing I knew, he'd risen from the bed and was standing in front of me naked. His body was pale and scrawny, and he wasn't quite naked. On the lower part of his torso and the top of his legs was some sort of black leather bondage harness.

I turned my head away as quickly as I could, but he came towards me.

'No!' I tried to run from the room, but he caught me by the shoulder and pulled me towards the bed.

'Don't play the ingénue, Anne. I've seen the way Broussard looks at you.'

I struggled to get away, but he pushed his body against me, so I had to fall back onto the bed.

'Leave me alone.' My voice was high with fear.

Pinning me down with a hand on one shoulder, he used his other hand to rip open my blouse. The buttons flew off and skittered away across the floor. Above me, his leering face took in the sight of my breasts, encased in a plain, flesh-coloured bra. I reached up to scratch at his cheek, and his grin widened.

'Play nice, now.'

I wasn't expecting the slap. A harsh, glancing blow across my cheekbone that made me shriek with the shock and pain. I was blinded by stinging tears, struggling wildly to escape from underneath him.

The door crashed open and de Groot was dragged off me. I gasped for air like a landed fish, trying to understand what had just happened.

'What the hell do you think you're doing?'

Lucien towered above de Groot, who lay trembling on a worn Persian carpet at his feet.

'She came to me,' he said petulantly.

Lucien turned towards me. 'Is that true?'

I shook my head, speechless.

De Groot struggled to stand up. His prominent erection had disappeared, and he looked like a gangly teenager next to Lucien's muscled frame. Lucien punched him hard enough on the chin to send him back down.

Terrified by his apparent rage, I pulled the two sides of my ruined blouse together and stumbled towards the door.

'Where are you going?'

'I ... to my room.'

Lucien followed me into the corridor. Had he guessed the real reason why I'd gone to de Groot's room? He caught up with me within a couple of steps and then stepped in front of me, standing with his legs splayed and his hands on his hips.

'Why did you go to him?'

'I just wanted to check on one of the titles he was interested in.' It was obvious I was lying. It was past 1 a.m., and that was the sort of question that could easily wait until the next day.

'Whatever you were doing in de Groot's room, don't go there again. He's a man with dangerous tastes.'

Pot, kettle sprung into my mind, but I was more concerned with getting away from him. I tried to skirt around him to get to the servants' stairs, but he stopped me by putting a hand on one shoulder. My ruined blouse slipped, revealing the deepening bruises from my tussle with Mrs Cooper. He stared at them for a moment, shining his torch on them, before letting go of me. I pulled my blouse back into place, hoping that he would lay the blame for them at de Groot's door.

'Go and clean yourself up. I'll deal with you in the morning.'

For the first time ever, he sounded tired. The evening obviously hadn't gone to plan for him, and it was my fault. I scurried away to the servants' staircase, not daring to think what he meant by his final remark. I'd dropped my torch in de Groot's room, and as the stairwell door closed behind me, I was in complete darkness.

I wondered fearfully if I would ever see the light again.

32

It took me hours to fall asleep. The evening had been a fevered adrenalin rush, my heart battering my chest, my muscles tense and fear lurking like a tumour at the back of my throat. I lay on my back, eyes wide open, staring up into the darkness. Maybe I was looking for salvation, maybe I was looking for the devil. My thoughts were jumbled. When I closed my eyes, on the backs of my eyelids I saw legions of innocents marched into the fire, directed by Lucien, sitting above them on the back of a huge grey horse, with Robert Cooper as his standard bearer. The horse morphed into Loki, slavering and snarling, while Mrs Cooper sat knitting in front of a guillotine that turned into a witch burning. She laughed as the flames engulfed her.

I woke up coughing. Choking, in fact, the acrid taste of smoke flooding my mouth. I blinked and my eyes smarted, so I sat up quickly. The room spun around me and I gripped the sides of my mattress, almost vomiting as my lungs did their best to expel the filthy air.

My befuddled brain was slow to comprehend, but at last I realised this wasn't part of my dream. It was really happening. There was a fire somewhere. Smoke was filling my room and if I didn't get out quickly, it would choke the life right out of me. I leapt out of bed and straightaway opened my two windows as wide as I could. I sucked in great gulps of fresh air, craning my neck around to see if I could work out where the fire was coming from. Flames were licking at the frames of nearly all the ground floor windows, and I could just make out flashes of red coming from the library windows directly below me. I heard loud cracking sounds as the windowpanes burst in the heat. Good God, the library? All those books turning to ash? The fire must have been burning some time. Panicking, I ran to my bathroom and soaked a hand towel in water to wrap around my face. Then I pulled jeans and a coat over my pyjamas and slipped my feet into my trainers, hoping the layers would afford me at least some protection from the fire.

There was no time to waste. Wrapping the wet towel around my lower face, I grabbed at the door handle. It burnt my hand as I flung the door open. The wood panelling in the corridor was on fire on one side. Pressing myself against the opposite wall, I ran towards the grand staircase. One thing I hadn't expected outside my room was the noise. The fire roared and the house groaned and creaked in response. As I reached the top of the stairs, I heard a tremendous cracking sound, like a rifle shot. The crystal chandelier that hung above the sweeping curve of the staircase crashed down onto the black and white vestibule tiles, smashing into a thousand glittering pieces.

I ran down to the first floor. On the landing I paused, peering this way and that, but it was too smoky to even make out the doors of Lucien's room or the guest bedrooms. Did they know the house was on fire? Had they got out already? I dithered for precious seconds, wondering whether I should run to their rooms to make sure they were awake, but another huge crash somewhere else in the house made me realise I'd be risking my life if I did it, while they might have escaped by now anyway.

I looked down. The bottom of the stairs was engulfed in flames, and they were creeping up gradually, singeing the carpet, bubbling up the gold leaf on the banisters. If I didn't go now, there would be no way through. As it was, I would have to run through fire to reach the front door. I looked towards it and, through the swirling smoke, I could see it was open. Good.

I adjusted the towel over my nose and mouth. It made breathing difficult, but I'd be worse off without it. Then I ran, taking the steps two at a time, ignoring the pain in my injured leg and foul burning sensation tearing down the back of my throat.

I could feel the soles of my trainers going soft as they started to melt, and it made me run faster. For a moment I imagined myself in the wreck of a burning car, trapped by the seat belt, and staring at my dead brother. His head turned slowly towards me and his lips moved. 'Go, Annie, you can make it out,' and then I was back on the grand staircase, running through the fire. I took the last five steps at a flying leap, hurling my body through the flames, thrusting my good leg forward and hoping for a balanced landing. That was too much to ask for, and I sprawled full-length on the black and white tiles. They were gritty and hot, and covered with small shards of glass from the smashed chandelier.

I scrambled to my feet. Everything hurt. I must have sustained some burns, some cuts, but nothing mattered except getting out of there. I staggered through the doorway and the cold air washed over me. Malcolm had come to me in my moment of need and given me the strength to go on and, in that one second, I'd never felt so grateful or so alive in all my life. Clear of the flames and the smoke, I dropped to my knees and wrenched the blackened towel from my face. My eyes were streaming from the smoke, but then I started to cry. I don't know why, maybe the shock of what had happened, on top of the encounter with de Groot and the alcohol in my system. It had been such a long night.

The piercing cold of the fresh air, combined with the effects of smoke inhalation, was making me cough. My lungs went through paroxysm after paroxysm until I was afraid I would choke them up entirely. My rib muscles, my diaphragm, my guts, my back ... every part of me was being contorted as my body fought to replace poisonous gas with clean oxygen. A ripping pain informed me that I'd cracked a rib, or more than just one. I slumped down onto my side on the cold drive, convinced that having escaped the fire, I was still going to die of its effects.

After a minute of writhing on the cold gravel, I felt a hand on my shoulder.

'Hey, you're going to be okay.' It was Sherman Kennedy.

He helped me to my feet, and my cough started to calm down.

'Thanks.' I was able to get one word out at a time between bouts of coughing. 'Lucien?'

'Safe,' said Kennedy. 'And de Groot, too. And the servants.'

He helped me walk round to the terrace, where I saw Robert Cooper and Lucien standing by the balustrade, their heads together in urgent whispers. Loki was cowering at Cooper's feet, whimpering, but the two men ignored him. Mrs Cooper was sitting on the flagstones nearby, staring up at the burning building with an expression of horrified fascination. De Groot, at least fully dressed now, was standing beyond her. He looked as if he was trying to get a signal on his mobile. Someone should have told him not to bother. There would be no fire engine turning up here and no ambulances to treat anyone's burns.

I didn't want to go near Lucien, the Coopers or de Groot, so I disengaged myself from Kennedy's supportive arm and stood at the side of the terrace, where it bordered the rock garden. Kennedy seemed to understand, so he let go of me and went along the terrace to join de Groot.

Every breath was still painful, but I was alive at least. I stared up at the house. There were flames in nearly every window and black smoke billowed into the night sky, obscuring the stars and dimming the moonlight to a grey glint. It couldn't be saved. The fire had taken hold and, even if there had been emergency services available, they wouldn't have been able to bring this blaze under control.

My eyes travelled from window to window until eventually I was looking up at the tower. The windows at the top were dark. The fire hadn't reached that far yet. But then I was horrified to see the black outline of a figure in one of them. I'd done battle in my mind, trying to work out if the woman I kept seeing was a ghost or a figment of my own imagination. I didn't believe in ghosts, but equally I didn't think I was having visions. I heard her thin cry for help, and I realised she was neither. This was a real, live woman. A human being, not an apparition. Frances Sparrow wasn't dead. She'd never been dead.

But now she might well die.

I looked at Lucien, still talking in hurried whispers to Robert Cooper.

I ran towards him. 'What did you do to her? Why do you keep her here?'

He barely glanced up. The noise of the fire had drowned out my words, and I realised it was just as well.

I ran back towards the front door, and as I ran, my mind made calculations. The grand staircase would be impassable now, but the servants' stairwell was behind closed doors, which would maybe hold off the fire for a little longer. I kept running, past the front door, and round to the kitchen door. A huge backdraught of smoke and flames gushed out when I pulled it open. I leapt back, but it spent itself quickly enough. I pulled the damp towel from my coat pocket and dunked it into the rainwater butt. Wrapping it around my face, I ventured back into the house.

I was barely able to see. The kitchen was an inferno, but there was a door in the back vestibule that led directly into the butler's corridor. I yanked up the hem of my coat to touch the door handle, quickly slipped through it and pulled it shut behind me. I was in total darkness now, but that was good. There were no flames here as the butler's corridor was entirely tiled, the floor, the walls and even the ceiling. It was still thick with smoke, however, and I had to feel my way along, counting the doors I passed until I thought I'd reached the back stairs. The tiles felt hot to the touch, and I knew I couldn't spend long in this atmosphere. My lungs were already damaged. But I couldn't let the woman in the tower burn to death.

I opened the door to the stairwell, and I could see again. The flickering of flames somewhere above told me the fire had breached at least one of the doors, and there was a strong smell of charred wood and burnt floor polish. As I started up the stairs at a trot, I hoped there was still enough time. Each breath was like setting a fire in my chest, and it felt as if my heart would explode.

The doorway between the stairs and the first-floor landing had entirely burnt away. Smoke was being sucked into the stairwell like a chimney and the fire itself was starting to creep up the stairs. I peered out into what looked like a scene from hell. An orange glow bathed the entire floor. The flames roared and there was an endless cracking and thudding as parts of the walls and ceilings succumbed.

A movement at the far end of the corridor caught my eye and I squinted to see what it was.

I saw Lucien emerge and disappear again into the smoke. He must have belatedly seen Frances Sparrow at the top of the tower.

'Here,' I shouted. My voice was cracked and brittle. 'Over here. These stairs are safer.'

But my words fell on deaf ears. It was no surprise that he couldn't hear me over the rush of the hot air and the crackle of destruction. I waved an arm desperately, hoping to catch his eye, but he went off in the other direction.

Then I got it. He wasn't in here to rescue the woman at all. He was going to the library. And in my heart, I knew what he was going there for. Only Lucien Broussard would put saving a book above a woman's life. But I had his measure now.

I turned back to the staircase and ran up to the next floor. I had to get to the top of the tower and come back down before they became impassable. The servants' stairs ended at the second floor. I had to go back out into the corridor outside, the one on which my own room was located, and go along it to the door that led up to the tower. The door that had been locked ever since I'd arrived at Winterbourne.

Both sides of the passageway were alight now, and there were flames dancing across the floorboards, spreading the fire ever further. It was becoming hungrier as it spread, devouring the old house ever faster. Using one arm to keep the wet towel in place across my face, and my other hand to pull my coat tightly around my body so it wouldn't flap into the flames, I ran along the corridor. Every step was painful. My leg, my lungs, my ribs. There were burns on my hands and I could feel the heat coming up through the soles of my trainers. There was a sudden flare as a fluttering ember caught in my hair and I had to use the towel to quickly smother it. My eyes were smarting, salt tears streaming down my face and stinging my skin.

It seemed to take me forever to reach the door to the tower, even though it can't have been more than a few seconds. As expected, it was still locked, but the wood was warping in the heat and so I smashed my shoulder against it, hoping it was distorted enough to break free from the lock. It didn't work. I tried again, over and over, shouting in frustration, praying that Lucien would do the right thing and come to help.

But no one came. It was just me, on my own. If only I'd thought before running up here. Mrs Cooper must have the key and I should have got it from her before attempting the rescue. But it was too late to think about that now. There certainly wouldn't be time to go down and get it.

With one last gargantuan marshalling of everything I had left, I moved back, then stepped forward on my good leg and kicked my injured leg into the centre door. It was hardly ideal using my bad leg as a battering ram, but my good leg had more power to propel me forward. My foot splintered through one of the door panels as my body collided with the door and a sharp jolt of pain shot through my knee joint and up to my hip. I was now in the awkward position of having one leg through the top half of the door, and I had to lean back to drag it out. I could hardly straighten it, let alone put any weight on it, and if this didn't help me get the door open, I'd have left myself in an even worse position than before.

With flames licking at my back, I pushed my head through the gap in the splintered panel. It was too dark to see anything, so I felt for the door furniture with one hand. I found the door handle and tried it. It made no difference, of course. The door was locked, and I didn't have a key.

Crying with frustration and rage, I kicked the door again and again, this time with my strong leg, and finally the lock burst open, and the door swung aside. Shouting Frances's name, I galloped up the steep, narrow staircase to the tower. There was one room at the top, as yet untouched by the fire, but I didn't have time to take in the details.

Frances Sparrow was standing at the window, oblivious to my arrival, trying to make herself heard to those on the terrace over the noise of Winterbourne's death throes. I went to her and touched her on the shoulder. She turned with a gasp of shock.

'Frances? Come with me.'

She was a tiny woman, smaller than I'd realised, and she was terrified. I had to drag her across to the top of the staircase, and when she saw the smoke billowing up towards us from the corridor below, she grabbed hold of the newel post with both arms.

'I can't,' she said. Her voice was weak and tremulous.

'It's the only way.'

I tried to carefully loosen her hands from the post, but she struggled like a wildcat to grab hold again. We were running out of time. Drastic measures were called for, so I slapped her forcefully across the cheek. The shock did it. Her hands went to her face, I grabbed one of her arms and started pulling her down the stairs. She shrieked and pulled away from me, but I was stronger. I wasn't going to die for Frances Sparrow, so I propelled us down the stairs with stumbling speed.

At the bottom, the smoke was thick and black, stinging my eyes and leaving me virtually blind. Next to me, still in my iron grip, Frances was coughing. I pulled the towel from my face.

It was only just damp now, but it still helped to filter the smoke, as I realised when I took a shallow breath without it. I ripped it in two and wrapped one half around Frances's nose and mouth. She fought against me, until she realised what I was doing. Then her eyes widened with gratitude, and she deftly knotted it at the back of her head. I replaced the other half of the towel on my own face, coughing violently.

It was only a few feet to the servants' stairs, but it meant passing through an inferno. I grabbed Frances's hand, and we leapt through the flames. There was no point in her resisting anymore. We were in the heart of it, so all she could do was follow my lead.

I'd closed the door to the servants' staircase behind me when I came up to slow down the spread of the fire. When we reached it, I saw that it was burning ferociously, blocking our path to freedom with a wall of flame. I looked around frantically and snatched up a huge cloisonné vase from a console nearby. The metal burnt my hands and I nearly dropped it, but I gritted my teeth against the pain, and used it to smash away the burning remnants of the door. As I threw it to one side, the skin on my palms and fingertips which had held it was ripped away. I probably screamed, but by now I was running on survival instinct. It was get out or die.

We tore down the staircase into a huge cloud of smoke, and then through it I saw flames at the bottom. The roar of the fire was all around us, but this was almost drowned out by the screeching of timbers, buckling and warping in the heat. One wall of the butler's corridor had collapsed into rubble, making our escape route impassable. There was a door to our left, blown open by a rushing draught of burning air.

I tugged Frances through it.

We were in the ballroom. The parquet floor had buckled and was on fire in places. The glorious chandeliers had all smashed to the floor and the mirrors which lined the walls had cracked and burst out of their frames.

We only had to make it to one of the French doors on the other side of the room and we'd be out of danger. Just thirty feet. I pointed to the nearest door and shoved Frances ahead.

'Go,' I yelled in her ear.

But before we were halfway across, there was a horrifying cracking sound above us. I glanced up and my eyes met the ceiling coming down towards me. Winterbourne was collapsing around us, claiming Frances Sparrow and I as her victims.

You will never leave.

33

T HE FOLLOWING MINUTES AND HOURS are jumbled in my mind. Fragments of memories compete with things I must have imagined. Moments of searing pain are interspersed with stifling black silence during which I could barely breathe. Music plays, people speak. Something cold across my forehead. A bright light shines in my unseeing eyes.

As if in another world, I see the skeleton of Winterbourne in the grey dawn. Just the bones of the house remain. A stone chimney. Crumbling walls. The old iron range in the kitchen, blacker than ever before. A gargoyle from the tower on the ballroom floor. Curling wisps of smoke dance a slow gavotte in the cold air. Everything is smouldering and then, as a veil of soft rain sweeps in from the sea, a hiss of steam joins the twirling smoke, blurring my final image of the house of the Broussards.

All is lost.

Fifty-thousand books gone, the good and the bad.

Reality slammed in and I was being bumped along rough stones, dragged by my shoulders that felt like they would dislocate at any moment, which only added to the pain and burning, to the confusion and fear. The noise was deafening. The howl of the fire ripping the house to shreds, the scream of long-dormant timber twisting in agony, men shouting, a dog barking and, just barely there, a woman crying. I could taste the smoke inside my mouth, bits of cinder or broken teeth, salty blood. Taste merging with smell, my senses burning, my stomach churning at the stink of singed material and the smell of scorched flesh.

And everything was black. I could see nothing, but I was alive.

'Stop here. We're far enough from the fire now.' It was the American's voice. Shouting orders and taking control. 'We need blankets and a first aid kit.' A hubbub of voices. 'You, Mrs Cooper, yes? Do you have stuff at your cottage?'

Loki barking, barking, barking.

I drifted in and out of consciousness. Sometimes I was moving, sometimes I was lying still. Sometimes I was cold, sometimes I was burning with a fever. The pain made me befuddled. I lost all sense of time or place.

Eventually, strong hands lifted me, and I think they placed me in the trailer behind the quad bike. Every bump in the track felt like a sledgehammer to my bones. My mouth was dry and my throat raw. I coughed and coughed, but that meant I was alive. Every ounce of pain bore testament to the fact that I was still alive. Winterbourne hadn't beaten me.

There was someone sitting by me in the trailer.

'Frances?' My tongue caught on the roof of my mouth and my lips were cracked and tasted of smoke.

'I'm here.' I felt a hand take my hand and I winced. My hands were burnt and broken, like the rest of me.

I was given water. I was drugged. Later I felt the motion of the sea. Enough light filtered through my eyelids to tell me it was daytime, but I didn't know which day, and I didn't know where I was. My perception of the present was unreliable. My memory was unreliable. And I couldn't trust my senses.

Eventually the fog lifted, and I emerged. I could make sense of what I was hearing, sense enough to realise I was in a hospital ward. Monitors bleeped, curtains were pulled back and forth, voices murmured. I raised my hands to my face, but there was no touch of skin upon skin. There were bandages, across my eyes, wrapping my hands, and other parts of my body. A cannula in the back of my left hand, with a tube stretching away.

I tried my voice. *Hello. Help. Water.* My mouth seemed unwilling to form the words, but then I heard someone moving close to my bed.

'Anne, you're awake?'

I think I nodded.

'Water.'

They must have understood, because I felt the pressure of something cold and hard against my bottom lip. The rim of a cup. I drank the water and it felt like an achievement.

I slept again.

When I woke up, a male voice spoke to me about my injuries. Broken bones. Burns. A skin graft on my arm, already performed. My eyes had been hit by falling, burning debris in the ballroom. I was blind. The prognosis for the recovery of my vision wasn't good. Concussion. Severe lung damage due to smoke inhalation. Smaller burns and abrasions all over my body.

I coughed when he said this, and everything hurt despite the industrial-strength painkillers.

Later, a nurse told me I had a visitor. I couldn't think who it would be. As far as I knew, no one had informed my parents about the fire, and I had no friends.

'Anne?' A woman's voice. She sounded nervous.

'Who are you?'

'It's me, Frances. I need to thank you. You saved my life.'

Of course, it was Frances. She was the only person who would come to see me, and now I recognised her voice from the aftermath of the fire.

'I don't remember much of it. Were you also hurt?'

'Not so badly. A couple of burns and some bruising. And the smoke in my lungs, of course …' Her voice trailed off.

'I thought you were dead,' I said. 'When I saw you at the lighthouse, and later at the tower window, I thought you were a ghost.'

'A ghost?' She gave a short laugh. One of her hands sought out mine. 'No, I'm very much alive, thanks to you.'

That first visit only lasted a few minutes, but she came every day after that. Slowly I got to know her, and gradually I was able to piece together the story of what happened to her beyond what I'd read in her diary. She'd come into Lucien's employment in very much the same way I had, answering an advert and being subject to a short telephone interview. I think he selected us for the same reasons. We were both quiet girls. Vulnerable girls. Girls who wouldn't be missed if something went wrong. I suspected Janice Allard had investigated my background when I applied for the job, and from the start they must have known what I was running away from.

Frances said little about her relationship with Lucien, but I knew enough to read between the lines. After her pregnancy had ended in a miscarriage, he had shut her up in the tower, with the promise that she'd be allowed to leave once the new librarian had finished the catalogue.

'Why didn't you carry on with the work?' I asked.

'I refused. I resigned from my post, but still he wouldn't let me go. And there's no way off the island without Robert Cooper's help.'

'Have you spoken to the police?'

'Lucien is dead. He went to save his books and he never emerged from the fire. The Coopers will simply claim ignorance, so what's the point?'

Between her visits, I would think of other questions. Why hadn't she warned me the day we encountered each other by the lighthouse? She said she wasn't meant to be there. Mrs Cooper had smuggled her a spare key to the tower so she could go outside on the days when Robert Cooper went across to the mainland. 'Cooper is Lucien's man, through and through, but Mrs Cooper didn't agree with the way they treated me. Until you came, I had the run of the house at night, and my freedom when Cooper went for supplies.'

This admission explained some of the noises I'd heard in Winterbourne, the slamming doors and creaking floorboards. Frances would sometimes venture down to the library or the kitchen in the small hours when she thought I was asleep.

On the day I went to the lighthouse, she'd sneaked out even though Cooper was on the rock. Mrs Cooper had told her Robert would be busy doing repairs at the cottage all day.

'But when I saw Loki with you, I was scared. I knew Robert Cooper wouldn't be far behind. I had to get away.' She'd run back to the house, intending to be back up in the tower before Mrs Cooper had realised she was missing. She cried as she told me this. 'I'm not very brave, and I was frightened of Robert Cooper. He used to watch me, before I was in the tower. All the time. Spying on me. He tried to touch me once, in the butler's corridor, when he thought no one else was around. He couldn't control himself.'

She told me he had a peephole into the yellow room's bathroom. He could watch from the next-door room. She'd stuffed it with soggy paper when she'd discovered it, but no doubt he'd unblocked it when I arrived at Winterbourne. It made my flesh crawl. So the creaking floorboards could also have been Robert Cooper, creeping around in the next bedroom. I felt sick. Even though Frances also told me that Robert Cooper had charged into the ballroom and pulled me from the wreckage at considerable risk to himself, I was still repulsed whenever I thought of him.

We didn't just talk about Craigsea Rock. Sometimes she read to me and other times she talked of her childhood in the Midlands. Her family were dead now. I asked her what she was going to do, and she said she didn't know. She had a small nest egg of money she'd saved and a small inheritance from her parents, but eventually she'd have to go back to work. She kept me up to date with world news, though some days I'd rather not have known, and of the changing seasons. Christmas came and went, with small gifts and a hospital Christmas dinner, and I think we celebrated more when she was able to tell me she'd seen the first snowdrops of spring.

Surprisingly, she wasn't my only visitor during my weeks in hospital. A police detective and a fire investigator came to see me, to ask about the evening of the fire. I told them what I could remember, but I don't think it helped them very much. They said they didn't believe it was an accident, but didn't say why.

'Who do you think started the fire?' I asked Frances, on her next visit.

She shrugged. She seemed strangely disinterested. I expounded theories that it must have been one of the Coopers or Kennedy or de Groot. Not Lucien.

'It was me,' she said simply, when I'd run out of steam.

'But ...' I was at a loss for words. 'You were locked in the tower.' It didn't make sense.

'I set fire to the books in the secret chamber. I thought it would be contained in there, and I went back to the tower and locked it behind me. I assumed you would get the blame, because Lucien didn't know I had a key and could come and go.' She took one of my hands in hers. 'I'm truly sorry for that.'

I wondered what would have happened if the fire had been stopped and Lucien had blamed me for it. I suspected I wouldn't be alive and back on the mainland.

'It spread so fast,' she continued, 'and then I realised I was trapped. You saved my life, Anne. I owe you everything.'

It was a lot to take in and process, but her motives were clear. She'd found Broussard's special collection as abhorrent as I had.

The police report was inconclusive. The fire had burnt so ferociously that there was no evidence left as to how it had started and who might have been responsible. The Coopers were still on Craigsea Rock, Kennedy was back in America and de Groot had returned to the Netherlands. Frances Sparrow and I were hardly of consequence, so the matter was dropped.

After that, Frances was constantly by my side, dealing with the doctors, reassuring me in moments of anxiety, making sure I had all I needed to make my stay in the hospital more bearable. 'Don't worry about anything,' she'd say softly. 'I'll sort it for you.'

Eventually, the doctor told me I was ready to be discharged from the hospital. He asked me what my plans were. I was blind. My body was recovering slowly, but I would continue to need physical therapy every day. I would need a carer, at least temporarily, until I had adapted to my life-limiting injuries.

'Let me look after you,' said Frances, when I told her what the doctor had said. 'I owe you that much at least.'

34

So that's how we ended up here, me and Frances, in our tiny but in every way perfect flat, chosen for its very urban location, as far away from Craigsea Rock as we could manage. We live frugally. I receive disability benefit, which is next to nothing, and Frances is my paid carer. She also has a part-time job and her own dwindling nest egg.

It's more than a year now since Malcolm's death, and three months since the Winterbourne fire. As I recover slowly, I'm coming to terms with being blind. I'm relearning how to do all sorts of everyday things for which I once would have relied upon my eyes. I can move around the flat. I can find things in the cupboard that I need for making a snack or a cup of tea. I can fill the kettle and boil it. It sounds pathetic, doesn't it? But these are now my daily goals and achievements. Just to do the things that, prior to the fire, I absolutely took for granted. Twice a week I have physical therapy and, once a week, a Braille teacher comes to the flat for an hour. I've entered a world of voice activation and audiobooks, and I can dictate emails and have my computer read them back to me. Not that I have anyone to email, apart from my therapists.

It's a new life, and a very different life. I get frustrated some days. Angry. Exhausted. Sad. I've been warned to expect depression, and to get counselling when I need it. For each small win, there always seems to yet another, even bigger mountain to climb. They tell me that eventually I'll be able to get a job of some sort. And then when I do, I'll feel useful again. I suppose that's something to look forward to, but there isn't much on my horizon, and I fear that anything good might be a long time coming.

I think about writing down all that happened at Winterbourne. But who, apart from Frances, would believe me? She doesn't want me to. We made a pact, when I left the hospital and we came here, not to speak of Winterbourne ever again. To turn our faces forward and build new lives. She says that if I write about it, I'll be mired in the past. Of course, she's right. And who would read it?

Instead, I find refuge in listening to audiobooks. I can lose an afternoon or a morning while Frances is at work. She picks them up for me at the library. But I've told you this already, haven't I?

Spring is well underway now, and I'm looking forward to warmer weather. Frances says she'll take me to the park. I haven't been out much at all since we moved here. I'm still shaky on my feet, and getting used to walking again with my trusty stick. The thought of being out on a busy pavement, with people rushing past me and roads to cross, fills me with trepidation. But I suppose I'll get used to it.

Frances is at work now. She should be back in an hour or so. I check the time using Alexa, my little helper when Francis isn't around.

'Alexa, play BBC Radio Three.'

'Streaming BBC Radio Three from the BBC,' she replies.

Music fills the flat, sweeping violins in a mournful crescendo. I think it's music from a film. A thriller, I think, but I can't quite remember.

'Alexa, turn the volume down.'

I detect the start of a migraine flickering in my peripheral vision. Another hangover from my injuries at Winterbourne. Bright lights flashing behind my eyelids. I feel a little sick. It gets worse, so I make my way to the tiny bathroom we share. I lean over the toilet and vomit, and as I do a hammer-blow of pain shoots from one side of my head to the other.

I gasp.

This is worse than any of the migraines I've had so far. I'm sick again and the pain comes back as a snake, coiled, writhing inside my skull, forked tongue as sharp as a needle, piercing the back of my eyes. I reach for the side of the basin and pull myself up. Feel for the tap. Turn on a blast of cold water and splash my face. Swill my mouth out with water. The pain is agonising, as if my head is about to explode. I press my knuckles against my eyeballs, practically crying.

What's happening? Has an aneurism burst? Am I having a stroke? But the pain makes it too hard to think. I bite my upper lip. I breathe deeply through my nose, trying to quell my rising panic. My eyes are screwed tight shut, tears squeezing out between my lids. I splash my face with water again and feel to one side for the hand towel, instinctively opening my eyes at the same time.

There's a blur of light.

I wipe away the water and the tears. The blur ... sharpens ... There are colours. A shadowy figure comes into focus. I'm staring at myself in the mirror.

OhmyGodIcansee. I can see. I can see again.

I'm shouting in jubilation.

I blink. It's still a bit fuzzy, but it's getting clearer.

But how? What's changed?

The doctors told me it was highly unlikely I'd ever see again. I took this to mean I definitely wouldn't see again, that the 'highly unlikely' was just their way of softening the blow. But ...

I look around the tiny bathroom. It seems even smaller now I can see how close the walls are, and the window, and how tight the shower cubicle is. I look back to the mirror, at my face. It's changed. Instead of one scar, I have several, most notably a deep red welt across my forehead that has cut away part of my right eyebrow. Where the scar disappears into my hairline, there's a wide swathe of white hair that wasn't there before. But it's definitely me. The face I know, and I don't care about the changes, the new scars. It's just good to see it again.

The pain's still present, but it's changed to a dull throbbing. I open the cabinet behind the mirror and find some painkillers. I can read the packet myself. I don't have to wait for Frances and rely on her for things like this.

Then I'm suddenly scared. What if it goes away again? If this is an irregular blip brought on by the migraine? I tell myself not to think like that. I must take this as a blessing and appreciate it while I have it. Who knows what tomorrow will bring?

I return to the living room feeling a bit shaken, and it's so strange to see where I'm going, rather than having to feel my way around. There's my chair, by the window. I go to it and sink down, my body recognising its familiar contours in a way which my eyes don't. Despite having sat here every day for the last couple of months, I'm staring out at a view I've never seen before. The street, the houses opposite, the trees, the cars ... It's not how I pictured it in my mind. I turn back to the room and I realise it's getting dark. I've never bothered to turn on the lights in the afternoon, although I'm always aware of it when Frances gets in from work and switches them on.

I don't know where the light switches are.

They're not hard to find, of course. With the lights on, I study the living room. Frances arranged the furniture and chose the colours, but I like it. It's cosy, with a colour palette of green and mustard, and there are house plants on every surface, in planters and hanging pots. There's a small dining table set against one of the walls, where we eat our meals. Bookshelves, of course. A sofa and a coffee table piled high with my audiobooks. But then I see something else, just beyond them. A larger book, with a red cover. I recognise it.

Unease comes slowly at first. An uncomfortable fluttering deep inside. A sharp intake of breath. A shiver as the hairs on my arms stand to attention. But I know what I'm looking at, and then fear rushes through me like an avalanche.

What's it doing here? Why would Frances have brought it? For that's the only explanation as to why Lucien's abomination of a journal should be sitting on our coffee table.

I'm drawn to it as iron filings to a magnet. I don't want to touch it, but I can't help myself. I sink down onto the sofa in front of it. I put my fingers on the cover, feeling the grain of the leather in a way I would never have done before I'd experienced blindness. I open the book, and there's the symbol of chaos on the first page. I stare at it. It's not moving. I breathe a sigh of relief. It's not moving. But then I see that it is, so very slowly it hardly shows. There's nothing wrong with my sight now and I can detect its movement.

I turn the pages frantically to get to the end. The entry I read on the last few pages, the future foretold, has gone. Those pages are blank. Could I have imagined them? The last entry is as it was before. The wheel at the front isn't turning. It was just my mind playing tricks on me. The whole thing was imagined, a fever dream while I was ill on Craigsea Rock. This is nothing but a work of someone else's overactive imagination. It's a fake. Nothing to be afraid of.

But as I close the cover, I spy a movement. Words are streaming across the page, appearing and disappearing too fast for the eye to read. I throw it open again and watch Lucien's beautiful copperplate flowing across the page, like the moving trace on a heart monitor machine. Line after line of it.

My eyes catch up with it and I read.

untochaosasonwillbebornuntochaosasonwillbebornuntochaosasonwillbeborn

'Unto chaos a son will be born.' I read the words out loud. Just once, to be sure of what I was reading. I feel a movement in my belly in the same rhythm as the words and in one horrifying second my world is turned upside down. Nausea. Indigestion. A lack of periods. An array of small symptoms I'd put down to the after effects of my injuries ... How could I have not realised what's now glaringly obvious?

I'm carrying a child. Lucien's child. The child of chaos.

... untochaosasonwillbebornuntochaosasonwillbebornuntochaosasonwillbeborn ...

I slam the ledger shut and stagger to my chair by the window. The baby stirs inside me and I don't know how to feel about it. Lucien's child. For a split second I imagine terminating the pregnancy, but I could never do that, because it's also my child. I close my eyes and breathe deeply, trying to calm down. I need to work out what's going on.

I think back to my time in the hospital. Why didn't the doctors tell me I was pregnant? I recall a time when, drowsy and drugged, I heard Frances in whispered consultation with my doctor in the doorway to my room. 'Let me tell her,' she'd said, 'It'll be better if I tell her.' It was all I could make out from their interchange. 'Tell me what?' I remember saying as she came to my bedside. But she'd hushed me. 'It'll keep.' And then I'd forgotten all about it, and never asked her what the doctor had needed me to know. Presumably, that I was pregnant. Why would Frances not have told me?

More questions come piling in. How did the book get here? When I brought Frances out of Winterbourne, she brought nothing. She'd set the secret chamber alight specifically to destroy Lucien's journal. I'd last seen Lucien disappearing into the burning library and my presumption had been that he was going to save this book in particular, and maybe others. He'd never emerged from the fire and had subsequently been declared dead. But did they ever find a trace of his remains in the ashes? Could he have survived? What did that make him, a man who could walk through fire unscathed?

The thought is so horrifying that I start to hyperventilate. I run to the bathroom and throw up.

If Lucien survived the fire and rescued the book, it still doesn't explain what it's doing here in our flat, lying casually on our coffee table. Frances must know it's here. She's never mentioned it. And it was her who insisted that we never talk about Winterbourne and all that happened there. Things don't stack up, and the longer I think about it, the stranger it seems.

The only way I can make sense of it paints a very black picture of Frances Sparrow. She must still be in contact with Lucien, and if she is, I can no longer trust her. Has she known that he's still alive all this time? Are they working together?

The baby stirs again deep inside me and now I know what their agenda is. It might be Lucien's child, but it's also mine. He shan't take it from me. I'm breathing heavily. My head still aches, and now I know there's another lifeforce within me, I feel sick and scared about what the future holds. But I also feel energised. Everything has changed. There is everything to fight for. My life, and this child's life.

I hear the key turn in the lock. Every muscle tenses and the hair stands up on the back of my neck.

'Hi, it's me,' calls Frances's voice from the hall.

I stand up and instinctively move towards the open window.

The living room door opens. But it's not Frances who comes into the room.

It's Lucien, and he realises in an instant that I can see him. His mouth curls into a spiteful grin. He's no longer debonair and handsome. I see him for what he really is . . . all of human ugliness distilled into one creature.

I grip the window frame, shrinking away from the presence of evil in the room.

'No need for pretence anymore then,' he says, in his own voice.

'No,' I say, 'no need for pretence. What did you do to Frances?'

He gives a small shrug. 'She's gone.'

Women like us are disposable.

'You killed her?'

He gives a small shrug as if Frances's life is just collateral damage. 'She'd outlived her usefulness.'

'She was my friend.'

'You barely knew her. You know me better. I've been here for weeks, using her voice.'

How did he do that? Inside, I'm reeling, but I can't let him see that. Instinctively, I place a protective hand across my belly. His eyes follow the movement, and I can practically see his mouth watering.

'I won't let you have it.'

'You can't keep what's mine. He'll come to me, anyway.'

Somehow Lucien knows I'm carrying a boy. Of course, he does. It's what the ledger says.

'Why didn't you let Frances keep her child?'

'She wasn't a virgin. The son of chaos must be carried by a virgin.'

He takes a step towards me. I'm not afraid. He won't hurt me while I'm carrying his son. Once the child is born, I'll be disposable. But for now, I'm safe.

There's a small writing desk near the window. A glint of silver. Among the clutter of bills, notebooks, pens and pencils, I see the paperknife from the library desk at Winterbourne, the one with the blue enamel handle. As Lucien takes another step towards me, I grab it and stab him in the face. It hits him in the eye. He lets out a roar of pain and raises his hands. I let go of the handle and turn back to the window.

Below it, there's a small porch with a sloping roof. I clamber quickly up onto the sill. Lucien has one hand holding his eye, from which the knife still projects. He makes a grab for me with his other hand. But the injury makes him falter and I'm too quick for him. I launch myself out of the window and drop down onto the tiles. They're slick with rain and slippery, but I don't care. Anything that helps me get down quicker is a good thing. I tumble to the ground and land with a parachute roll. It knocks the wind out of me momentarily, but I push up fast and start to run, not caring about the darts of pain that fly up and down my injured leg. It doesn't matter. I'm putting space between us.

Above me, behind me, I hear Lucien shouting from the window, but I don't care for his words, so I don't turn to listen.

I'm running now and I'll run forever, as fast and as far as I can. I'll take this child and I'll never give up. I'll run forever as if the devil's at my back.

Because he is.

Epilogue

Six months later

I CRADLE MY SLEEPING BABY IN my arms. He's travelled so far for one so young. We're on the other side of the world, as far away from Winterbourne as I can imagine. It's hot and humid here, and a fan turns lazily on the ceiling above us. Outside, I can hear the splash of water, unfamiliar birdsong and the quiet sounds of a village going about its business. Through the small, high window all I can see is the sky, azure blue and cloudless, as it is every day here.

Malcolm stirs and I guide his mouth to my breast. He has his father's black hair, but my brother's soft grey eyes. He suckles greedily and his tiny hands curl into fists and open again. I place a finger on his palm and he grips it. I'd never imagined motherhood could be so fulfilling, so all-consuming.

I wonder if we'll ever feel safe. I live here using a different name. I support us by working online under another different identity. I avoid going out except to buy food, and when I do, I cover my head and my face. I watch. All the time, I'm watching. For Lucien, and for Robert Cooper. I realise now, Cooper didn't risk his life coming into the fire to save me. He was saving his master's child. And I feel certain that he will have been dispatched to find us, wherever we're hiding, however long it takes.

It'll be time to move on again soon and I'm already thinking about where we'll go.

I look down at Malcolm and he stares up at me. Will he really search out his father when he's older?

'Beware the one-eyed man,' I whisper in his ear. And, 'I'll keep you safe, my darling.' I tell him this every day, always wondering how many days we have left together.

I treasure each one, as I'm under no illusions.

The storm is coming.

Acknowledgements

As always, the process of creating a book, from the initial glimmer of an idea to the printed version being in the shops, requires the input of many people besides just the author. Writing may be a solitary pursuit, but publishing is certainly a team effort, and I'm indebted to everyone who has been involved in *Winterbourne*'s progress.

Huge thanks go to my agent, the inimitable Jenny Brown, who has championed *Winterbourne* from the very beginning, and was fully supportive of my switch of genres from crime to gothic.

Having moved to Edinburgh some nine years ago, I'm thrilled at last to have a Scottish publisher, and Black and White, as well their parent company, Bonnier Books, has been brilliant. My editor, Rachel Morrell, is a joy to work with – no one can match her enthusiasm for the project, and she edits with a light but deft hand. Thanks are also owed to the rest of the publishing team, in particular to Lucy Rose for designing such a gorgeous cover, and to Sandra Ferguson, copy editor, and Alice Fewery, proofreader, for spotting my mistakes and errors. If there are any clangers left in the book, they are all my own responsibility. I'm also grateful to Emily Langford (Senior Designer), Beth Whitelaw (Publicity Manager), Sophie

Raoufi (Marketing Manager), Thomas Ross (Publishing Manager) and Ali McBride (Publishing Director) – as well as anyone else who's had, or will in future have, any role in the publishing, marketing and selling process. My thanks also go to Olivia Caw for the brilliant job she did narrating the audiobook.

Although I'm writing this before *Winterbourne* is published, I'd like to thank in advance all the bookshops and booksellers, and libraries and librarians (I made my heroine a librarian, after all!), who will play an integral role in delivering the book into the hands of readers. And of course, I appreciate every single person who buys or reads the book – and especially those of you who are generous enough with your time to leave a review or recommend the book to another reader.

Every writer needs the support and friendship of other writers to see them through the good, and sometimes not-so-good, times. I'm grateful to Jane Anderson, Suzy Aspley, Kristin Pedroja, Hannah Kelly and Sheena Cook for their friendship, wisdom and humour – I always get a big lift whenever I see any of them.

Finally, a word of appreciation for my family – thanks for being there, Mark, Tim, Rupert and Alyina.